"Powerful, pitch-perfect."

—Elle

"Melanie Rae Thon's accomplished fifth book rushes forward on the steam of the author's spare poetic writing. . . . Thon manipulates the pieces of her story like colored gems at the end of a kaleidoscope."

—The Plain Dealer (Cleveland)

"In SWEET HEARTS, Melanie Rae Thon's characters listen carefully for ghosts; sometimes dead or lost souls rise up out of the contemporary Montana landscape, tapping on window panes, leaving footprints in the snow. . . . [Thon] has an arresting prose style, confrontational and searching. . . . Most telling is her use of the question-and-answer form to comment on cultural change. . . . It's a graceful way of showing how one god replaces another, how religions and histories of vanquished people are effaced over time."

—Newsday

"Thon is an immensely gifted prose stylist and storyteller."

—The Washington Post Book World

"SWEET HEARTS reminds us that redemption is not, as it was for St. Paul, a revelation in the form of a thunderclap, but rather the steadying end to an imperfect faith. . . . Thon's novel is itself an act of faith, Marie's narration a silent but testifying song of protest which urges, but never begs, for us to look, listen, and try to understand."

—Another Chicago Magazine

Books by

Meteors in August

Girls in the Grass

Iona Moon

First, Body

Sweet Hearts

SWEET HEARTS

A NOVEL

MELANIE RAE THON

WASHINGTON SQUARE PRESS
PUBLISHED BY POCKET BOOKS

New York   London   Toronto   Sydney   Singapore

This book is a work of fiction. Names, characters, places, and
incidents are products of the author's imagination or are used
fictitiously. Any resemblance to actual events or locales or persons
living or dead is entirely coincidental.

 A Washington Square Press Publication of
POCKET BOOKS, a division of Simon & Schuster, Inc.
1230 Avenue of the Americas, New York, NY 10020

Copyright © 2000 by Melanie Rae Thon

Reprinted by permission of Houghton Mifflin Company

ISBN: 0-7434-3679-2

First Washington Square Press trade paperback printing February 2002

10 9 8 7 6 5 4 3 2 1

WASHINGTON SQUARE PRESS and colophon are
registered trademarks of Simon & Schuster, Inc.

Cover design by Regina Starace
Cover photo © Fred Hirschmann

Printed in the U.S.A.

Selections from this work first appeared in *Antioch Review*, *Ontario Review*,
Colorado Review, *Mid-American Review*, *Bomb*, *Iron Horse Literary Review*, and
Five Points. The author wishes to express her gratitude to the editors of these
magazines.

for my mother who taught me to swim,

and my father who gave me the water

Unless we are willing to escape into sentimentality or fantasy, often the best we can do with catastrophes, even our own, is to find out exactly what happened and restore some of the missing parts.

—Norman Maclean, *Young Men and Fire*

CONTENTS

1. Ghost Brother · 1

2. Unburied Boy · 6

3. Small Crimes · 10

4. The Deaf Girl: Notes for a Play · 17

5. In Uncertain Light · 19

6. The Disappeared · 23

7. Cowbirds · 29

8. Dixie and the Crows · 32

9. The Long Way Home · 35

10. Children's Games · 38

11. Snow · 39

12. Ghost Girl · 42

13. The Hunchback · 43

14. Dreams, Death, Desire · 46

15. Birdsongs · 56

16. Instructions for Extinction · 58

17. Blind Fish · 60

18. The Lake · 62

19. On Drowning · 72

20. Catechism · 73

21. Testimony · 81

22. Mother: Final Instructions · 85

23. The Rainbow · 87

24. In Another Lifetime · 90

25. Mysteries · 110

26. The Coyote and the Crow · 111

27. A Wounded Cow · 115

28. Little Woman · 118

29. Other Mysteries · 120

30. In the Photograph · 122

31. With Hearts Like Awls · 123

32. Another Winter · 128

33. First Winter · 132

34. In Summer · 134

35. A Child of Two Fathers · 136

36. The Stowaway and the Lover · 143

37. The Evening News · 147

38. Home · 150

39. Lost Children · 155

40. Twilight · 158

41. Morning · 164

42. In Another Country · 170

43. Catechism · 176

44. Miracles · 178

45. Our Saviors · 180

46. Catching the Coyote · 190

47. Whose Child Is This? · 193

48. On Bleeding Out · 195

49. Catechism · 197

50. The Lives of Birds · 207

51. Catechism · 216

52. Snow in August · 217

53. The Birdman · 230

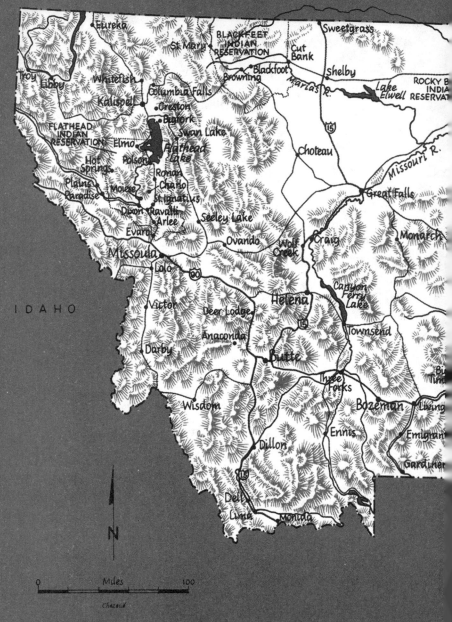

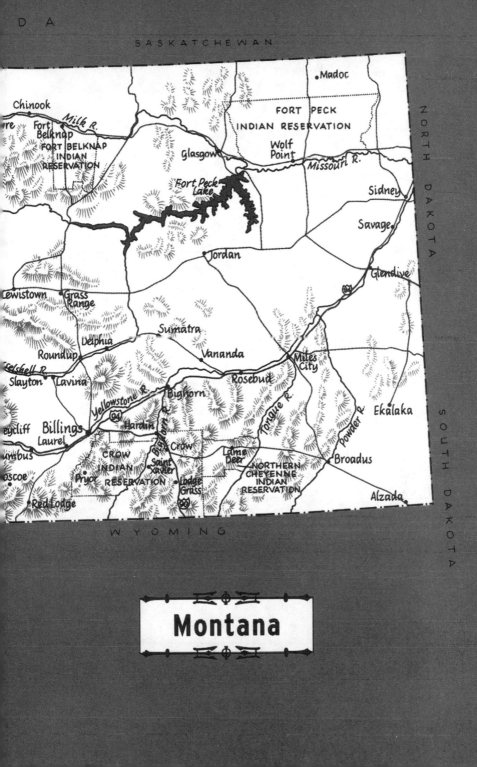

Montana

FAMILY

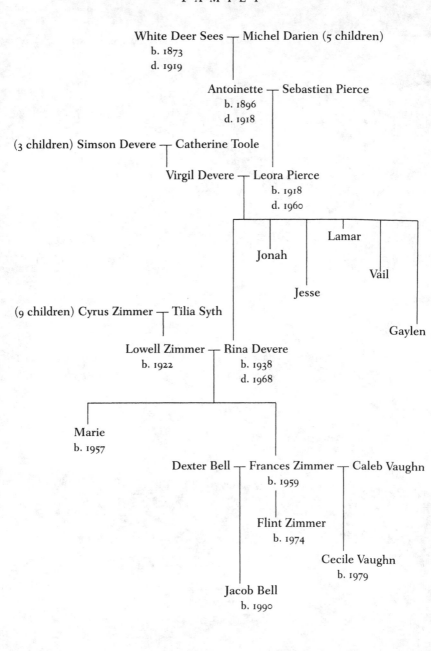

White Deer Sees — Michel Darien (5 children)
b. 1873
d. 1919

Antoinette — Sebastien Pierce
b. 1896
d. 1918

(3 children) Simson Devere — Catherine Toole

Virgil Devere — Leora Pierce
b. 1918
d. 1960

Jonah

Lamar

Jesse

Vail

Gaylen

(9 children) Cyrus Zimmer — Tilia Syth

Lowell Zimmer — Rina Devere
b. 1922   b. 1938
                 d. 1968

Marie
b. 1957

Dexter Bell — Frances Zimmer — Caleb Vaughn
b. 1959

Flint Zimmer
b. 1974

Cecile Vaughn
b. 1979

Jacob Bell
b. 1990

❊ 1 ❊

GHOST BROTHER

I am the daughter of a drowned woman.
I have stories to tell but do not speak.
Who will trust me?

When I'm afraid of what I see, I pretend it's a play. The dead
will rise for applause. We'll all go home. I promise.

First there's the girl, Cecile Vaughn, ten years old.
She stands barefoot in the muddy yard.
Montana in March, the earth just thawed.

Why is she the only one to know Flint's home?

Ghost brother, she smells him in her stepfather Dexter's
truck — wet fur, rags, blood — something the dog might dig
up.

These are my sister's children.

The missing boy brings bad weather and bad luck. Rain turns
to sleet, then snow; his mother Frances singes her hair; Dexter

passes out by the porch and wakes five hours later, left leg so numb and cold he thinks he's paralyzed himself.

Chained to a tree, the dog howls and howls.

Flint leaves his mark on Cecile's bedroom window, smears on the pane — fingers, nose, open mouth — a map of his body on the glass shroud. From inside, Cecile measures him against herself.

No ladder, no trellis — how did he climb to the second floor?

At dawn, bare trees burst with squawking crows.

Dexter loads his .22, hates the birds, wants some damn peace in his own house.

But crows watch us through our windows, see us loading guns and setting traps, lacing bait with poison. Any farmer knows this. You have to be smarter than a crow to kill one.

Dexter Bell is no farmer. He owns a tow truck and a snowplow, lives by other people's troubles.

By the time he gets outside, the crows have vanished.

Dusk. Clouds break. Wind rocks the pines and pink sky glows between branches. In the woods, coyotes cry while hundreds of boys try to slip their own shadows, all of them hungry and lost, like Cecile's brother.

Under the porch Cecile finds the rolled-up rug where one boy has been sleeping. She leaves him a jar of milk and a box of chocolate raisins.

All week, that rain.

The yard becomes a shallow lake and keeps spreading. Beneath the porch, the ground turns spongy.

Even the invisible boy can't sleep. He sinks. Cold mud seeps inside his scrap of carpet.

If the weather had been warm and dry, would he have stayed outside forever?

The little girl forgets to ask him.

The eleventh day, early morning.

A shivering child taps lightly at the kitchen window.

Dexter grabs his rifle, opens the back door, blocks the entry with his body.

But the boy is quick.

Fast as breath, he's in the house.

He's with them.

His mother giggles, inching backward. He's small for his age, but harder than Frances remembers. Dark-skinned or only dirty? There they are again, two brothers in a field, fingers sticky from cotton candy. They follow Flint everywhere. Their shadows can't be cut and peeled; one of them must be his father. He's grown from child to little man, skinny in that way that shows every vein and tendon. He could be either one of those boys from long ago. One summer night Frances Zimmer ditched her deaf sister and twirled in a mad teacup. The Kotecki brothers paid for all her rides at the carnival. Ponies skewered on poles rose and fell while the carousel played its bright tune over and over. Those boys left fingerprints and the smell of sugar on her thighs and throat and stomach.

Flint, she says; and Dexter says, *No wonder.* He means his bad luck, the numb leg, snow that melted too fast for him to plow it. He says, *Feed him, give him twenty bucks — if he's gone when I get back, I'll pretend I never saw him.*

Outside, Dexter fires three shots at empty branches, then unchains Dixie to take her with him. Dixie: half mutt, half boxer, sixty-two pounds and dumb as a rock but absolutely faithful. *My girl,* that's what Dexter calls her.

Cecile crouches in the hallway. When her brother was a ghost, she liked him better. Now he's flesh and mud. Just like Dexter. And the two men before Dexter. Just like Grandpa. And Cecile's father, who always smelled of blood and was blood-spattered. A butcher, he couldn't help it, but all the same, that's why Frances left him. *The blood,* she said, *I couldn't stand it.* Caleb Vaughn wanted his young wife to work in the shop beside him. But no, she'd rather go back to her own father, Lowell Zimmer, live cramped in one of his motel rooms with Cecile and Flint; she'd rather scrub floors and scour toilets than stay with Caleb.

Did Cecile's father beg? The child can't remember.

And Cecile doesn't remember Daddy's hand under her back, Daddy teaching her to float in the bathtub, Daddy singing *hush, little baby* in her dark bedroom.

All this she forgets on purpose.

She remembers instead his stained apron, the marks of his hands where he'd wiped them, all the good reasons Mother had to leave him.

Cecile can visit her father any day she chooses. Can ride her bike to town, a gravel road Creston to Kalispell, nine miles. Cecile Vaughn can walk past Caleb's shop and see Daddy through the window. Sometimes she does this when she's supposed to be at school. When the man looks up, does he know her? She watches Caleb's new wife hack through bone with a cleaver. This wife doesn't mind slabs of beef hanging in a cold locker. They have three daughters, plump girls, soon to be good workers. Not like Cecile, Caleb's first mistake, skittery child born of a delicate mother. *Look at her wrists, Caleb.* If his mother had been alive when he'd made his choice, she would have warned him.

Free or runaway? Frances doesn't need to ask Flint this question. Superintendent Beckett phoned last week. *Most of them come home,* he said. *When he does, you call us.*

He's hitched six hundred and twelve miles across Montana, a jagged route to find them. He keeps the map in his head, can name every town where he wasn't arrested: Rosebud, Sumatra, Slayton — the beginning of his journey. He's slept in barns and unlocked cars. Wolf Creek, Choteau. Once he walked all night to keep from freezing.

Frances says, *You must be hungry.*

She fries eggs and pork chops, gives him toast and jam, then coffee. He tries to eat it all, but can't — swallowing is work; his stomach's shrunken. He smokes. That's easy. Frances lights her own cigarette from the flame of the gas stove, and he says, *You shouldn't do that.* He knows. The day her hair caught fire, he was a crow yammering at the window. He beat his wings against the pane, but couldn't help her. She spun and flailed. Mother, burning. That night he turned all boy again, arms and legs, no wings to lift him. He climbed the maple high enough to see his mother naked in her bedroom. He watched her lips move; he read her body. So he knows this too: she's pregnant, breasts and belly rounded, hipbones fading, not that far along really, but too late to end it. Dexter's forbidden her to drink or smoke, has named his boy Jake, *Jacob, a good name, from the Bible.* His dead father's name, and his father's before him. A name too good for Dexter or his brother Gerry. When Frances said the baby might be a girl, Dexter looked befuddled. *No,* he said, *you have one of those already.*

Frances tells Flint she can spare a hundred dollars; and Flint says, *How far do you think that will get me?*

He means he's tired. He wants to eat every day, stretch his stomach, take a bath, sleep under blankets. *Like a person.*

When he says this, his voice is high, the voice Cecile remembers. He's her brother, and she comes into the kitchen. He stares. She's too big; that's what he's thinking. *It's me,* she says, *really.*

☀2☀

U N B U R I E D   B O Y

Four A.M. Dexter Bell can't get his key in the lock though he's left his headlights blazing. He kicks the door, yells for Frances. *You've got exactly ten seconds to get your ass down here.*

He's counting fast, but Frances stays deaf as her deaf sister.

That's when Dexter starts shooting. At trees, at stars, at their bedroom window. When glass shatters, Frances finally hears him.

Why lock a man out when he's got a rifle?

Flint lies next to Cecile. His mother has given him tonight, has made a bed on the floor of Cecile's room with two sleeping bags and a pillow. After all his nights on the ground and all his days of walking, he can't stand the hard floor. Wood bruises his

bones. Ten sleeping bags couldn't protect him. So he's in Cecile's bed where he can stroke her arms with one finger, where
he can feel her soft legs against his legs. The heat of her sur-
prises him, thin-skinned girl, all her blood rushing to the surface. He whispers, *Don't listen*. He means to guns and glass
and Dexter. He means don't listen to the moaning dog; don't
listen to our mother.

He's taken a bath, then a shower. Clean, he smells like her,
is that smooth, that familiar. He kisses her eyelids. He says,
You kept me alive. He carved a heart in concrete with his fingernails, chipped her name and his — and God's and Mother's.
Six weeks of nightwork, maybe longer. What else could he do?
His fingers bled and he sucked them. *That's how I knew I had
something inside me*. He pretended she was there, in the windowless ice box. *The quiet room*, the guards called it. *Time-out
in the loss-of-privilege modulo*. They had the power to name
things. But no matter what they said, days turned to weeks in
isolation.

What rule had he broken? Did he steal a cigarette or walk
too fast in the courtyard? Did he have coins in his pocket, con-
traband, enough quarters to stuff in his sock and use as a
weapon? Did he refuse to answer an officer's question; did he
raise an eyebrow, silent and insolent? Did he mutter? Muttering is forbidden, a sign of defiance or mockery. For this and
other signs, you must be disciplined. They put you in the hole
for strangling another boy or for talking after lights out. If they
catch you with a sharp, they make you strip and bend; they
look inside you. Their tiny flashlights have brilliant beams.
What do they find under your tongue? What do they know
about your ears and nostrils? When you bend, are you dark inside, or are you pink and tender? No trials here, no lawyers,
only the guards to witness. There's a list of your crimes in
Beckett's office, too numerous and small for you to remem-

ber. So it's the punishment you recall, minute by minute, the room underground, the mat on the floor, the nights without blankets. You remember your broken wrist, your cracked rib, the officer who said, *He just went wild.* He means you did this to yourself: you flung your body to the floor; you beat your own head bloody. What good is truth when facts are simple? Your bones are the ones left marked, your body the one that can't forget it.

Flint shows Cecile ten tiny scars on his hard stomach — not a guard this time, but three other boys who pulled Flint into a closet, who jabbed their shivs and twisted, who left him crumpled by the mops and buckets. He hid these wounds, though they took weeks to close and left his shirt spotted. Telling meant naming his attackers, waiting for vengeance. You can wait forever. In this place, anticipation, not blades, will kill you. He washed his shirt each night. Another rule broken: Your clothes belong to the state; they will be washed in the state's laundry.

So he liked the hole, *the module;* he laughed alone in his spaceship. No gravity here. You float or fly, upside down, wrong side out — no difference. He became incorrigible on purpose. *Incorrigible,* his favorite word of all the words he learned at Landers. Down in the box, the other boys can't touch you. But sometimes you dream them. They jump you in your sleep, shove a dirty sock in your mouth, call you *pretty boy* and *darling.* Their little hands thrill or cut you with the same gesture. They hiss in your ear, so softly no one hears them.

He says he's been out since last September. Lie or wish — it doesn't matter. Telling it that way gives him months of freedom. He says he stayed buried in the yard all winter, under leaves and snow, waiting. Cecile imagines dozens of lost children living in tunnels. Unborn or thrown away, they seep into the ground. They flow to the river.

They come back when water rises, hoping to find their missing mother. They remember her footsteps — not as sound, but as vibrations inside her.

All her life, Cecile has heard the lost ones digging. Small and blind, they scratch through dirt; they crawl under floorboards.

Years since Flint left her, but Cecile remembers the last meal he ate in their mother's kitchen. Peanut butter and marshmallows melted on crackers, a quart of milk, five Kools after. *You'll make yourself sick,* Mother said. And Flint said, *I hope so.*

He's sixteen now. Two days ago, under the porch, he celebrated his birthday. The boy was eleven when the men in the green van took him. All this time he's lived at the Landers School for Juvenile Offenders. *Last chance,* Judge Dorinda Jarvis said. *Learn the rules now, son, and maybe you won't end up dead or in Deer Lodge before you're twenty.*

On the plains the wind blows and blows, day and night, summer, winter. Flint says, *It's the wind that makes you crazy.*

Your keepers tell you: If you run, there's nowhere to go, no town, no place we can't find you. If you run, you're presumed armed. Do you understand the consequences?

Pencils are sharps; sharps are dangerous. There will be no unsupervised writing.

You will receive two pieces of paper per week and one roll of toilet paper every three weeks. Guard them. There will be no replacement of lost items.

They don't say: A fat boy with flabby breasts will hang naked in the same shower where you and others mocked him. You will not see his body, his tongue sticking out, his face purple. Except in dreams, where he keeps swinging.

You will learn a game called strobing. Will steal bits of metal from the shop to play it. Instructions are simple: ten boys hold hands in a line while the boy with the metal plugs himself into a socket.

Hand to hand, the charge passes.
A tick, a trill, ten little hearts stuttering.
It's the boy at the other end who absorbs it.
If there's water on the floor, the rush will kill him.

Before Cecile sleeps, these are the things Flint whispers.

⚜3⚜

SMALL CRIMES

Flint knows his own life by his crimes on the outside. Age four, first theft; age six, first fire. In between, Mother married the butcher. Caleb Vaughn taught Flint to drive the new Mercury: the man worked the pedals while the boy turned the wheel. Mother's long light hair blew out the window, and Caleb said, *You're a natural.* Did they really do this? Sometimes Flint tries to forget, because he hates to see himself happy. Caleb Vaughn wanted to adopt him. *Give him a name, make us a family.* But Mother said, *He has a name.* Yes, *Zimmer,* her name, and Grandpa's. Later she said, *The sweet ones, they kill you with their good intentions.*

Age seven, first assault, the school playground.
Flint yanked Kyle McCormick from the monkey bars,

nicked his cheek with a jackknife, and said, *Next time I'll really cut you.*

He had reasons he couldn't explain, an afternoon alone with that boy — ropes cinched tight around his wrists and ankles, a tree he should have climbed, a dirty garage he couldn't quite remember.

For possession and use of a dangerous weapon, school policy demanded expulsion. No state law required anyone to provide alternative education. Mother said, *Maybe your aunt will teach you to read.* A private joke. Let the woman who won't talk instruct the child who won't listen.

Free all day, Flint stole other boys' bikes. And why not? His own bike had been stolen. So these exchanges were simple logic. Blue, silver, black — they had five speeds or twenty. He lost each one, ditched it in the river or heaved it down the gully.

He learned to drink. The first beer of the morning always tasted bad, but the second went down easily. After three, he could lie on the floor till afternoon, not sleeping but drifting, buzzing body not quite his, humming brain not quite thinking. Patterns of light shifted through blinds and amused him for hours. If he rested now, he could sneak out later, ride one of the bikes down the dark highway. He liked the risk, rocks and holes in the road, ice that sent him skidding.

In November, a weaving car grazed his rear tire, and the boy flew into a field of frozen weeds. Nobody stopped. He lay on his back, very still. Colors burst behind his eyes, red into blue, a violet flood pricked by stinging yellow. *Dead,* he thought. The earth beneath him opened. When soft snow fell on his face, he was amazed to feel it melting.

In February, Mother wrote Caleb a note: *Gone to the lake.*
Took the children.

They lived in a room at Grandpa's Starlite Motel. *Just a few*
weeks, she promised. But they were still there in June, and still
there in August. Then one cool night Flint Zimmer made himself famous.

The headline said: EIGHT YEAR OLD ADMITS TO ARSON.
No need to print his name. Everybody knew who torched
Royce Beauvil's boat. *With deliberate intention.*

Flint Zimmer doused the canvas cover with kerosene.

Flint Zimmer tossed three matches.

A miracle. This boy made flames rise on water.

Estimated loss: twenty-two thousand.

Where was Mother that night?

Gone to town.

Among the missing.

Now he was a Delinquent Youth, a serious offender who
showed no remorse, gave no excuses. So he did not go back to
second grade in September. Judge Jarvis committed him to a
group home for troubled boys, forty miles from the border of
North Dakota. *Merciful,* she told him. *If I ever see you in my*
court again, I'll send you to Landers.

He served eleven months, one week, three days. No one
came to visit. Mother said, *It's a thirteen-hour drive. You'll be*
home soon.

When he came back, home was Columbia Falls, the edge of
town, just south of the tracks, a two-room flat above a laundry.
Mother had a job at Sloan Fetterman's pawnshop. CASH FOR
GUNS, the sign said. A stuffed grizzly roared in the window.

Flint tried to be good, but boys followed him after school. They knocked him to the ground: three to one, no chance of winning. They flicked lighters close to his face; they said, *You like this?*

Now he was nine, flunking second grade. Words spun off the blackboard, nothing but swirls and scratches. He thought of his mother's letter, the sentence he did read: *Too far, I can't afford it.*

What good were words?

Who wanted to know them?

He was a failure at ten. Grandpa said, *The boy needs skills, not learning.* Lowell Zimmer glimpsed himself long ago, one more child with no gift for language. He forgave Flint for his crimes, but left those words unspoken. He taught his grandson how to use a saw and hammer, how to drive a nail straight, how to start it at an angle. That summer, they repaired the porch together. They chopped wood after dinner, and when the work was done, Grandpa rode shotgun while Flint drove the El Camino up and down the gravel road, motel to highway.

Grandpa offered mild instruction: *more gas,* or, *tap the brake gently.*

Grandpa bestowed extravagant praise: *good eye, quick reflexes.*

Flint imagined his future as a carpenter or mechanic, as a man alone in the woods with an ax and a chain saw. He was a spiderman, swinging limb to limb, trimming the treetops.

Then it was fall, no more trips to the lake, no more lessons in the El Camino. The boy couldn't spell the words he loved: *silhouette, arson, merciful.* Though Mother said he was Wednesday's child, he couldn't get the name of the day on paper without reversing letters. He saw the perfect slant of the nail in his mind, but couldn't make sense of clean triangles drawn with a ruler. He needed to touch the things with his hands — hammer, wood, nail — he needed to strike hard enough to feel the blow from wrist to shoulder. He wanted every angle to have a purpose, to be part of the porch or the birdhouse he was building. His teacher whispered, *hopeless*.

He didn't need to hear: he read her.

Flint Zimmer skipped school to develop his other talents. The boy had a special gift for breaking and entering. It was one of the things he'd learned at his private school, that group home near the border where every child was an expert of some kind.

He showed his sister how to tape a basement window so glass wouldn't shatter, how to tap lightly with a rock or hammer.

Cecile was the first to check each house, to be sure no one was asleep or hiding. If she found a dog, she'd calm it, speak in her little-girl voice till it licked her legs and fingers, till it followed her gladly. She'd lead it to the smallest room, lock it up, open a back door for her brother.

They shaved the hair from dolls' scalps, then stripped their tiny clothes to examine plastic bodies. Sometimes the bodies felt hard, sometimes rubbery. Their legs came off; their torsos were empty. When you pulled their heads from their necks, they just kept smiling. The children left pieces of bald, naked babies stuffed under pillows and hidden in cupboards. They dropped china. By accident at first and then on purpose. They stood on chairs. They stood on tables. Cups exploded on tiles.

They loved that sound. Forbidden noise. No one slapped. No one threatened. No grandpa here, no judge, no mother. No deaf aunt to clean up your mess in silence.

Once they took a bath because the tub was round and the white towels thick as blankets. Mother didn't have a tub in the flat above the laundry. Only a shower there, and in the motel room before that. But Cecile remembered a tub somewhere. She floated with her eyes closed. She was very small, inside herself, inside the water.

One day they started taking. A watch on a chain, a silver locket. Inside the locket's heart, they found a tiny tooth, some precious baby's. Later they stole a revolver and a trumpet. Flint met an older boy who knew how to sell things. Maybe he sold them to Frances at the pawnshop. They had money at last. Flint said, *We can make a living.*

In a brick house, Flint wore a man's big boots and sipped his whiskey. Cecile ate three bowls of butterscotch pudding. They were happy here, giddy at first, then warm and drowsy. The heads of animals on the walls watched them: elk, moose, big-horn. Their eyes were glass, their skulls empty.

Sten Gunderson came home sooner than expected, saw his fishing pole and hunting vest, tool box and snowshoes, all his favorite things piled by the door, ready to be stolen.

Standing at the bottom of the stairs, Gunderson heard something scramble above him. Little rodents. He caught Flint in the bathroom and held a pistol to the boy's head while Cecile hid in the shower. Fingers stuck in her ears, she still heard the man say, *I know you, boy, your grandfather and your mother.*

Then the police came, and Sten Gunderson said he'd follow them to the station. *To be sure you keep the little bastard.*

Bastard, yes, everybody knew this. Cecile wanted to lie down, wanted to sleep there under pounding water — she was that tired, but she remembered the man's hand, the gun trembling. *I know you.* He'd kill her. So she crawled, down the stairs, to the basement, out the broken window.

She was five years old, Flint was eleven. He never told anyone she was with him — not even Mother.

The headline said: STRING OF THEFTS CONNECTED.

That bad boy again, Cecile's brother.

The newspaper Cecile couldn't read said: LOCAL BOY HEADED TO LANDERS.

Two men shackled Flint and locked him in the cage of the green van with three other boys — car thief, sheep killer, rapist. They had one more stop, two hours west, in Libby. This child was twelve, but skinnier than Flint, pale arms white as a doll's porcelain belly. He'd tried to kill his stepfather, had paid a nineteen-year-old man fifty dollars to do it. But the man was a bad shot, and the stepfather was only wounded, his arm, not his heart, all this for nothing.

The horizon turned fiery orange, then rose and lavender. The lights of little towns disappeared behind them. When the talk stopped, when the boys were sore and tired from hours of bouncing on metal benches, Flint heard one child sobbing, a sound so close and hard it filled the van and rocked each body.

Gone for good this time, seven years detention. The judge remembered Flint's history, that burning boat, its mysterious value. The boy had failed to learn from his mistakes; the mother had failed to provide a stable environment. Seven years. When he got out he'd be full grown, eighteen, a man at last and old enough for Deer Lodge.

Cecile thought if she'd confessed her part, she might have saved him.

Now Flint's back, in Dexter's house, in Cecile's bed, warm beside her. When his fingertips read her ribs or spine, when he touches the bones of her ankles with his toes, does he blame or forgive her? He whispers, *I know things; I'll teach you.*

⊰4⊱
T H E   D E A F   G I R L :
N O T E S   F O R   A   P L A Y

There's no safe place in this story.

I don't want to be the mother of lost children.

I don't want to be the boy raised in a cell, or the sister who loves him.

I don't want to be a good samaritan, one of those kind strangers who tries to help us.

The deaf girl, me, the children's aunt, their mother's sister. In the play that is our lives, I stand stage left, signing to the audience. I can speak if I want to. I don't want to. I sound ridiculous. My father never makes me speak. This is how he proves he loves me. He lets me hold my tongue, thick in my mouth forever. This is the sign for *drowned*. Unsaved. This is the sign for *mother*. Nobody reads signs in the dark. Lungs fill with water. This is my father's house. Show me the sign for *prison*.

I could leave him.

I could be the quiet maid in any motel, some other man's silent wife, mute and obedient. But I stay for this reason: when my father's lips move, he has a voice I remember. Today he said, *I'm going to town. Need anything?* Six words. Every one, music. When he says *town*, he means Bigfork, not Kalispell or Polson. I know this. I make the sign for sugar, *sweet, kiss,* a code between us; then *chocolate, bitter. Flour,* I sign. *Five.* I mean pounds. He smiles. He says, *Is it my birthday?*

Once, I had a lover.

Yes, even me, imagine.

Seven times we met in one of my father's motel rooms. He had a soft beard and a long ponytail. His chest was white, his shoulders narrow. *Like a boy,* I wanted to tell him. I traced him, forehead to ankle. He had bones like mine, close to the surface. I knew him, this way. He looked for work but couldn't find it. I read his lips well enough; he said, *Come to Alaska with me.*

His words had shape but no sound — high or flat, his voice was a mystery, not like my father's voice, rippling inside me. In my father's house, I am a hearing child. Windowpanes rattle. I feel storms in my fingertips. Boards creak in the hallway. That's Daddy moving room to room, always restless. He's worn a groove in the wood with his pacing.

On this lake, gulls flap, woodpeckers hammer. Pines pop, their sap freezing. In winter, the snap of brittle limbs wakes me. What I see triggers sound; what I hear comes from memory. If the ice melts fast off the lake, it fractures, each crack, low thunder. Stones tremble. Everything has a voice, and I know it.

Sometimes the thinnest ice is slow to give. Then one bright morning, the lake begins to ring. Glass bells chime, high and delicate, until one perfect note shatters them in a stroke of sunlight.

A poor excuse, you say.

There is ice in Alaska, birds to flap hard against the cold sky, a boy to read my body.

I hear what I want to hear. I suppose I lie. I would speak the truth if I could make sense of it. I can't make you listen. If you want to understand, you'll have to watch. You'll have to learn my language.

Who can justify a child's love for a father, or a sister's for her brother? This is the sign for *passion*: clenched fists crossed over the heart then pulled away. I mean *suffering*. I mean *desire*.

Ask Jesus; he'll explain.

⊰5⊱

In Uncertain Light

Let us say it is a late afternoon in October. Five months ago, or five years — what is time to a girl who has lived always in one place, on a lake wide as a sea, in a white house with a green roof, in a room down the hall from her father?

Imagine golden light slanting through dark pine and yellow

tamarack. The father emerges from the woods wearing a red flannel shirt and carrying a hatchet. His blue shadow falls behind him.

Another day: this time it's deep winter. An old man slips on a patch of ice and flails like a clown, struggling to regain his balance. He hunches against wind-driven snow. Would he be ashamed or angry if he glanced toward the house and saw his daughter watching?

This is my father: short white hair, stubble of white beard morning and evening. He stays smooth only a few hours. He rubs his hand over his face. All these years, the same, but the sudden growth still bewilders him. He says, *I don't know why I bother.*

My father. Thin legs, chapped hands. He keeps a dozen pairs of gloves in a drawer in the hallway, scratchy wool or supple deerskin, lined with silk or fur or cotton. He has no preference. Though his skin cracks, he forgets to wear them. The black leather ones lined with the fur of a white rabbit lie wrapped in a silk scarf, both saved for some special occasion. Perhaps he imagines his deaf daughter married at last. Perhaps he hopes to give her away some chill afternoon in January or November. With gloved hands, he will guide her.

Father. He looks like a tall man in the distance. Strong, sturdy. For example: when I am in the kitchen of the house and he stands high on a ladder propped against the motel, repairing the gutter. He can repair anything — the dock, the boat, the roof, the plumbing. He can replace a broken window, cracked tiles, blistered linoleum.

He can pull a double-sized mattress out the narrow door and up the muddy hill, then heave it into the back of the El Camino. Once he carried his limp daughter out of the woods. If he found me that way again, I do not doubt he would still attempt to lift me.

He'll let me help him unload the new mattress. But I have to ask. I have to guess what he has in mind, or I have to catch him.

Hours later, when we stand in the same small space, he seems shrunken. Maybe he is washing his hands at the kitchen sink and I am putting plates and glasses into the cupboard, maybe I am close enough to measure, to see that the daughter he once carried is now half an inch taller than he is, that his faded flannel shirt hangs loose across the chest and shoulders, that his belt is cinched a notch tighter than it was when I looked the last time.

And when was that? A month, a year? Is this shrinking slow or sudden? Does he know? Is he sad or grateful? Often I have thought he would be glad to leave me, his small crime, his silent burden.

If my mother had awakened my father, if one of them had called good Doctor Dees in time, paramedics might have rushed me to the hospital in Kalispell, sent me speeding down this dangerous road in an ambulance; they might have sensed how serious the fever was and called for a helicopter to take me all the way to Missoula. Some thought-troubled doctor making night rounds might have envisioned the mysterious way each infection leaves a child vulnerable to another: encephalitis, pneumonia, meningitis. No drug or human hand could have spared me from the first, but murmuring nurses quiet as nuns might have pumped my veins full of antibiotics, swaddled me in white sheets, and stopped the second disease before it moved through blood from lungs to spinal fluid.

Then my family would have a different story, and I would be able to hear it. Imagine.

My father and I live like ones long married. Ones who have learned not to touch, no matter how closely their bodies pass as she makes the tea and he stirs the oatmeal. Ones who know what the other wants — salt, butter, wrench, mallet — without asking. Ones who read lips and hands and eyebrows. Ones whose tenderness is a ghost between them.

When I think of his touch, when I dream it, it is the rough hand cupping my face that I most wish to feel. His eyes are not closed. He is not afraid of me.

Daddy.

Now he is here. The air in the house shifts, a faint, cold wind traveling from the living room to the kitchen where I stand chopping onions and celery. He leans in the doorway watching my back, my long dark hair in one braid dangling, my large hand on the knife chopping. I am a tall woman, thin and bony. Wide in the hips and at the shoulders. Not delicate like my blond sister Frances. Not supple like my smooth mother Rina. Not lovely, this daughter who hacks vegetables so swiftly.

The father pretends the deaf girl is oblivious, though they both know if he raised one hand or made one word, she would somehow feel it. But what word would it be? This is an ordinary day. Let us say June, or March, or September. A day like today, a day like any other. There is nothing to swear or confess, nothing to forgive because all is forgotten. There is no reason to be particularly kind, no reason now or ever to be cruel.

The good daughter, the false wife, slices carrots and shreds chicken, then scoops them into the pot of bubbling broth with the celery and onions. She will not turn until she feels space open behind her, until she is certain the doorway is empty.

When I imagine my father making the sign for love, he paces the beach, shaping the word *penance*.

Consider two houses, the one on the lake where I live with my
father and the one in Creston less than twenty miles north
where my sister Frances lives with her husband, Dexter Bell,
and her daughter, Cecile, Caleb Vaughn's child. The other
child, the boy who slept under the porch, the wet one, the
dirty one, the one unwanted in this or any house, this one is
the son of no man who will ever claim him. His name is Zimmer, Flint Zimmer, and sometimes I think of him as ours, mine
and my father's, though we have failed him miserably, though
we do nothing that saves him.

If he had come to our door last night, if he had knocked politely, would we have hidden him from his own mother, from
the police, from Superintendent Beckett at Landers? Would I
have washed and dried his muddy clothes while he lay in the
hot bath water, half floating? Would my father have boiled
potatoes then whipped them with milk and butter until they
were smooth as cream and not too hot and easy for a starving
boy to swallow?

None of this happened. My father and I ate alone in our
familiar silence. The chicken soup burned our tongues, but
of course neither the man nor his daughter mentioned it. I
washed the dishes while he paced the porch, smoking. He
rapped on the window and mouthed the words: *It's my turn.
Leave them.* But I kept washing and he kept smoking, and
when he came inside, he looked at the plates and glasses in the
drainer as if they accused him.

I do not accuse him.

He knows this. And so the bowls and pot have voices. This
would make sense if you knew us.

Frances did not call to ask our father's advice. She wouldn't. For all we knew, the boy was still shut away, safe in a cell, locked in our memories. Now I think we should have read the signs: that fierce wind all day, rain that blew in every direction. Clouds hid the mountains until water and sky became one element, the same smudged gray where they met at the horizon. Waves foamed, green and black, breaking into spumes of white as they battered stones and docks and sent gulls flapping.

But this has happened a thousand times and meant nothing. The old man and his deaf daughter remember very well that a blue lake, a warm summer day, a clear sky are the most dangerous.

We welcome waves and wind: when the lake is wild, it warns us to keep our distance.

This morning, the rain has stopped, but the dark limbs of pine and fir are still dripping. I imagine it is the same in Creston, that anyone awake in my sister's house can hear it.

That house is made of logs stained dark, two stories high, the third house of seven on a road that stops at the edge of the foothills. Each house is separated by a thousand feet or more so that each family can preserve the illusion of privacy. You might hear your neighbor's dog barking or his cock crowing. Sometimes you hear howling and you wonder: the dog again, or is that a coyote? Often you hear a truck rumble down the road, heading toward one of the other houses, and you think, *It's late,* and you know there will be a fight in one of those bedrooms, questions someone will fail to answer, curses. But even at the height of summer when every window in every house is open, voices are muffled by trees, and cries lost like dreams misremembered.

In March, those windows are sealed, shut tight since early

November. The only voices you have heard all winter are the shouts of children, the ones who run down this road after the school bus drops them.

What I mean to say is that this is a place where your neighbors will help dig you out after a blizzard, where they will share their dinner and let you spend the night on their floor if your house loses power and theirs doesn't. They will dress in the dark to come jump your battery at five in the morning. If they pass you on the road today, they will roll down their windows to ask about the gunshots last night, but they will accept your explanation, will believe you when you mutter, *damn coyote*. These neighbors respect your silence; they let you keep certain secrets. I mean that a boy could hide here for weeks if his mother would let him.

Creston, an hour before dawn, the little girl's upstairs bedroom. This room is at the end of a long hall, the back of the house, as far away from the bedroom on the first floor as possible. Crows caw. A square of gray sky in the window begins to lighten. Frances Bell enters the girl's room and sees her children in bed together.

She wants to slap the boy. It's his mouth, soft with sleep, that angers her. It's his arm, thin and heavy across her daughter's stomach. She shakes him. He burrows down, pulls the blanket over his head, but she tugs it back, says, *When Dex wakes up, you can't be here.*

Flint knows it's true. He's seen the .22 cocked and aimed. In every room, the man is ready. There's a little revolver stuffed in a canister on the kitchen counter, a 9 mm semi-automatic pistol in the drawer of the nightstand, safety on, magazine fully loaded. The Winchester 25-35 in a leather case under the bed is big enough for elk, an old gun, but fast and accurate. Dexter claims he killed a bear once, made a rug from the hide and head but had to sell it.

The house itself is dangerous, full of forgotten ammunition. If you torch a place like this, it can detonate, blow apart in three minutes, kill everybody inside when all you meant to do was scare them. A boy from Chinook taught him that. The kid was doing his first five at Landers. When he turned eighteen, he'd go to Deer Lodge for another sixty. No wonder he tried to run. And he said three hours of freedom was worth three months in the ice box.

If Dexter sees him today, Flint knows exactly what will happen: the call, the chase, the long ride back to Landers. If three hours of flight gets you three months in the hole, how long will he be down there? No time to figure. He's dressing in the dark. Mother's washed his clothes; she gives him new socks and a wool sweater. Does this mean she loves him? He can't be certain. She says, *There's a green jacket in the closet by the front door. Dexter never wears it.* He understands her now: he can take what she won't give him. She hands him a leather pouch fat with a roll of bills. She says, *Be careful.*

When he counts the money, two hundred and seventy-four dollars, he'll have his answer: she wants him gone, as far as this will take him.

Spokane, St. Paul, Denver?

Last night she said he could disappear in a city. *Start clean in another state. New name, no record.*

He can sleep under a bridge, like a troll, make people pay to cross it.

He'll chew leaves and grass, the soft petals of flowers. He's eaten worse. He'll strip tender bark and gather fallen apples. In garbage cans he'll find fins and tails, old bread, tiny hearts, and the bones of chickens. He likes these: snap them open, suck the marrow. People who live in houses never do this, so it's always there, for you, sweet and filling, but it gives you bad dreams. A bird flutters in your face — broken breast, severed wing — she becomes you, a creature without feet, and you realize you've splintered your own shins in exchange for one meal.

Six years of sixteen in lockup. What does Flint Zimmer know of survival? He can make a knife with a stolen pencil and a sliver of metal. He's resourceful. He doesn't need matches to spark a fire. When he was six, he discovered that sunlight striking glass made dry leaves smoke and crackle. Patient boy, he saw one small flame start a whole field blazing. An accident that time — he tried to stamp it out; he tried to smother it with his jacket.

He's smashed enough windows and been in enough houses to know the strange places people hide what's precious. In unlit rooms, he's smart as a blindman: he finds one loose brick with his fingers, hears the single board that wheezes beneath him. People on vacation stash jewelry in the freezer. An emerald ring with tiny diamonds, there, wrapped in plastic behind the corn and carrots. He feels it. Long guns lie quiet between towels under folded linen. Do you think he won't smell them? He has a nose for oil and leather, worn wood, residue of gunpowder. He smells the soft white doeskin in the hallway closet. You saved this for twenty years. You meant to sew a vest and wear it hunting. Now some stray boy nuzzles the animal in his sleep, uses her smooth skin as his pillow.

He's heard of other crimes, but hasn't had the chance to commit them. Boys brag. Some can hot-wire a car in less than a minute. Of this skill he's most jealous. He knows so little that's useful. In the van on the way to Landers, that sheep killer from Evaro said he gutted the animal while she was still living. Roasted the flesh but ate the liver raw, still warm from her body. A lie, no doubt — one bite, perhaps, to taste, but more than that, how could he stand it? Just his bad luck not to know the cost of killing a breeding female in Montana. Flint thought this boy had talents he didn't possess. A sheep killer could eat any time he was hungry. How do you catch a scared animal? How does a small boy pin four legs while he opens the belly? If you want her dead, do you jab the throat, then pump the leg to bleed her? How long will it take? His teachers, those boys at Landers, were always weak on details.

Flint can pop most locks with a thin file. Can enter your car and knows how to drive, but can't start it. All his knowledge now seems worthless. He remembers how much pressure it takes on a boy's chest to make him stop screaming. He's learned to keep quiet no matter what happens. But silence is a gift that doesn't always save you. For instance: the hanging boy with flabby breasts never screamed. He couldn't. And Flint wonders now if that boy changed his mind while he dangled. If Evan Jewell had been stronger, not so thick and clumsy, maybe he would have grabbed the rope, pulled himself up, stopped his own strangling. Were there burns on his palms? Flint wishes he knew this. But what would be worse: believing the boy tried to live, or understanding that even as he choked, he never doubted his decision?

Barely a mile from home and Flint's hungry already. There's a diner at the edge of town where he could eat pancakes and bacon. But he needs to save his money: in that city far away, everything will be expensive. An Indian boy at Landers claimed if you washed a cow's teat, you could drink straight from her udder. He showed Flint how to kneel and squeeze with one hand, how to aim the hot liquid. Seven miles from home, Flint tries to do the same. No luck. When he squats underneath the cow, he sees sharp hooves and huge belly. One kick to stun, then she'll lie down and crush him. Her udder bulges and she moans, ready. The teat is clean, but he's too scared to take it.

Almost noon, south of Bigfork.

Flint hitches a ride with a trucker wired tight on Dexedrine and coffee. He's headed for Wyoming. Casper. *Like the ghost,* the man says. *Friendly.*

That's good, Flint says. But he gets out in St. Ignatius, thirty-seven miles from his grandfather's motel, still deep in Montana.

He's stolen the trucker's pills and slipped a tiny flashlight into his pocket. He tried not to take them, but they rolled on the seat. Of their own will they slid in his direction.

⇥7⇤

C O W B I R D S

Every spring, my father shoots cowbirds. Perhaps it is moral purpose that guides his bullets, making his aim exact and deadly.

He does not explain. Cowbirds are robbers of the worst kind. I know this.

Long ago, they followed bison across the plains, but neither bison nor bird could cross the mountains or find their way through the dense forests of Montana. Then the whitemen came to open the world with their axes. Though the great herds vanished, though the hunters slaughtered them by the millions, the clever cowbirds in their drab feathers lived unnoticed and learned to rove coast to coast, nothing to stop them.

Cowbirds have no wish to do harm — they are opportunists, and we help them: we pave their roads and clear space for them to feed; we leave just enough woodland for them to mate and multiply. Perhaps my father thinks he can compensate, that one man on one lake can save the songbirds from extinction.

In late spring, the female cowbird calls her suitors to the forest. She searches for nests while hopeful males sit high in the treetops, whistling. I am spared their noise. For small mercies, I am grateful.

Cowbirds have no heart for home or family, no fidelity to mates or offspring. The female lays her eggs one at a time in the nests of smaller birds: finches, warblers, vireos. A vireo nest is hard to find, camouflaged by bark and lichen, but it is soft inside, and strong, woven from grass and fiber, lined with the silky web of a spider. You won't find it if you're human. Nor will you find the warbler's nest, a cup of grass and weeds built in the tallest spruce or lodgepole. If you're lucky, you might see a little bird flit through the woods like a butterfly. If you could hold a warbler in your hand, you'd be amazed by its markings, bright yellow breast, green back, black hood and ear patch. You could feel its whole body trilling. The finch builds its nest of twigs and rootlets, and though the nest is high, the cowbird somehow finds it.

She removes one egg from each nest and deposits her own in its place — just in case any songbird is counting. Her scattered children hatch big and early, peck their hungry way out of their shells and start squawking. Why don't the warblers notice the difference between these impostors and their own children? Are they deaf and blind? Can't they smell, can't they taste the deceptive flesh of the usurper? Perhaps the scent of young cowbirds is sweet; perhaps they taste like water. The vireos exhaust themselves feeding strangers. They do their work, the curse of instinct. The finch's nestlings starve. My father and I find them in the woods, featherless and pink, pushed from their own nests by false siblings.

As soon as young cowbirds fly, they join flocks of vagabonds, their own kind. Though all their mothers have deserted them, though every father is long missing, they recognize the ones they must follow. They know themselves.

A mystery, a blessing.

And so my father is ready. In late May, in June, in July, he will stand on the porch and fire into the trees. It will make no difference in the end if he shoots three or ten or two hundred. The cowbirds will thrive. So his act is futile, a gesture, a sign, a fist he shakes at God, as if to say, *Watch me*.

In the long shadows of morning, I will see my father walk into the woods, searching for the songbirds' starved nestlings. If by some miracle one is alive, he'll carry it home in his pocket, feed it crumbs of bread soaked in milk, give it water from an eyedropper. He knows this is hopeless. They never survive without their mothers' protection. He might give one fledgling a day of suffering if he's lucky. By evening, I'll watch my father dig another hole, deep enough to bury a small bird where coyotes and ravens won't find it.

DIXIE AND THE CROWS

Three days now Dixie's been yelping. She runs in circles, wraps herself around the tree till the chain is short and the collar gags her. Dexter Bell's filthy girl. Her nose and paws are black with mud, her pale hair mud-speckled. The flock of crows swells by the day. They hover at the edge of the woods in bare birch and maple. Too soon to rob other nests of eggs, too soon to pluck insects from the orchards. Noisy angels, they feed off torn animals on the highway or scavenge through garbage. No wonder they yap, bellies full of poison.

The crying birds make Dixie crazy, but Dexter says, *Something else is out there*. He feels it, bobcat or coyote. One sentinel crow sounds a warning to the others: stranger in these woods, hungry or infected. Last summer, a cougar killed a house cat on a quiet street in Kalispell. Nobody's safe. Maybe it's the boy already. Dexter doesn't say this. He wants to trust Frances when she swears he's really gone this time, a thousand miles south by now, heading for Mexico if they're lucky. Dex knows about the money, more than half of it his. She says, *I'll pay you back;* and he says, *Forget it.*

He loves her, in his way, and he's thinking about the baby, little Jake inside her, a miracle he never expected — so he needs Frances, and he needs the child who will change them. He doesn't understand how, or what he means when he thinks this. It's an act of faith, the first one he can remember: he has never felt this blessed, has never used the words *miracle, faith, holy*. He stopped going to Sunday School when he was seven. Took his air rifle down to the ravine instead, shot squirrels and sparrows, or tried to hit them. Once he shot his brother Gerry.

Nicked his smooth cheek and maimed the pretty child forever. Not on purpose, but Mother thrashed him all the same, made him drop his pants and bend in front of his little brother. She used a thin switch, wet willow. He cut the branch himself while she waited in the doorway. How many times did she strike? He can't remember — only five, or more than twenty? She hid the gun. *For a month,* she said, *until you've learned your lesson.* But he never got it back. She sold it. She said, *A woman alone can't have boys in trouble.*

Sometimes he wishes she were alive so that he could forgive her. He remembers lying on his belly as she washed him. Iodine stung in the welts, the cure more painful than the beating. Still, he didn't whimper. She was the one who cried, who said, *I know, I know; I'm sorry.* Her hand was soft, her fingers gentle. He rocked himself to sleep that night, thinking some woman he didn't know had done this: some witch had flown into his mother's body, grabbed the stick and whipped him.

All these years and now at last he almost understands her. Flint is his bad example, a vision of the boy he might have been if not for Mother's brutal kindness. The unborn baby is his new passion: he'd do anything to protect the child. That's why he leaves the .22 propped by the door. That's why there's a box of hollowpoints tucked in the canister with the revolver. He tells Cecile, *Don't you ever touch.* He tells Frances, *Let me teach you.*

But Cecile does touch the Taurus 85, .38 caliber, point and shoot, single action, no need to cock it. On Friday she cuts school at noon, goes home when she knows nobody else will be there. Long and heavy or tiny as toys, the guns tempt her. *Don't touch.* She loves what's forbidden, small lies, every secret. Anything she doesn't tell belongs to her only. There's a radiator and an open window in the school bathroom: it's easy for a girl her size to climb up and out of it. There's a path through the woods no one else uses. By one o'clock, her teacher will notice she's missing and call Mother at the pawnshop. Mother will lie too, will say, *Didn't she give you my note? I picked her up. She's at the dentist.* Later she'll swat Cecile's head, say, *I hate this.* But she won't tell them, those teachers or the principal, her judges, those concerned neighbors. All the people who whispered about Flint, all the ones who asked, *What kind of mother?*

So Cecile is safe; Mother hits, but not that hard. She can bear it.

Alone in the big house, Cecile slips the revolver into her pocket. It feels light as a squirt gun full of water. She glides from room to room, points out of every window. Dixie whines. Cecile goes outside to aim at crows. She loads each cylinder, only five in the little Taurus. The birds don't scatter. They don't believe she'll shoot them. She could drop them one by one, and still they'd sit, never believing the skinny girl has a real gun with real bullets. Some crows are too smart for their own good: reason makes them doubt the evidence.

But she doesn't want to kill birds. Noisy as they are, the crows aren't her enemies. She shoots at tin cans on a stump, keeps moving back, testing — ten paces, twenty. She has a good eye, the absolute concentration of a child. No sound, no thought distracts her. She's inside herself every moment, and the gun is just a part of her hand, not a separate object. Each can on the stump is her too: when she gets it in her sights, there's no space between them. Four times out of fifteen, she sends one flying.

She doesn't know that the blast of the gun is a voice that

calls her brother. She thinks nobody sees, and she's right: he's nobody, crouched behind the woodpile.

⊰9⊱

T H E   L O N G   W A Y   H O M E

He meant to go. The first day, he caught his reflection in a window, and his own image surprised him. He saw a stunted man in dark glass, narrow face pinched and worried. But he's not a man. He's a child who wants his mother to dig a cave under the porch to hide him. She's chosen Dexter and his house, a safe place, no bad boy living beneath the floorboards. *Cross a border.* He should have done this.

The second day, still buzzed on the trucker's Dexedrine, he got as far south as Missoula. He climbed a winding road into the hills until he found the house he wanted, a clean one built above the smog of the pulp mill, one with an unlocked garage and a metal ladder. The cracked window on the second floor was his open invitation, proof at last that somebody loved him.

A boy's room, yes, he belonged here. The clothes were too big, so he rolled the cuffs of the jeans and punched a new hole in the belt with a nail. This boy had everything Flint needed — hooded sweatshirt, denim jacket — he had wool gloves without fingers, beggar's gloves, perfect for smoking. He had a slender knife with two thin blades. Worthless, Flint thought, too small for gutting fish or birds. But the knife whispered, *Take me.* The soft, lucky boy who lived here kept a bag of dope stuffed in a boot, two packs of rolling papers and a lumpy sock full of pills stashed in the top drawer of his dresser. So easy to find, Flint wondered why his mother had never caught him, why this boy slept in a wide bed under a down comforter all the nights Flint slept naked in a windowless cell or rolled up tight inside a piece of wet carpet.

In a pale green bathtub down the hall, Flint smelled that oblivious woman. He felt her smooth tub: still damp. Just an hour ago she'd drifted in her own scent, drugged by the sweet oil of geraniums. She'd left him a bottle of orange pills. FOR PAIN, the label said. Yes, he had that, and he could read those words. Small as they were, they didn't spin or confuse him.

Downstairs, in another bathroom, he found shaving cream and razors, fat yellow pills and tiny blue ones, a spray to give him the scent of the man who owned this house, that animal scrubbed clean, musk beneath perfume.

Everybody in this family hurt, and Flint Zimmer loved them for their suffering.

Along the stairs, shiny faces behind glass floated free of pain. These people, his people, didn't judge him. Numb and unafraid, they stayed very calm, lips curved into half-smiles, hands folded in their laps forever.

No killers here, no real weapons — only a silver lighter the size and shape of a doll's pistol. Flint took his dirty clothes to the trash and shot them with flames till they sparked the garbage. Far from the house, he turned to see the oily swirl of his black smoke rising.

The fourth day there was a dust of snow on the ground and he was home, watching Cecile, watching Mother. The idiot dog howled. He slept in the Mercury, Mother's car, the one he'd learned to drive, the one Caleb had bought her. He smelled whiskey and mouthwash, moist grass, torn blossoms. The scent of her here made him remember a kiss in the dark, long hair brushing his face, one of those things that must have happened in another lifetime.

He smoked her cigarette butts down to the nubs. Would she feel his imprint? He smoked a joint rolled from the boy's dope, then used Mother's whiskey to swallow one orange pill and two pale blue ones. His sleep was dreamless, safe from memory, no crushed petals falling on his face, no flowery kisses. He lay submerged, beyond thought and feeling, a perfect sleep, like being dead before you were born, like being nothing.

He woke groggy and thirsty, small inside his baggy clothes, shrinking. In the cold, his left wrist ached, joint stiff, those broken bones poorly mended. His body recalled what his brain didn't: a child's history was here if he ever wanted to read it. Today he only wanted the wrist to stop hurting. He tried the boy's pills, emptied two shiny black capsules to snort the white pellets. His nose burned. He tasted blood at the back of his throat, then the drip of bitter fluid.

Lying in the car, he was almost warm, almost hidden. He wanted to stay here all day. She could take him to town, bring him home in the evening. He'd sleep, drowned, unharmed and harmless. But the pills made him jittery. He ran toward the woods, started Dixie yapping. He climbed a tree, fast, straight up the trunk, clinging to fragile branches. He had the hollow bones of a crow. Weightless, he laughed and dangled. He hung upside down from his knees. If he fell, nothing would break him.

When he crashed from the speed, he was too weak to walk. He wanted sugar, Coke and Twinkies, sweet cakes full of cream. Nothing to chew, easy to swallow. He lay curled on the damp ground, shivering, hands pressed between his thighs. Long after dark, he crawled to the car. Locked. So he rolled underneath it.

CHILDREN'S GAMES

They played a game, Mother and Flint. One night she remembered the doors, the next two she didn't. Twice she filled her pint, and twice he drank her whiskey. The blades of the knife were too short to jimmy the door. Mother knew this. He saw himself as a bad dog with muddy paws: *You can't come in here.* He wanted to explain, but words turned to barks and howls, and only Dixie answered.

Today he squatted behind the woodpile to see his sister. She aimed her little gun out windows, upstairs and downstairs, the kitchen, the bedrooms. She aimed at Dixie. *Yes, shoot her.* The dog tugged at her chain, straining to break it. He wished the silver lighter were a real gun. He'd do it himself. Once in the head, painless. Stop that ridiculous yelping. Could he? The thought made his jaw lock, started his left eye twitching.

His sister came outside, wearing yellow boots but no jacket. Why didn't the cold sting her? She pulled the trigger five times, tearing the stump with her bullets. Each burst erupted from Flint's own belly, hard spasms that hurt his lungs and filled his mouth with acid. She reloaded and put a bottle on the stump, walked back twelve paces, then turned like a dancer. No pause to aim, she fired: glass sprayed, a green shower.

⇥11⇤

S N O W

The roads between the Starlite Motel and the house in Creston have turned slick and deadly, but Dexter Bell is a happy
man today, blissfully ignorant, joyfully busy. Last night's storm
dropped six hours of March snow, wet and thick, then hard
and icy. It's Saturday afternoon, just past five, but in every town,
the streetlights have popped on already. Their light diffuses.
Through the yellow haze, Dexter Duane Bell, that resourceful
rescuer in a black tow truck, spots a gold Cadillac teetering at
the edge of the gully. Inside, a white-haired woman grips the
wheel, afraid to move. He has to talk her out. *We're okay,* he
says, *I've got you.* Dexter Duane: a tall man, a man with a good
face, a quiet voice, a soft mouth — a lean, slow-talking man
with flecks of snow in his scruff of beard and mustache. She
trusts him.

He tows her home, though the car is undamaged. She tries
to give him fifty instead of twenty-five, says he's saved two lives
tonight, hers and her husband's. Dexter imagines that old man
inside his warm house, rigid in his bed with bars, gasping. An
efficient nurse clears the tube in his throat or brings his bed-
pan. She wears latex gloves. She is not unkind, but her skin
never touches his skin. With rubbery fingers, she pats his arm.
There now, all finished. The old man needs his wife, somebody
with small, cool hands and a voice he remembers.

Dex won't take the fifty or even twenty-five. *End of the day,*
he says. *Let me do this.*

A virtuous man? *The rescuer lives on grief.* That's what his
mother told him. He'd like to argue with her now: did she
blame doctors for heart failure and lungs full of fluid?

I don't make snow; I don't cause accidents.

Frances says, *We could have used the money.*

She's at the stove, stirring macaroni with double cheese and sausage. His favorite. He thinks of the cash she gave to Flint; they could have used that too, but he doesn't mention it. He's flush tonight, pockets bulging, four hundred and forty dollars richer than he was this morning. He'll make another three hundred by daybreak. He promises Frances a new dress, steak and candlelight, a night out, dancing. *Baby?* She won't answer, won't turn to face him. He runs one finger down her spine, says he'd like to save her when he gets home. *If you'll let me.* Frances says, *Was she pretty?*

Pretty? *Yes.* He hadn't thought of it till now. He could soothe Frances with one word, *old,* but he keeps this secret. Purple coat, white hair — a lady. He keeps remembering her black leather boots, too loose at the top because her legs were so frail. He was staring at her calves when he decided not to take the money. How could he? He wants to tell Frances that the woman almost died today. It's true: five more inches and she would have rolled to the bottom of the gully. He pictures the car, upside down in the snow, engine steaming. Somebody kept her alive tonight; somebody helped him find her.

He doesn't say this. Frances would laugh, scornful, not amused. *So, you're her angel?*

He tries to rock her in his arms, but she won't sway. *Not now, Dex, I'm busy.*

Dexter Bell. A handsome man? She thought so the night she met him. He was shooting pool at the Rainbow. Long arms, big hands — that's what caught her eye: he could wrap himself around her. Some skinny redhead brought him beers, but the look he gave to Frances said, *Say the word and I'll lose her.*

What is it about Frances that makes men want to love her?

She's slender as a girl, sweetly blond, dangerously pale. She brings out the rescuer and the savior. First Caleb, now Dexter, each one vain or innocent enough to think he will be the one to change her. You can't save Frances. She's a motherless child. She has too many secrets. She'll leave you if you're too kind. Dexter Bell must know this already.

He whistles for his girl — Dixie never refuses. She stands on her hind legs, dirty paws on his shoulders. Together they take tiny steps, a stuttery dogman waltz, two loops through the kitchen. She licks his face with her big tongue. *My darling,* he whispers.

What does Frances want?

To erase her life year by year, to fall backward, to become the barefoot child she was, standing on a bright beach, watching her mother swim toward her. She wants to say her sister's name. *Marie? Marie, are you asleep yet?* She wants Marie to hear her. Then they might have another life, and she might bear happier children.

Until time bends, until she finds the tear in the veil and steps through it, whiskey numbs the pain, tequila obliterates memory. I am not making excuses. I am telling you what it means to be Frances. I am reminding you how foolish it is to try to help my sister. I am deaf but not blind. I have known her forever. Still, I remain hopeful as a man, foolish as a lover. I imagine teaching her to sign. I imagine lying on a bed in our father's motel. We are supposed to clean this room, but the day is hot, and we are slow and lazy; we are telling each other stories; we are reinventing our history.

❄12❄
G H O S T   G I R L

Cecile Vaughn watches her image in glass. On this snow-muffled night, the living room reflected in the window floats and drifts, and the child sees a barefoot ghost girl talking to herself with her hands. This is the sign for *snow:* white rain; this is the sign for *spin*. Cars whip out of control. White rain blurs their tracks. While Dexter plows, Mother drinks whiskey and soda; Mother fills Dixie's bowl with beer. *I hate to drink alone,* she says.

Later, Dixie staggers to the living room, nobody's darling now, just her dogself again. She sprawls and tics. In a dog dream, Dixie runs, chasing weasels and rats. Mother slumps at the kitchen table. *Just need to close my eyes,* she says.

Cecile wants to stay awake till Dexter comes home, till everybody lost in the snow has been saved and delivered, carried to his own front steps. Trees waver in the woods, bending beneath heavy limbs. They seem to move toward the house — slowly, slowly — she feels them closing in. They murmur in voices she cannot catch, swirls of wind, frigid breath. They touch her with their cold limbs. *Lie down,* they say. She hears this. They bury her in a white cell, pack the snow tight around her, turn it hard as glass with their spit. Air freezes in her throat, needles of ice sting her chest.

In the morning, she can't remember the face of the man who pulled her through the mouth of the cave as the ceiling collapsed. Daddy? He carried her upstairs to bed. He wore a down vest and a hat with earflaps. She can't recall the smell of him. Bloody apron, wet wool — were his hands clean at last? He unbuttoned her blouse. He rubbed her bare legs. *Like ice,* he said. She remembers his fingers — yes, like Daddy's, thick. He tugged the nightgown over her head, backward and wrong side out, but she didn't tell him.

Warm and half asleep, she feels very small, *hush, little baby,* two, not ten. But her body swells as she wakes till she's huge inside of it.

Now she knows where she is. In a log house across the old steel bridge. On a road that leads to the woods. In Creston, with Frances and Dex. Daddy will never be clean, and Mother will never love him.

So it must have been Dexter who saw her naked, Dexter who touched her body with his big hands, who changed her clothes, who put socks on her cold feet, who pulled the blankets to her chin. Did he blow snow out of her mouth? Fill her lungs with his warm air? This is the sign for *save;* this is the sign for *kiss.* Who can ever say what he did? She was deaf and dumb in the storm, so she had to read his lips: *Shush, just a dream, don't be scared.*

❧ 13 ❧

THE HUNCHBACK

Now this Dexter Bell, this not-father, stands in Cecile's doorway, haloed by the bright light of the hall. *Be a good girl,* he says. *Take care of your mom.*

Four days since the storm, and there's nothing to plow: along the highway, wet snow pocked with black mud melts into rivers of slush. But Dexter's luck holds. Last night his brother Gerry called, said he needed a load of Montana rock delivered to Seattle, wondered if Dex could make the trip, pick up the rock in St. Regis, and help him lay a flagstone floor. *Retired surgeon*, Gerry said, *lived in Montana as a kid, wants to own a piece of it now. Five days, six thousand, how does that sound?*

It's worth ten good snows. Dex won't have to cut trees this spring, won't have to dangle fifty feet above the ground with a chain saw.

Cecile counts: five days in Seattle, one in St. Regis, two on the road. *Be good.* Eight days. She can do what she wants.

She tucks the little revolver inside the pocket of her yellow coat. The hammer's bobbed and won't snag, a smooth glide in and out. All day at school, she imagines the places it might go off: the bathroom, the playground, the bus.

Her teachers have expected this all along. Bad girl, bad blood. Last year, they blamed her for a fire in the trash and a window broken after dark. Did she strike the match? Did she throw the rock? She can't remember, so it doesn't matter anymore. What they believe comes true: she fulfills their hopes.

But the gun stays quiet, inside the closet, inside her coat. At recess, no whooping boys fall from the monkey bars. No pretty girl crumples, suddenly silent in a bathroom stall. Squirming children tempt Cecile on the bus; now and forever she could make them sit still. But this day she spares herself: four stops and a mile from home, Cecile Vaughn slips out.

Twin boys make signs through the back window. They flatten their faces against dirty glass. They open their mouths. Sweet Deirdre Highley, every teacher's pet, flips Cecile off.

In the soggy woods, she hears someone behind her, quick footsteps echoing her own. When she stops, he stops. She shows him the gun. She speaks to the damp air: *Don't come*

too close. He scares her now. Brother, bird, hungry ghost —
his ragged breath hurts her lungs. She runs, faster than he
can run. He stumbles. He falls. The starved child can't chase
her down.

Late afternoon. Cecile builds a lumpy snowman in the yard:
no mouth, no hat, no arms. Light fades fast behind purple
clouds. The snowman drips in the warm wind, too pale to
scare crows.

Mother calls from the Rainbow Bar. She'll be a little late,
she says. *Lock the doors.*

Ten, eleven, twelve.
The house in the distance.
Two windows glow.
The boy who watches from the woods knows his sister is
alone. She aims a flashlight out the kitchen door. With her
bright beam, she blasts the snowman's skull. Her hunchback
shrank till dusk, melting fast, but tonight he's frozen hard.

Lying in her narrow bed, Cecile dreams her brother into the
house. He's a baby's whimper in a tiny room, cries she hears
through two closed doors. Later he's a squirrel trapped in the
wall. Impossible to find. Impossible to pull out. Finally he's
an owl whose wings make no sound. He hears every breath
and scratch: Cecile twitching in her sleep, a mouse tunneling
under snow.

Feathers become fingers.
Wings become arms.
A dirty hand covers her mouth.
Please, he says, *don't yell.*
She nods. Why scream? Who can save her now?

She wakes alone. Mother's car is in the drive. A miracle. Some angel must have steered it home.

Cecile looks for her brother behind the woodpile and under the porch. She smells him in every closet of the house. He molders somewhere: a burlap bag filled with wet feathers and hollow bones. He's scattered himself: peeled off his own skin, plucked his hair, shredded his clothes. A boy like this can't be found. She sees mud tracked up the stairs. Proof. But the only handprints on the wall above her bed are a perfect fit, the exact size and shape of her own. She's looking for a boy lost long ago, the soft one who slept beside her all those nights in all the identical beds of Grandpa's motel, the one whose fingers smelled of chocolate and whose breath smelled of milk.

Not the sour boy he is now. Not the one with matted hair. Not the one whose gritty hand covered her mouth.

That boy finally understands he can't come home. That boy waits for her in the woods after school.

He has a plan.

He needs her help.

⚘14⚘

D R E A M S ,   D E A T H ,   D E S I R E

Children who learn to read their own dreams sometimes save themselves and all their people from destruction.

If my sister Frances would come to our father's house, if she would watch my hands long enough to remember the secret signs between us, I could remind her: the daughters of our grandmother's grandmother have never been so lucky.

There are no wise ones left in the tribe of our family, none alive who will warn Cecile: *The owl who rises from a heap of feathers is your blood, but not your brother.*

That lost boy is gone forever. My sister must understand this as well as I do.

When our mother Rina was a child, she dreamed in the languages of animals: hoots and howls, snorts and clicks. If the buffalo chirps like a cricket, he sees you, beware. Kneel if you want to live, stay still, let him pass. He is twelve feet long, great head to whisk of tail; he might weigh three thousand pounds; he stands six feet high at the shoulder.

Do not be deceived: the buffalo is quick. To keep us safe, our mother taught us.

One night long ago, when I was still a child who listened, Rina and I heard the cry of a moose explode from her chest. She couldn't wait, and her bull on the opposite shore groaned, as if he knew her pain, as if the sound that tore her throat hurt him. He plunged into the cold lake, ready to cross the bay to reach her. With his heavy bones and branching antlers, the bull's long swim at twilight seemed impossible, but the splash of his stroke was his reply, and he came in the near dark, strong with desire. He amazed us. From the edge of the lake, the shivery music of loons offered torment or comfort.

Before our mother spoke the words of men, she was a clever child who trusted the voices of birds and bears. So when the sturgeon sang her underwater name, our Rina gladly followed him.

Frances, a dream can be a vision or a trick.

Once upon a time, there was a father who was not our father. He was Plenty Coups, Aleek-chea-ahoosh, last great chief of the Absarokees, known as Crows to the whiteman. Because the sons and daughters of his wives never lived, he called himself father to all the Children of the Raven. Distant and diluted as we are, I cannot claim him. Look at us: we are white girls without a tribe, children bred pale through a century of forgetting. We are Scottish, Irish, Norwegian, German. That's our father, son of a Presbyterian and a Lutheran. His people were ministers and miners, loggers or soldiers. They came to Montana to find gold, to convert heathens, to fulfill their duties. They slashed forests and burned prairies. They plowed the earth and carved their own country. They killed Indians when they were afraid, when they wanted the land, when they were told to do so.

We are Crow, Cree, French and Chippewa. That's our mother, a child of the wandering Métis, the landless ones in their Red River carts, herded from one side of the border to the other, unwanted in Canada or America, refused refuge on any reservation, driven to the edges of towns where they lived in tents made of rags, where they camped under their carts or dug caves in the hillsides. They took women from every tribe — I mean, some women chose to go with them.

Our grandmother's grandmother was born a Crow and could have been one of the many daughters Plenty Coups adopted. Why did she disappear with the dirty band of mixed-bloods that camped at the edge of her village one summer? Their wooden carts with huge wheels screeched across the plains: you could hear them for miles. These people carried guns and wore the black hats of the whiteman. Ponies and oxen pulled their carts. When they had to cross a river — the Tongue, the Milk, the Musselshell — they removed the wheels and floated. They used their crossbreed dogs, their half-wolves, as pack animals. They strung necklaces of porcupine quills and elk teeth, sewed shells and beads to buckskin vests, but loved most of all their delicate cotton shirts dyed brilliant green or red or violet. They marveled at perfect seams stitched tight by tiny needles. Some tied their hair with white weasel fur, some with satin ribbons. They lived between, neither white nor Indian. In winter, they wrapped themselves in buffalo robes or wool blankets. A few were vain or foolish: they made themselves hats like the French, from beavers and foxes — a luxury, a lie — they were poor as dirt; they were dust blowing.

Nobody fought them because they were everybody's people. But no one trusted them in times of trouble. If you were a Crow, they'd tell you they saw the Sioux camped in your country. But if they met the Flatheads hunting buffalo in the Valley of the Greasy Grass, they'd tell them how to hide from the Absarokees.

Later, there were no buffalo for any hunter to find, so it didn't matter. Later, each tribe was safe on its own reservation, under the benevolent protection of the United States government.

But not our mother's people. They had no land to negotiate. So they kept moving. They scavenged from garbage cans and ate what they found in the dumpsters behind slaughterhouses. They dug turnips and camas roots and potatoes. They plucked corn. They didn't steal: the land was their mother; they gathered what she offered. They snagged trout and pike and salmon. They caught small dogs and rabbits — nestlings, snakes, squirrels. They dried kinnikinnick and smoked it like tobacco. People in towns feared their diseases. Relatives on the reservations had too little food for themselves. They held up open palms and offered the homeless ones nothing.

What did our grandmother's grandmother see in her hungry lover? Was she tempted by his bright blue shirt, or his French accent? Perhaps she only wished to escape the man her father had chosen. Was the girl bound at fifteen to be the third wife of her oldest sister's husband? I cannot tell you. White Deer Sees left no word, no diary, no picture chipped on stone to tell me — only the fact of her choice, the mystery of her rebellion.

She and the Frenchman shared no common language except signs in the dark, mouths on each other's mouths, hands on each other's bodies.

In the morning, the girl called White Deer Sees saw what she wanted and took it. She spoke once, then was silent. Her word was *yes* in every tongue, no need to translate.

So she married Michel Darien, and began to wander. Their fifth child, the third to live, was Antoinette, who married Sebastien Pierce, who was mostly French, but perhaps also English and Assiniboine, a man who belonged nowhere, who could have passed as white but didn't want to.

Our grandmother Leora was their first and only child, born in the winter seven died of influenza, Antoinette among them.

So it was.

So it is, Frances.

The children of our family shall be motherless. Your son is not the first to beg or wander; and though he does not know his people, they speak to him as wind speaks to leaves and blood speaks to body.

When I was a hearing child, Rina recited this prayer, our history, a litany of names, so that someone would know, so that I would repeat them.

Our grandmother Leora lived in the Red River cart with her father Sebastien. Who was more betrayed, the widowed man or the abandoned child? Ask yourself, Frances; ask our father. Leora learned that a pretty girl can scrub her skin and hair with sand and water. A homeless girl can shine if she rubs herself with leaves and grass and flower petals. A pretty girl can wash her clothes with stones at the river, dry them in the sun, then walk to town at dusk and meet a whiteman.

So it happened one night in Helena. The man was Virgil Devere, and Leora found him swallowing both pride and sorrow. That day he'd learned how the dead still touch you: Simson Devere, his good father, had willed the ranch and all his cattle to Virgil's younger brother Edlin. Now Virgil — wayward son, never beloved — owned nothing but a scrap of land on the Flathead Reservation. This father sent his curse from the grave; he let the ground speak for him. Simson Devere must have bought these acres from a starving Indian, must have traded cows and whiskey, persuaded the hungry man to numb his pain while he signed away his children's future. The meat the whiteman offered lasted a single winter.

Was this plot of earth a gift to Virgil? One last chance, or one last lesson? Either way, the scorned son meant to have his hill and make the best of it.

Leora, in her clean clothes, in her shining skin, saw that she could marry the whiteman without living in his country. A private joke. She would hold one corner of a reservation at last, though every tribe had refused her people.

Frances, those who lose their history must re-create it.

⟨ I move through time; I watch the water. ⟩

Today, sun slanted through high clouds and the surface glittered, silvery gold, bright and false as mica.

Later it turned hard and green, chopped by waves, a lake of stone breaking.

At sunset, the lake grew still, and our father paced the high, narrow deck along the roof. He leaned far over the railing to stare toward the Island of Wild Horses. After all these years, I do not know what he hoped to see there. Were the ghosts of the Salish still swimming their horses to that island, still hoping to hide the animals from Blackfeet raiders? Was our mother swimming too, unnoticed by the warriors, strong as the ponies? I saw nothing, no wave rising in the arch of a horse's back, no froth becoming mane, no curve of a woman's body. The water lay blue and flat, reflecting nothing but the clear, dark sky above it.

Does our father know our mother's history? Did she confess to him, or to me only? If her life was our secret, passed woman to child, Rina had no idea how long this daughter could keep her silence. Imagine our father's confusion. To be saved, we must give up all our secrets. How could he know his young wife if Leora's story was a tale Rina never revealed?

In our grandmother's body, enemies met; in her veins, the blood of betrayers swirled.

Leora Pierce married Virgil Devere and anointed herself with the whiteman's holy water. She drank it from a tin cup. She drank it straight from the bottle. It burned the throat but warmed the belly. It engorged the liver. This holy water hardened each cell until her thin body flooded with its own poison. In the cage of her ribs, the spirit broke open; and with each breath, she felt it leave her.

Frances, if our grandmother's grandmother had stayed on her own reservation, the good chief Plenty Coups might have loved her as a man loves his own child. Once upon a time he must have touched her head to give his blessing. Was it his fault she turned away? No, of course not. Like all the women in our family, this girl couldn't endure too much kindness.

Long before he was the leader of his people, even Plenty Coups was a child, a boy who chased yellow butterflies to learn how to run fast and far as a warrior. When he caught one at last, Grandfather whispered: *Rub its wings over your heart, and ask the butterflies to lend you grace and swiftness.*

He swam in every season, willed himself strong, then dove into rushing rivers where ice still floated. He ate from the raw heart of a bear, so that when he said, *I have the heart of a grizzly,* he would not be lying. This child didn't understand the purpose of deception: a man alone is himself only; courage comes in the act itself, not through the telling.

He struck and dodged a charging buffalo. And yes, it was true: the calm, strong heart of the grizzly beat slowly inside him.

He was just nine when the Sioux killed his brother on the Powder River. He became a man that day. A child's heart fell to the ground and stayed there forever.

He would not speak his brother's name. The names of the dead are sacred, and only the Father, Ah-badt-dadt-deah, shall say them.

Before Plenty Coups turned ten, he walked himself weak in the Crazy Mountains and dreamed a dream to save his people. For three days he climbed alone, neither eating nor drinking. His tongue swelled, so dry and thick he wished to cut it out of his mouth, but no Person came, no Helper offered a vision. In the cold, pink light of morning, the weary boy carved off the first finger of his left hand, then beat it against a log to start the blood flowing.

He staggered, thoughts howling inside him, each breath a roar, each pulse a torrent. At last the vision came: Plenty Coups saw a Buffalo-bull change to a Man-person wearing a buffalo robe. He followed this one down a hole in the ground where buffalo stood *without number.* They pressed close, huge and hot, hair prickly with burrs, smell of musk so strong he thought it was the scent of his own body forever. They pawed the earth with sharp hooves. They chirped and snorted.

Be not afraid, the Man-person said, and the boy who was afraid walked naked among them.

When they climbed out of the hole, into the sun, the buffalo followed, so many the plains turned dark *in every direction.* Still they thundered — cows, calves, bulls — as if the hole had no bottom. But the child blinked once, and they vanished. Gone, every one — the countless buffalo became ghosts of themselves in an instant.

Look again, the Man-person told him. Now a new kind of creature leaped from the hole. These were small and spotted, no two the same color — they were black with white faces or brown with pale speckles. They were the color of bleached skulls, and through their pale hair, Plenty Coups saw every bone of their bodies. They came from another world, from the future, from the whiteman.

Later, the boy stood alone in a thick forest and felt the Four Winds gather their strength to blow as one. The dark sky swirled, violent green, then orange and yellow. Plenty Coups pitied the trees as they snapped and twisted. When he smelled their torn bark and thick sap, he knew how they suffered.

The Four Winds left only one tree standing. In its branches was the lodge of the Chickadee, a tiny bird, strong in its mind but not in its body. He lived because he listened. When others spoke, he stayed silent. When others fought, he kept his own counsel.

The child could not imagine the power of his own vision, but when the Wise Ones heard what Plenty Coups had seen in the Crazy Mountains, they knew that the boy's dream was a great one.

Yellow Bear, wisest of them all, said, *Plenty Coups will live to see a day when the buffalo disappear from this earth. The whiteman and his spotted animals will hold our country. Plenty Coups must listen as the Chickadee listens. He must learn from the mistakes of others. Tribes who fight the soldiers will perish. All who resist will fall before the Four Winds, broken. The Chickadee alone shall survive because he makes peace with the ones who cannot be stopped, who are too many and too greedy, who hatch like giant birds in the east and flock toward us, who eat the fat, who sit on the water, who desire the land in a way that destroys it.*

So it was, Frances.

The people of Plenty Coups knew that this vision was the dream by which they must travel. They would point their guns with the whiteman. This did not hurt their hearts. The Sioux, the Cheyennes, the Bloods, the Piegans — the Arapahos, the Blackfeet, the Flatheads — all these tribes were their enemies, all these people wanted to steal their beautiful country. When the whiteman came with his promise of protection, the Absarokees wished to believe him.

And some of us died, and we lost many horses.

They lost the Absaroka Mountains, the Beartooth Plateau, the Upper Yellowstone River Valley. But the land they did keep — the Pryor Mountains, the Castle Rocks, the Valley of the Greasy Grass — this land was their own, and they loved it. When the buffalo died, they learned to plant corn and raise cattle. Plenty Coups who had chased butterflies, who had eaten the heart of a grizzly, who had cut off his own finger, who had scalped many Sioux and swum many rivers, became a statesman, a leader the whiteman could trust, a proper gentleman who would one day lay a wreath at the Tomb of the

Unknown Soldier, who would be proud of all the Indians who fought in the Great War, the First World War, before anyone knew there would be a second one.

This Plenty Coups, who was once Aleek-chea-ahoosh, was baptized Catholic and given the name Max on the same day his adopted daughter was given the name Mary. He built a two-story house with sharp corners. His adopted children memorized the Lord's Prayer in Crow and English. But the great chief whose dream had saved his people refused forever to speak of his own life after the death of the buffalo.

He told the sign-talker, the friend who would one day write his story: *You know that life as well as I do. It is not mine. When the buffalo vanished, the hearts of my people fell to the ground, and they could not lift them up again. After this, nothing happened.*

Frances, even those who dream the future cannot change it.

❊15❊

BIRDSONGS

In summer, chickadees land in my father's palms. I am telling you the truth. He is not a man with visions, but he can sit this still; he can be this patient.

Chickadees sing their own names. Warblers trill in two phrases. Nuthatches toot like tin horns while the red-eyed vireo asks and answers his own questions.

I try to remember these songs, but I was foolish as a girl and did not always listen. What child has the wisdom or courage to imagine her own losses? I recall the squeal of gulls, their shuddering cries, but the sweet call of the meadowlark, a gurgle of breath becoming the music of a flute in the distance, is one more voice I've forgotten.

In another life, a girl and her mother heard a noisy jay stop its squawking to mimic the tremolo of a loon at twilight. Did he wish to fool us, or was he having a dream of becoming?

When my father speaks the chickadee's name, his lips flutter in a language I cannot read, and I turn away so unremembered music will not hurt me. Yes, Marie Zimmer was once a child who lived in a world of separate sounds: walking in a field one cool morning, I heard the first, long note of the thrush, a cry too beautiful to bear, and I thought if I broke the bars of my ribs, I would find the bird singing inside me.

Silence might be a blessing now, but even my deafness is imperfect: trucks rumble down the highway while airplanes roar in circles. The television is a shuddering box, bombarding me with senseless noise. I despise it.

Sometimes when my father is not home, I bang the keys of the piano he gave me. My fingers are fast to find a single rippling pattern. I quiver like the wires struck, and my body rings, but vibrations through bone are the cries of broken birds who make no music.

⊰16⊱

Sturgeons: Use steamboats. Imagine these lakes and rivers are bottomless. Trawl for the great fish in numbers beyond counting. Smoke their flesh. You and your passengers will find it delightful. Feast on their salty eggs. Use the fat of the fish to fuel your engines. Catch, eat, render — what could be more efficient?

Songbirds: Slash forests, pave highways, build railroads. Expand suburbs. Create the perfect environment for usurpers and vagabonds. Give the cowbirds plenty of space to rove and feed; leave them just enough woodland for breeding. Watch them lay their big eggs in the nests of warblers and vireos. Close your eyes. Count to ten. Finished.

Wolves: Use aircraft to spot them. Hunt them with dogs, their own cousins. Set steel traps, even where these are illegal. Use high-powered rifles with scopes. Follow their movement with heat sensors. Poison the carcass of a deer and leave it in the snow when the winter is hard and the wolves hungry. Lure a nursing female from her den. Shoot her. Crawl down the burrow to find her young. Be quick. The other wolves are hunting and might return soon. Do not be afraid of the pups. They are blind and toothless. You could keep one alive with half a pint of milk a day. Don't do this. Put all five in a burlap bag, twist it tight at the top, sling it over your shoulder. These wolves are not heavy yet, only seven pounds between them.

When you reach the bridge, drop three large stones into the

bag. Do not be distracted by cries or whimpers. Knot the bag tightly; use a rope if necessary.

As you walk to the center of the bridge, take time to enjoy the view. Imagine the long plunge to swirling water.

Heave the bag over the side.

Drop it.

Variations: If you suspect wolves have killed your livestock, you may prefer more intimate methods. Take the bag to the river's edge. Some find comfort or satisfaction drowning the pups one at a time. You may wish to feel them struggle.

If you live in Montana, if you are a stockman obsessed with the idea that the wolf, that wily thief, takes money from your pocket, you are invited to resort to extreme measures: the state veterinarian will inoculate any wolf you capture with sarcoptic mange. Give him your tired, your poor, your famished wolves, your trap-torn cripples. He will provide the needle full of mange, and his infected wolves will carry new death to all their brothers and sisters.

Advice: Do not be deterred by the knowledge that your precious cow died from disease, that the three wolves you saw at twilight were scavengers, not killers. Do not consider the likely possibility that your sheep was pulled down and gutted by your neighbor's sleek black Labradors, those skillful hunters with strong jaws and powerful haunches. Ignore any blood you see tracked through the house by your own Irish setter.

Remember: The wolf is dangerous. He leaps into your dreams. He steals your children. He disguises himself as your grandmother. Trust me. Your actions are necessary. Small and helpless as the pups are, your rage and your fear are justified.

⁂ 17 ⁑

BLIND FISH

My father says nobody whose word can be trusted has pulled a sturgeon from this lake since 1927, but divers searching for drowned children and drowned mothers swear they've seen fish bigger than themselves hiding in the lake's deepest trenches.

A freshwater sturgeon can grow twelve feet long. One old fish with barbels that look like whiskers might live a hundred years if no hungry human hooks or spears her.

They resist change.

Their Jurassic ancestors would find them sweetly familiar, still recognizable, though there are a hundred fifty million years between them.

They resemble sharks, or mermaids, or monsters.

Their snouts are flat, their skulls bony. Swim bladders in their guts allow them to breathe air for several hours. Long enough to roll in the shallows and spawn over rocks. Long enough to flop on the beach while they wait for the fisherman with a club to kill them. In courtship, they tumble and leap near the bottom. Or so we are told. What human has ever seen this?

They are loved for their delicate flesh and even more loved for their delicate caviar. You can kill the female and eat all of her, or you can catch her to strip the eggs, and this is said to be more merciful.

They are bottom feeders but not scavengers. This distinction is important. With their barbels they search the sediment for living prey: insect larvae, snails, worms, crayfish.

They are not vicious.

Big as they are, they won't attack you.

Hours after it is caught, a half-frozen, fifteen-inch pike can bite hard enough to draw blood as you try to gut it. But a sturgeon will look at you with its sad eyes as if to say, *I'm older than your grandmother. What are you doing?*

They are not blind after all; they see you. When they surface to feed in the shoals, their vision miraculously returns to them. Amazed, they understand that loss of sense is a choice of environment, a fact in the lake's treacherous canyons, but not, in the end, irreversible. Seeing you, they are not grateful for sight. They think, *We did not miss much.*

Don't be deceived by the scales. A sturgeon is soft inside, and delicious.

Some claim there are monsters in this lake. They have pictures to prove it. But the pictures are always grainy, out of focus, so the monster might be a log tossed by a wave, a trick of light, a sturgeon breaching.

The monster might be your own memory, wild horses, your mother who can breathe air but who doesn't want to, who goes down instead, who seeks the deepest trench, the one unmeasured, carved by the glacier that dug this lake, then melted to fill it.

If you fall in the water, you're safe where it's white. That's the foam, near the surface. Where it's green, you have hope. Swim toward the light. Keep your faith. Imagine all the people on shore who still love you. If it's black and you're blind, you can lose your direction, make mistakes or grow weary. That far down, the weight of water is oppressive, which is why, I suppose, the sturgeon's scales are hard as enamel, why its body is flat and has five bony ridges, why it rises out of the lake to swim miles upstream where it spawns in the dangerous river.

⚹ 18 ⚹

THE LAKE

This is the lake: twenty-eight miles long, fifteen miles wide, Blue Bay to Elmo. When my mother swam away, I learned its greatest depths: four hundred feet in the jagged trenches where sturgeons open their eyes but can't use them.

My sister's children don't need to know their grandmother to feel her cold pull. Rina has ice instead of bones. Rina melts every time we try to save her.

When Flint said, *I have a plan; I need your help,* how did Cecile answer? When he said, *the lake,* did he hear his grandmother call him?

Imagine driving.

The east shore. A dangerous road in any season.

Narrow, winding.

Watch for falling rock. Watch for ice as late as April. Keep both hands on the wheel when truckers hauling logs roar past you.

Think of rain.

So hard the highway flows, looks molten.

Only four-thirty, but clouds are low; it's dark already.

I'm following the children — not on the road, not today, but in my mind, in the future, in a story I tell, though I do not speak and nobody listens. I have no choice. But you don't have to watch. You can go home and lock your doors any time the scenes I sign scare you.

Cecile's the bait: frail girl in a blue dress — I see her. Flint hides in the woods. He keeps his sister's yellow coat tucked inside his own jacket. Easier to catch you, my dear, if the little one waits, bare-armed and shivering. She's been standing in the icy rain almost half an hour. She doesn't care who stops now. Killer or savior, you could be either one — old man with a fondness for little girls, jittery boy, gentle nun.

She's not sentimental. She'll take what you've got: wedding ring and stethoscope — hunting knife, silver cross.

Doctor Nathan Dees, a kind old man, a good samaritan. It's his business to help children. With scrubbed fingers he probes for dangerous swellings: tender glands or internal bleeding, an appendix about to burst and flood a tiny body with poison.

When he sees the girl, she blurs, his sister's watery ghost come back to haunt him.

Good Doctor Dees, deaf in one ear. I know him. Once he touched my face with his clean hands. He said, *Marie, can you hear me?* Perhaps he thinks of himself as fit, but in truth he's brittle. Skin dry, bones porous. Still the best pediatrician within a hundred miles. So people say. So he believes when his dead mother stops muttering.

This morning he soothed the fevered daughter of a woman he delivered thirty-seven years ago. Before noon, he stitched a screaming boy's split forehead. Nineteen stitches in all, but by the fourth one, the child was quiet, mesmerized by the doctor's pale fingers moving above him. Strange blessing. He was a priest with a needle, and the child surrendered. When the mother said, *How did you do that?*, Doctor Dees couldn't hear her question. His eye was on the wound. It delighted him every time he did this — he could tape or sew or even glue the skin, and the cut would close because the body wants to heal. He whispered to the boy; he said, *You're a brave one.*

—— ≡✦≡ ——

He's almost home now, to that house on the lake where a log fire flares and crackles. It's warm inside those rooms and quiet. A motherless girl might dream a house full of flickering light and muffled music. On the table: crystal goblets, silver candlesticks, ceramic plates made by a potter in Whitefish.

Imagine the wife who waits: slim and elegant, devoted to her husband. She glides through the kitchen. How can any living creature be this graceful? Her coral lipstick matches her coral blouse. There are spaces in this house, and lost children might fill them. There's a room upstairs, a small bed never used, a door Jeannette Dees no longer opens.

She chooses wine, Pinot Noir. She has two tenderloins in the refrigerator. She'll mash potatoes with a hint of nutmeg, sauté yellow squash, steam fresh broccoli.

The doctor slows down when he sees the girl on the road, though at first he does not trust his vision. He's afraid he's conjured her, pulled her from the lake with guilt and memory.

Long ago, his mother told him: *One always dies, no matter what you do to save her.*

He keeps a black bag in the car — for emergencies. For any friend or stranger who might need him. Last August he saved Willard Kemp at a picnic, gave him a shot of epinephrine when his throat started to swell from a bee sting. A simple cure, really, but it kept the man's windpipe from closing. Three months later, Will Kemp keeled over in his garage, dead at fifty-two from a heart attack. Miracles are temporary. Hearts stop; doctors fail. One child survives an hour in an icy river; one dies in three minutes. Who can explain this mystery to their mother?

Nathan Dees has never found an answer to the most important question: why he lived, why his sister didn't.

The good doctor has been driving toward Cecile Vaughn his entire life. They share a history of drowning. Her grandmother has brought her to this road. His sister has burdened him with sympathy.

The girl in blue is delicate, standing there like a little woman, one hand on her hip, impatient. Even as he stops, he thinks she might vanish in the sudden glare of headlights. But she's solid. The rain strikes her skin and does not pass through her.

When she tugs the door, the lock jams, and Doctor Dees has to reach across the seat to jiggle the handle. He's slow, stiff from driving. He has time to see her face, wild in the rain, a shiny animal. He has time to change his mind, time to heed some distant warning: his mother's complaints or his dead sister's murmur.

But he wants this girl, her strange company. A real voice in his good ear will make the others quit pestering.

The lock gives. He's got it. She jumps in the car, slams the door quickly. A rush of cold air swirls around her; she drips mud and water. Stains the leather seat. Stains the carpet. Not the tender child he imagined. She swears. *Fuck this.* The only words he'll remember.

She leans across his lap, wet and writhing. She tries to unlock his door, but her fingers are cold. Like him, she's clumsy. Too late he understands: she's not alone; there's another one out there. That one is furious. He moves like black rain, a dark place glittering across headlights. He pounds on the window with one fist. He waves a crowbar. Doctor Dees thinks, *Shift and hit the gas,* but the message ticking in his brain doesn't move his muscles.

The boy swings, howling in pantomime. The first blow cracks the window; the second caves it. Through a web of spidery lines, the child and the man see each other broken.

Doctor Dees raises his hands, a silent plea.

The boy steps back — not to retreat, but to regain his balance. He whirls, a full spin, gets every pound of his skinny self behind the crowbar.

Shards spray, glass and rain, a brilliant explosion.

Fragments pierce the doctor's cheek and arm. Somebody whimpers in his own voice, and he's ashamed, but can't stop it.

Then the wet girl has her cold hands inside his shirt, in his pockets, down his socks. She licks his finger to slip his wedding band off. She takes bills and coins, throws his wallet on the floor. The other one unzips the black bag, finds gauze and alcohol, Digoxin, Benadryl, Trilafon, syringes and tourniquets, forceps, scissors, Pitocin. What good are these things? The names on the little bottles are mysterious. He wants something to kill the pain. Demerol. At last, a word he knows. He takes this bottle and the stethoscope.

4:33.
The green numbers of the clock glow.
They're gone. It's done.

The doctor sits by the side of the road, trying to dig splinters of glass from his face and arm. But his hands shake, and the blood flows. He can't see anything now. He thinks, *I need the blanket from the trunk; I'm going into shock.* He wants to wash his wounds, bandage himself, but even the black bag on the back seat is too far.

He'll be rescued, of course. Someone will spot the car, call the Highway Patrol. The headline will say: LOCAL DOCTOR TERRORIZED ON LAKE ROAD. These are his last thoughts, slipping down.

——　══◆══　——

He's right. By six-fifteen he's in the hospital in Kalispell, listening to his wife say, *Please go. My husband can't tell you anything else.* She's whispering to a sheriff's deputy at the door. Doctor Dees sees the cloud of her light hair, her perfect coral lips, her perfect silk blouse. He thinks of her lovely dinner. Perfectly ruined, no doubt.

The old man is a bad witness.
The girl's dress was blue.
Maybe her hair was blond.
She was wet and cold.
Fuck this.
The other one must have been a boy. Or a slender man. Or a woman in a man's clothes.
He remembers this one's voice. *Like someone under water trying to talk.*

Days from now, when the children are caught, Nathan Dees will learn that his attacker, the girl who molested him, whose fingers he feels around his ankles even now, this girl, Cecile Vaughn, age ten, stands four foot seven, weighs fifty-eight pounds.

Flint's victim or accomplice?
Nobody knows.

They lie in a junked car, pink and rust, no tires, one door; it's been a target for decades, is riddled with holes. Flint remembered the steep path through the woods. With the narrow beam of the trucker's flashlight, he found the ruts of an old logging road. They heard the creek beside them, rushing fast with melted snow.

Rain beats the roof. Flint holds the flashlight in his mouth and uses his tiny knife to dig slivers of glass from Cecile's cheek and palm. She doesn't cry; it wouldn't help. She spits out the window, but still tastes the man robbed hours ago, salt and sweat, the sting of antiseptic under gold. She coughs, feeling again that long finger down her throat. The wedding ring on her thumb is loose, a wide band — worth something, she hopes.

When the battery fades, darkness is complete and full of sound. Cecile hears rain in the trees and rain on the roof. Flint listens through the stethoscope. His lungs roar; his heart implodes.

As the crow flies, the children are twenty-two miles from their mother's house. Cecile slaps her legs to keep them warm. She wears her yellow jacket now, but it's wet inside and out. They should have taken the doctor's coat, waterproof, lined with wool. Flint holds her close, says he can feel her heart beat, twice as fast as his own. He's crashing, coming off the speed he ate hours ago. Muscles cramp in his calves and arms. He dropped the Demerol somewhere on the road. If he had those pills, he could stop everything else: hunger, thirst, love, remorse. Staying awake takes all his will. She wants to sleep too, but he says, *No.* He's seen this before. One night a boy at the Landers School climbed through coils of razor wire and wasn't sliced apart. He slipped his own skin and left no scent for dogs. The next day the other boys told stories of the ghost soldiers who would return to show them how. But at dusk three guards carried the boy back in a tarp. In this way the others learned that a thin child damp with sweat could freeze to death on a mild night in June.

They have to walk. Flint promises they'll find Grandpa's motel. Down the hill, to the water, not that far.

Listen, he says, *waves, the shore.*

Who else can she trust in these woods? The huntsman, the wolf? Her small self? She thinks of the plan gone wrong, the new car Flint imagined he would be driving south by now. She was supposed to be the bait, then go home. *Distract the driver,* he said, *and run.* Did he really intend to let her go? A lousy plan. Stupid to break a window if you want the car. She understands that her brother has no skills, only words, instructions from braggers and liars, bad boys like himself.

A fourteen year old at Landers showed him how to jack a car. Dale Geyde was shorter than Flint, but stocky and strong. He danced his crime in jumps and jerks. He whooped. Dale Geyde did a high kick, said, *Get the fuck out.* He pulled a terrified woman from her car. *Scared of me,* he said. He was so proud.

This little car thief drove three hundred and seven miles before the gas ran low. He forgot to play that scene, forgot to mime the part where the car sputtered and sirens howled. He sprinted across a field, but two patrolmen ran him down. One leaped; they all fell.

Each man outweighed the child by almost a hundred pounds.

Nobody ever asked Dale Geyde why every finger of his right hand was broken. The use of the men's boots to subdue the thief was justifiable force. Dale Geyde was the one presumed armed; he was the one who was dangerous.

Cecile feels for the ring, but it's gone. The stethoscope is in the woods, left behind in the pink car. They have nothing to show. No reward, no proof. Seventeen dollars in cash, that's all. They could have stolen more from Mother's purse. They could have stayed home.

The lake at last, a black hole.
If there were stars tonight, this is where they'd fall.

Grandpa's motel is another mile and a half down the road. She squats to rest, but Flint whispers, *We're close.*

The parking lot is empty. The sign says: CLOSED TILL APRIL 1ST. A string of lights through trees shows the way from the motel to Grandpa's house. Inside, every room is dark. But that doesn't mean Grandpa isn't awake, pacing the hall. Cecile's afraid he'll hear them scuttle, the way he hears rats under the porch. She knows his rule: *Shoot to kill.* A wounded animal is dangerous, no matter how small. Grandpa should know. Once a squirrel with a broken spine bit him four times. When the old man was a child, he learned his lesson well.

She's seen him shoot cowbirds from the trees. Five rats in five days, under the porch. A sick red fox, foaming at the mouth. Unlike Dexter, Grandpa is a deadeye shot. He has strong fingers and thick palms. Grandpa could snap her ribs, one by one, break her, *yes,* to touch the inside part. The night Flint burned the boat, she saw Grandpa lift her brother with one hand and slam him to the wall. He raised his fist but didn't strike. Grandpa must have scared himself. He dropped the boy and walked away. Was this worse? Grandpa who loved them left Flint crumpled on the floor.

Sometimes she's afraid of Aunt Marie too. Aunt Marie's body is the place where women drown. Marie's hands say: *water, shimmer, rocks, hot.* If Cecile learns too many words, she'll know.

With two inches of stiff wire and a slim blade, Flint pops the last lock of his grandfather's motel. They don't need light: this is home. When their mother decided she'd rather wash strangers' sheets than scrub Caleb's spattered clothes, they lived in rooms exactly like this one. Except those nights when the motel was full. Those nights they packed their bags and changed the beds and slept on Grandpa's floor.

Mother told Cecile, *Daddy's still your daddy but not my husband anymore.*

They strip in the shower, under the hot flow. Flint washes blood from Cecile's face and hands, then washes himself. When he wrings their clothes, he's amazed by the blue dress, limp, so small, the material worn thin, only this between his little sister and everything else.

He wraps her in two towels. She remembers scratchy cotton, the smell of bleach, chipped tiles, the cold floor. Their fingers read the stubbled plaster of these walls. *Home.* In the kitchenette, they'll find tea and salt, but no food. In the living room, two plaid couches that fold out. In the closet, a pile of blankets, all wool.

They lie naked in one bed. *Waves, stones, rain, blood.* The sounds outside their bodies come inside now. At last, their skin is warm. Pressed against her brother, Cecile can't tell where he begins and she stops. She tries to breathe when he breathes; she tries to slow her heart. He sleeps first, and she wants to be asleep too, beyond all thought, drowned.

My mother swims and drowns and swims and drowns. I do nothing to stop her. These things happen forever. Blistering sun, green waves — she's not tired. She strokes toward the Island of Wild Horses, as if the horses call her. *Rina.* My sister and I gather wishing stones, smooth as eggs, dinosaur birds. Careless girls, we forget to watch. *Mother.* So we'll never know where or when we lose her. Each stone has a band of white, a seam of quartz, but not a place you can break open.

These are my hands, the lines on my palms. The black-haired woman in the carnival tent says broken lines mean bad luck. As if I need her to tell me. She leans close; she speaks slowly. The nuns say Mother is an angel. I dream of her, fins instead of wings: this mother grabs my ankles; this angel drags me to the bottom of the lake, where the temperature is always thirty-four degrees, summer and winter. Her long hair tangles around my throat. She kisses my eyelids. Nobody will find us.

Searchlights swing at dusk. Fools. Our mother who sinks in heaven laughs with her mouth full. Light does not penetrate water. Don't they know this? One by one the men return. But not our father.

The moon reflects: its silvery image shimmers and stretches. This long, bright path could bring my father back to shore where I stand waiting. I cannot call. He cannot see me. He rocks in his wooden boat, still believing Rina might rise up and want him.

❧20❦

The stories our parents tell answer none of our questions. My
father whispered tales of fish that grew older than men. I
didn't believe him! I thought it was a fairy tale, but when my
mother swam in the lake, I was afraid for her, afraid of the
creatures who might call, afraid she might wish to answer.

Mockingbird, our Rina could mimic anybody's language,
song of the loon or the priest's precise Latin. She knew her
catechism in French and English. Sometimes she prayed in
her great-grandmother's tongue, and this prayer was a song,
and it carried her backward. She came to my room late at
night when my father and Frances were sleeping, when I was
still a hearing child, when I was the one she trusted. We were
safe in the dark. Nobody else was listening. Often her hands
were cold from the lake, as if her body had come back to land,
but her spirit hadn't.

She offered instructions. She made me answer her riddles.

What were Custer's real names?

Son-of-the-Morning-Star, Long Hair, Ouchess, Creeping
Panther.

Where did he die?

The Greasy Grass.

Who killed him?

Nobody knows.

What were his last words?

Nobody lived to tell us.

What did he want?

To be the president.

Why did he choose to die?

He was desperate.

Why was he not scalped?

Because his hair was short and so thin on top it was not worth taking.

Why was he not mutilated?

Because his child was Yellow Bird, and the child's mother was Monahseetah, and the other women refused to touch his body.

Why was he not mutilated?

Because he shot himself, and the Indians saw this.

What is truth?

That depends on where you stand, on the bluff or in the river. That depends on what you wear, your wolf's hide, or your sheep's clothing.

Why did Mahwissa puncture his ear with her sewing awl?

Because he ignored the warnings of the chiefs, because he broke his peace with them after he smoked the pipe, because he found their ritual amusing and not binding, because he did not believe the Everywhere Spirit would let them kill him, because Mahwissa, the aunt of Monahseetah, wanted Long Hair, Ouchess, the Creeping Panther, to be able to hear better in the Spirit Land.

What is hope?

Having the right to speak in your own language.

What is grace?

Having somebody else understand you.

What is mercy?

Ceasing to fight when the battle is over.

What happened to the ones who looted the bodies?

They began to covet the things of the whiteman.

What are the unpardonable sins?

To permit anyone to go hungry, to lose one's oldest child in battle, to permit the baby of a dead mother to cry from hunger, to return alone from the war after one's comrades have fallen.

What are the cardinal virtues?

Generosity, bravery, moral integrity, fortitude.

How will we find redemption?

Mourning for our dead enemies.

Brilliant girl, once upon a time my mother had been the darling of the nuns in St. Ignatius, the one child of a hundred with a gift for learning, the one girl quiet and serious enough to follow in their patient footsteps. The good women of St. Ignatius would have been amazed to hear the catechism we recited.

When her teachers praised her, she never bragged, never said, *I'm going to college.* This secret was too strange and too valuable. Nobody she knew had ever done it. When the nuns whispered that she was the smartest student they'd ever taught, they didn't add the words *female* or *Indian.* They didn't qualify her intelligence.

She didn't confide in her girlfriends who refused to study, who were not as clever as she was. She didn't tell Baptiste Thomas, who was Baptiste Little Knife, the boy who made love to her in the grass by the river.

They would laugh; they would taunt her. *Junkman's daughter.*

So she must have been surprised by the trap of her life, how quick it was, how soft and painless.

Frances, the dead long to move in the air between us. I can teach you to sign. I can tell you our story.

One summer day, our seventeen-year-old mother hitched toward Kalispell. She meant to get a real job in a real town, save her money for college in Portland or Seattle or Missoula. An Indian woman got her as far as Ronan, where Rina started walking. Two miles up the road, a trucker stopped. He could take her all the way, he said, but she never made it. She saw our father's sign at the motel: MAID WANTED. She told the driver, *This is it; this is where I'm going.*

She was pregnant by October.

Did she love our father?

She married him in March. He was thirty-four and respectable, a whiteman who could support her. She was eighteen now, a reservation girl. Nobody asked about love. Nobody asked Rina Devere if she was happy.

I was born in June. I destroyed her.

She worked for our father. She learned that the difference between being a wife and being a maid was that he didn't have to pay her.

She hated the guests. They were loud and dirty. They clogged the sinks and flooded the bathrooms, forgot empty pans on the hot stove in the kitchenette and burned the furniture with their cigarettes. They left heaps of soggy towels for her to wash. She carried me on her hip or on her back while she gathered their soiled laundry. She was not far from the reservation, not far from the clothesline where the ghosts of her five brothers floated. Two years later, she carried you, Frances, the same way she'd carried me. I followed her room to room. Watching our mother work, I came to understand the sorrow at the beginning of my own life.

Did she love us?

She carried us, Frances. She let us follow her.

She had no friends that I remember. She had nothing in

common with people who owned orchards, who played bridge, who gossiped. Floris Beauvil lived next door but never once came to visit. Never once sat in our kitchen.

Floris Beauvil and our mother didn't exchange recipes. They didn't whisper about their husbands and smile, amused as mothers, tolerant.

I'll tell you, Frances, there was silence in our house long before I learned to perfect it.

I do not remember seeing our parents touch, though our existence is proof of something. He watched her. We all did. She was as tall as I am, five foot nine, not delicate. Where I am bone, she was muscle: a swimmer, a woman built for long plunges. She was smooth and dark. She glistened. When she comes to me now, she is always beaded with water.

I am not deaf in my dreams. I hear myself when I say, *Tell me*. I mean, *I am ready*.

But she will not explain. She will not whisper, *An accident, I swear it*.

She wore her black hair in one braid, thick as a tail. It had its own life. It looked dangerous.

I believe she was almost happy in the late afternoons, sundazed, becalmed by water. In that blessed hour, the work in the motel was done for the day, and it was too early to start dinner.

When my fever spiked one summer night, our mother never considered calling a doctor. She never took my temperature. She felt my head and neck with her cool hands. I glowed like embers, soon to be ash, soon to be nothing.

Afterward, Rina believed I could hear what I wanted to hear.

She who had taught me to love words, to recite the catechism, to answer her riddles. She who had whispered night after night, *Stay curious*. She who had learned prayers for the priest. She who could sing a high, mournful chant, the endless story of her wandering people in words that were not words, in sounds without edges. She could not believe the whiteman's God had punished her for her dreams by giving her a deaf child.

At first, I tried to please her. I pretended to hear when I was only reading lips. I remembered the echo of language. When I spoke, anybody could understand me. I read your lips, and hers, and Daddy's. It was enough to have three voices inside me. I was not bad, not stupid. I could read anything on the page. I loved to read. It was silent and secret, mine alone. I was not that damaged. When I read to myself, Mother didn't have to blame herself for what had happened. For the doctor she didn't call while I lay burning. Why would she think to call? No doctor had ever come to her house on the reservation. Children were not rushed to hospitals in the middle of the night. They survived — or they didn't — while mothers and sisters sat beside them. She had no other example.

She thought about this later: what she hadn't done, how she'd failed. My presence was a rebuke. I was constant. She yelled, but I couldn't hear, so she couldn't break me. I forgot how to speak. Vowels had no shape; I lost the cadence of language. I scared children and birds. I mumbled like an idiot. I saw pity on people's faces and read shame in the simple words they used when they spoke at me. They thought I was too ignorant to understand. I stopped speaking because I had to. She who had given me her love of words never forgave me. When she raised her hand, I didn't duck; I let her strike me. Then she was sorry, and she held me too tightly and she rocked me and she was hot and tired and she went swimming and I couldn't go with her because of the fits, because I might drown, so I stood on the dock; I watched her open the dark water with her hands; she swam far away and she swam home and she shook her hair when she stood on the shore and the water flew in bright beads refracting golden light to green and red and blue and violet before they splattered black on the rocks around her. Her wet skin glistened and she shivered, not from cold, but from exaltation.

Did she love us?
She taught me to read.
She taught you to sing.
Sometimes the three of us danced together in one of our father's motel rooms when we were supposed to be cleaning it.

I remember a winter afternoon, Christmas Eve, dark at three-thirty. You were singing, *Silent night, holy night.* Your dress was red, crushed velvet. You had ribbons in your yellow hair, little sister. Rina must have sewn your dress and curled your shiny ringlets. Nobody on earth could have been more beautiful.
Did she love you?
I can't answer; I can't be certain — but I can tell you this: nobody could have loved you more than I did.

I played the piano. I was eight years old. A hearing child. I'd taught myself. By ear. *By ear.* Imagine.

Frances, you were the first to understand, to believe it. Doctor Dees came at last. He and our mother hovered over my bed, asking that stupid question. *Marie, can you hear me?* But you knew already. You didn't wait for me to fail; you didn't wait for them to prove it. You rode away, swift on your blue bike. Like your son years later, you loved the dangerous highway. Seven years old, but you'd been quick to learn and had perfect balance. Cars roared past you and you heard them and you screamed into the wind as they sped by, and you heard yourself and this was your only comfort.

Nobody called your name.

Nobody looked for you.

When you came home after dark, Mother didn't scold because she never knew you were missing. But I knew. You came to my room, Frances, white blouse torn, legs and arms scraped by brambles. Dried blood pearled along a hundred tiny cuts. And this was the beginning, a glimpse of our future. You had learned the first and most valuable lesson of our new lives together: if you ditched your bike by the road, nobody would notice; if you ran down by the river where the rosehip briars grew thick and tangled, nobody would look for you; if the thorns cut your arms and legs, if they snagged your clothes and ripped, if they scratched your face, you could yell into the night and nobody, nobody would hear you.

⚜ 21 ⚜

TESTIMONY

I would like to testify in my sister's defense. She's a bad mother; I don't deny it. The facts are indisputable. Her children run wild. But this is not a court of law. This is a play. The law depends on facts, on the rules of admissible evidence. The play depends on the courage of imagination, mine and yours together. I confess: I am an unreliable witness. I do not hear your questions. I read lips, it's true. But it is more correct to say I read hands and bodies, the wrinkled brow and averted gaze, the lie of your eye's focus. My art is inexact. My father's lips are familiar, his words precise and clear to me, but a stranger's mouth can be inscrutable. Most times I am guessing, reading pause and gesture, pouring my words into your spaces. I lie to tell the truth. Those who turn away from me have no voices.

Still, I believe I know something about motherless girls, black lakes, summer nights, carnivals. My sister and I saw a man chained in a tank of water. He was too white and almost naked. He pleaded to us through the glass. He mouthed the words: *Help me.* We saw a red-haired girl without arms lift a goblet of wine with her toes and drink it down with unbearable dignity. A toothless man ate fire. He had a woman tattooed on his pale chest. He closed his eyes and stroked her. He knew her lines without looking. He said, *She loves me.* Behind one of the tents, the bearded lady nursed her baby. A graceful man with leather gloves walked on his hands. His torso stopped below the ribs, and he used his arms like crutches to propel him. He moved faster than I did. When he stopped to rest on the stump of his body, he pulled off his dirty gloves one finger at a time to reveal the elegant hands of a gentleman.

The fat man couldn't stand up. He lay on a bed in a tent, and we stared through a hole in the canvas.

We saw a miniature woman in a box. LITTLE GLORIA, the sign said. Her husband charged us fifty cents to step behind the curtain. There she was, body and head, stubby arms and legs flapping from her torso. Little Gloria sat on her little chair, watching her little television. She sold us postcards with her picture, a dollar each, and we paid, gladly, penance for the crime of seeing. The postcard said:

HELLO. MY NAME IS GLORIA RHODEN. I AM FROM DRESSIKA, JAMAICA. I AM MARRIED AND HAVE ONE DAUGHTER. MY HUSBAND'S NAME IS SONNY, AND MY DAUGHTER'S NAME IS LYNITH. I AM 29 INCHES TALL AND 49 YEARS OLD. GOD BLESS YOU.

She'd signed the card by hand: *Little Gloria*.

God had sent her from Dressika just to shame us.

In the barn, a dozen shoats tried to suckle their mother. They were quick and pink, and I wanted to free them, now, before they grew fat and tempting, before the farmer could sell them by the pound and make his profit. I heard their squeals. Yes, *heard*, because the high yips of pigs are sounds I remember. Their cries made sense to me. Our losses converged: my past was their future.

While the gypsy read my palm, Frances disappeared in the field with two brothers. I wasn't there, it's true; I didn't see. But she's my sister, and so I can imagine the dry grass scratching her arms and legs, the blue sky going black above us. I feel the miracle: wine turning to blood in the body, a terrible exchange if God isn't with you.

I remember the boys watching my sister. She rode a wooden pony — hours before, when nothing had happened.

I see the horse's carved mouth, hard mane, stiff tail. Frances has chosen the one with wild eyes, glimmers of white showing. Its body is black and shiny, the paint surprisingly smooth, the saddle slick and cool. She rises and falls as the carousel turns. She lets go of the pole to wave at the boys. This wild horse can't bolt away from her.

On the ferris wheel, the younger brother kisses her neck, under her hair, the softest place. Sweet boy, so tender. This one is Clayton. He's fifteen and slender. When the ferris wheel stops, Frances hangs high in the night air. Sorrow is on the ground, beneath her. Lights everywhere twinkle. Red and green, violet and yellow. Up here it's very nice and almost quiet. Little Gloria is far, far away, watching her silent television. The tattooed fire-eater sleeps, passed out under his trailer. The bearded lady buttons her blouse, and all the pigs stop squealing.

Frances pretends the Tilt-A-Whirl is a mad teacup: sounds blur; every noise is her own blood roaring inside her. The spin stretches her face, opens her mouth so wide she can't close it. She's squashed between the boys, and Rudy, who is almost twenty, touches her thigh. An accident? On the roller coaster, she screams. If I'd been there, I would have heard her.

I want to tell you the truth. But the truth is not a house made of words, not a safe place with walls and ceilings. The truth is a wide field and a deep lake. Anybody can die here.

I will not speak, even for my sister. The voice I have left to me would not convince you. Long ago, I spoke out loud in the woods, and the birds flapped away, frantic. I put one hand on my chest to feel the vibrations. I was discord and static.

Perhaps I ask too much, asking you to watch, asking you to learn these signs, shapes vanishing in air, unwritten. Who believes messages in the sand? When they blow away, who remembers? You want the past to be hard and knowable, a fixed place, defined by unyielding words that do not change every time you use them. Sometimes my signs are small, close to my body; sometimes I am almost dancing. I wonder, Does anybody ever understand anybody else's language?

Please define *love*.

Please define *compassion*.

Here is another list: *assault, theft, desire, arson*.

I ask you to withhold judgment.

I remember the doctor, the good one who seemed old even when I was a child. He came to the house too late to help me. He clapped, he spoke, he rang a bell. These sounds hurt in a new way. Mother leaned over the bed. Doctor Dees whispered, *Marie, can you hear me?* I laughed. I knew their game. I said, *Why are you shouting?* The doctor said, *She's reading our lips. She remembers voices.* He told my mother to cover her mouth and speak, but Rina who loved wild horses, who loved cold water, who feared nothing and nobody, our mother Rina wouldn't do this.

MOTHER: FINAL INSTRUCTIONS

Consider the words of Lieutenant General Phil Sheridan: "The only good Indian is a dead Indian." I hear my mother's voice, my mockingbird, my teacher.

You can kill Indians one by one, risk your own life, suffer discomfort. Or, you can wipe them out from a distance. Use your diseases: malaria, measles, influenza, cholera, smallpox, syphilis, tuberculosis.

To speed the process: eliminate the buffalo. Again, Sheridan offers words of inspiration: "Destroy the Indian's commissary, and you will destroy him."

The buffalo is everywhere and everything, sixty million strong from the Atlantic to the Rockies, from dusty Texas to the Great Slave Lake of Canada. He moves as one beast, an impenetrable mass of muscled animal twenty-five miles long and fifty miles wide. He cannot be counted. He cannot be domesticated. The only thing that stops him is the quick rise of the Rocky Mountains. He speaks a language you might understand if you were wise enough and patient. He squeaks, bellows, clicks, hisses — at dawn and dusk you hear him moaning. He has a voice like God's, or a cry like your mother's.

In a silent catechism, my mother asks, *What is your uncle's name?*

Pte, buffalo.

What does he become?

We are good Catholics, Rina and I; we believe in the miracle of transubstantiation.

I say, *His flesh is my body; his skin is my tipi. His hide is my boat, and his dung is my fuel. I worship his head. I sharpen his shoulder blades and swing them like axes. Hooves become glue, bones become needles. His sinew is thread, and his horn is my ladle. With his blood, I am dark: I am painted for battle.*

Rina says, *If he is everything to you, why did you kill him?*

White girl, betraying daughter, I am to blame for this and other crimes against my mother and all her people.

Starvation is slow, but finally effective. I know what Rina wants to say, but she has stopped talking. She mocks me with her final instructions: Give the Indians whiskey to dull the pain. Call yourself merciful. Give them your God and forbid them to dance. If they disobey, if they wear their ghost shirts to Wounded Knee, slaughter them in the snow and leave them to freeze where they've fallen.

For the few who endure, assimilation may prove useful. Send their children to your boarding schools far from the reservations. Burn their filthy clothes. Teach them to love boots that squeak and pants with pockets. Give them your language with hard edges and your wide rooms with sharp corners. Soon they will laugh at the ways of their parents. Change their ridiculous, incomprehensible names to Moses, John, Sheldon, Harvey — to Mary, Elizabeth, Anne, Catherine. Teach them to scrub floors and shuck corn so that they will be useful.

Remember: Leave enough land at each school for a cemetery. These children are dirty. They spread their infections.

When the old ones left behind on the reservations are desperate with grief and hunger, when they weep for the children who have died and for the children who scorn them, offer up your Black Robes who will teach them that the whiteman's

God has strong medicine. If they need proof, remind them of all the diseases your people survived and their people didn't. Those who embrace the Savior will never question his preference.

Erase any pictures you find in the sand. Memory is dangerous.

During times of plenty, the bodies of the dead will fatten the land. During times of drought, farmers and ranchers will be grateful to find all the bones you have left in their fields. The pulverized pelvis of the buffalo will make your fine china, strong buttons, smooth necklaces. The long leg bone of an Indian or his most excellent arm may be carved into the handle of a hunter's knife or a letter opener for a delicate lady. In Dodge City, a single Indian skull brings a dollar and a quarter. Reduced to powder and shaped into elegant combs, the bleached bones of the faithless Indian will last the whiteman almost forever.

Mother whispers, *How can you sleep, my daughters, while the world you know vanishes?*

⊰23⊱

T H E   R A I N B O W

My sister Frances sleeps alone in her cold house in Creston. Even if you gave her a hundred clues and a hundred chances, she would never guess what Flint and Cecile have done, or where they are hiding. She sees no children in a dream, no good doctor, no rain-slick road or motel shower. Last night, she stopped off at the Rainbow. *Just for one.* Maybe she had three or four while Gil Wiley lit her cigarettes and touched her knee under the bar.

What time did she leave?

No later than twelve.

She's lying to herself. She ordered a shot of tequila with a chaser of beer at last call. When she kissed Gil Wiley in his cold truck, his big tongue filled her mouth.

A nice man?

Sure. Most of them are nice enough till you take them home and they're finally yours. But Gil Wiley is Dexter's pal, a decent guy: he didn't push his luck. At three-fifteen he said, *In another life.* They laughed. He let her go.

She should have been home by four, but sometime after five she found herself in the ditch, asleep in her car. She remembers a jolt. She must have dozed. She doesn't say, *accident,* doesn't say, *passed out.* Lucky this time, not hurt, not stuck, but it was almost six when she got to the house. She went to the bathroom first, saw the bruises around her eyes, felt the tender place where her forehead swelled.

She lay in the tub for almost an hour. With each breath, her body rose. So easy to float. She imagined her mother Rina not breathing, choosing instead to go down. How deep was the lake where she stopped? A hundred feet or more. Did she kick and gulp? Did she thrash, unable to cry out? As she sank, did she see her daughters gathering stones? How much water can the lungs hold? If Frances had looked up just once, would Mother have changed her mind and found the strength to kick to shore?

There was no need to swim so far. When you lie on your belly, an inch or two of water will do the job. But Rina wanted to hide herself. For seven days she stayed with the blind fish in the absolute dark.

Frances didn't understand then, but she does now. You can turn over any day, end it all.

She doesn't turn. She gets out, dries herself, wraps her hair in a towel, puts on her robe. Six-forty-five. Cecile should be up for school soon.

At last she climbs the stairs and walks the long hall to the other end of the house where she finds the rumpled bed unmade, but no little girl. Cecile must be in the kitchen, eating cereal and milk.

Stubborn as she is, Frances knows: the hope she holds is false hope. The kitchen's dark. The bowl is in the cupboard, the cereal on the shelf. All the spoons lie curved together like silver fish in the drawer.

The boy is back. Empty bottle, stale smoke — she read his signs days ago, a pattern of warning in his footprints, their future stamped in snow. Last night he took Cecile on some tempting escapade. *To punish me, no doubt.* So whatever happens today will be her fault. She should have called Superintendent Beckett the first morning she smelled Flint in her car. Beckett would have eased her mind. *Some boys need a cell.* Yes, to be contained, to keep themselves whole. *He wants to be caught.* Who will ease her mind now? Whom should she call? The police? Her father? Dexter? Gil? What will she say? *My children, gone.* How will she explain? *A bad mother.* The simple truth. *I had a bad start.*

She wants to talk to Marie, nobody else. She wants to confess to her sister over the phone. *Yes, drunk, of course.* Silent Marie, forgiving as a deaf priest behind a screen in a black box. When nobody hears, the words come out.

Her children are fine, she's sure. Didn't Flint hitch six hundred miles from Landers to Creston? They're stuck somewhere, that's all. The boy knows how to find shelter, break windows, steal food. She pours herself a tall shot. What harm can it do now? She wants to get in the car and find them before dawn, smack their butts, bring them home, make them hot chocolate and toast. She rocks on the couch. It's wrong to sleep, but she can't stop herself: the sofa moves like water and her body floats like wood.

⇥24⇤

IN ANOTHER LIFETIME

Frances, I am afraid. Your children are as motherless as we were. How can we understand their crimes if we fail to imagine Rina who broke the wave and dove deep, who became younger than her daughters forever? When the sturgeon sang, she tried to answer. But her human lungs filled. Her black hair flowed and tangled. In the image of her own death, our mother has remade us.

Frances, all our people will disappear unless we find a common language. Only the stories we tell can save them now. I will teach you my signs. I can read your lips if you'll let me.

Once upon a time, in another life, in a fairy tale, a girl named Rina had five brothers, all younger: Gaylen, Vail, Lamar, Jesse, Jonah. Her father, Virgil Devere, is a whiteman who owns a junkyard just outside Dixon. This is what he's made of the hill his father gave him. When Rina thinks of home, she sees a battered car high on a metal scaffold overlooking the Jocko River. The flying Pontiac Torpedo, once red and now rusted, is her father's advertisement. Virgil Devere can rewire your lamp or fix your radio, patch your tires and change your oil. He'll pound out and repaint that dented fender from the accident you never reported. He has faith in motors: he seems to start your engine just by laying hands on it. When your radiator springs a tiny leak, Virgil Devere will be the man to find it.

He's the junkyard genius.

He doesn't drink like other men. He doesn't smoke or chew tobacco. His voice is soft and rough at the same time, as if words in his throat scratch him.

Imagine he's your neighbor. On the reservation, a neighbor is anybody who lives within forty miles. You're closer than that, just down the road, outside Ravalli. Imagine you're a man his age, not a friend, but an acquaintance. Does Virgil Devere have friends? Not to your knowledge. He came to your house one morning to jump your battery. Six o'clock and still dark, ten below zero. Wind howled; funnels of snow swirled like ghosts around him. Your wife brought him coffee, but refused to invite him into her kitchen. She can't say why. She just doesn't trust the junkman.

This is home. This is Rina's father.

In the shed he keeps saws and hatchets, doorknobs, cracked mirrors, a saber with an ivory handle, a bone cutter to dismember buffalo, three whips to sting your horses, a phonograph that doesn't play, a sewing machine without a treadle. All this he's salvaged from dumps as far north as Eureka.

Last year, he hauled a piano up this hill. Half a century ago, it must have come by train and then by riverboat, Baltimore to Montana. Warped by rain, crushed by snow, the piano was impossible to salvage. Virgil tightened the wires until the only sounds they made were high and tinny. He let the wood dry, then torched it.

Blistering mahogany sparked and crackled. Flames licked between the keys; smoke swirled. Hand-carved legs glowed, red-hot brilliant embers.

The piano blazed half the night, lighting Virgil's hill, visible for miles. Every neighbor came to see. Tonight the junkman would be famous. They came from Dixon, Moiese, Charlo, Ravalli. *Fire.* The word spread to Arlee and Evaro, Ronan and St. Ignatius. Revelers sat on the hoods of cars, drinking malt and whiskey. They brought old grandparents, frenzied dogs, crying babies. The heat of Virgil's piano was insatiable.

Children played a game: Who-can-stand-the-closest?

Strange music, that's what Rina most remembers, each wire popping in its own time, no human hand to control them. Seconds passed between notes, or five flung themselves into the sky together. This is a song that cannot be repeated. This is the Fourth of July on the Flathead Reservation.

In the smoky dawn, bright ember turned to pale ash and crumbled. All the snapping dogs and drunken boys lay silent. When the iron frame wavered and slowly fell, nobody on the reservation was awake to see it.

Home. In a trunk in her father's shed, Rina finds a dark-haired porcelain doll with a cracked skull, and a dimpled Shirley Temple with golden curls and broken fingers. Beneath them, wrapped in a wool blanket, lies an Indian whose eyes are beads, whose face is smoke-tanned buckskin.

Out back: a wood stove and a radiator, five bicycles with only two seats and six tires between them. Windmill, water pump, cuckoo clock, ice box — whatever you need, the junkman's got it. If a house burns in Idaho, Virgil Devere will drive a hundred miles to sift through wreckage.

Home. If you say it, Rina sees a hillside of crumpled metal, pieces of cars and plows and buggies; she sees her father, and later her oldest brothers, Jesse and Jonah, with grease on their hands and in their hair, grease smeared on their shoes and streaked on their coveralls, grease inside their ears, up their nostrils, and under their fingernails. They bring the junkyard home every night. And every night, Rina wants to get away from them.

Our mother who is not our mother yet, who does not know our father, who would never wish or imagine two daughters into being, lives in a little white house with a sagging porch. The roof leaks; wind whistles through the boards around the windows. She can't cover them with plastic, because the only heat comes from a wood stove, and a house too well insulated is dangerous. Last winter, a whole family suffocated in their sleep: mother, father, three daughters, two cats, one dog, and five happy hens that had been brought inside where they might stay warm enough to lay eggs through December. In the morning, all the little girls looked flushed and rosy. The father smiled in his sleep; his wife spooned against him.

So they died, faces finally still, all their dreams finally peaceful.

Rina's father is the junkman. She is the junkman's only daughter. There is not a single moment of her life when she can forget this.

Six days a week, Rina's mother Leora dresses like an Indian, like a whiteman's idea of an Indian, and drives to the Trading Post just north of St. Ignatius where there's a genuine frontier village, where she works for a very white man, Boris Brimm, selling souvenirs to tourists. She sells polished stones and bone buttons, sharp knives in wooden sheaths, tiny medicine bags with no medicine, deerskin pouches for ladies' eyeglasses or gentlemen's tobacco. She sells bows and arrows made by Boy Scouts in Missoula, beaded moccasins sewn by Blackfeet squaws in Browning. Squaws, yes. Genuine leather, genuine bone, genuine Indian.

There's a genuine wolf's hide hanging from the ceiling, its head still attached, so Leora can talk to it.

She sells postcards of all the chiefs and scouts and warriors who no longer care that the picture box might shorten their lives and steal their shadows.

There's Spotted Eagle, the Sans Arc, who escaped to Canada but surrendered in hunger. From his armband, bear claws dangle. What good did these charms do him? In the Grandmother's land, winters turned long and bitter; in the Queen's country, he found neither food nor protection.

Leora holds Red Armed Panther, broad and handsome, hoops in his pierced ear, long hair strung with shells and feathers. Hunter, traitor, warrior, liar — this Cheyenne scout helped General Miles chase the Nez Perce through Montana. No wonder Chief Joseph's heart was sick and sad. Even his allies refused to help him. Charlo the Flathead pointed an empty gun at the ground while Plenty Coups and his Crows pointed their guns with the whiteman.

This mercenary red-sleeved panther could be Leora's father's long-lost cousin. With her mixed blood and her weird luck, Leora never knows where she might meet another cousin.

Red Dog, Red Bird, Red Cloud, Red Leaf. Who can count the dead? Who remembers names like these?

Leora brings home Red Cloud the Oglala chief. Red Cloud

won his war against the United States, but still touched the pen to sign the treaty he couldn't read. Red Cloud traded sacred ground for dirt and coffee, dry riverbeds, white sugar, scraps of meat. Before he died, he asked to be buried in the black robe of a priest. No wonder his face is misaligned; no wonder the right side of the old man twists with grief.

Little Hawk, Little Raven, Little Wound, Little Big Man.

Leora Pierce steals postcards from Boris Brimm and brings them home to teach history to her daughter Rina. Here's Little Wolf before his exile in Oklahoma, before his daring exodus back to Montana, before Starving Elk seduced his wife and Little Wolf had to shoot him. For this crime, the Cheyenne chief was thrown away. Banished. Never again could Little Wolf eat or smoke with his tribesmen. At night he wandered, hooting with the owls and yipping with coyotes. Sometimes Leora thinks she hears her lover calling. The Little Wolf in the photograph is still strong and still determined, but his hands seem small and thin, and Leora wants to hold them.

She imagines White Bird in white doeskin. She heard his story from an old woman who camped with them one summer in a town of tents outside Helena. Her voice withered in the night, and Leora had to lean close to hear her. She felt the woman's breath soft as that white bird against her cheek, but neither she nor the old woman ever saw him. He soared over the Bear Paw Mountains. This birdman took two hundred Nez Perce with him. He left no tracks. *He flew, I tell truth, the soldiers never caught him.*

Chief Joseph stayed behind to find his women and children, the ones who couldn't fly, old men already dead, babies already frozen. He needed to carry the wounded out of the woods. *Because nobody we knew had ever heard of an Indian who recovered in the hands of a whiteman.*

Three hundred and thirty-seven prisoners of war were ferried by flatboat and hauled by wagon train to Fort Lincoln, herded into boxcars bound for the swamps of Leavenworth, and finally delivered to Eeikish Pah, the hot place, where Joseph watched his people sicken and die of heat and hunger and malaria, where the Indians kept a cemetery just for children. Ninety-seven, ninety-eight, ninety-nine. Welcome to Babyland in hell. Within a year, the Nez Perce marked a hundred tiny graves with sticks and sagebrush.

The grainy photographs of Joseph do not expose the bullet holes in his sleeves or leggings; no message on a postcard mentions bullet scratches on his wrists and back and forehead. The man once called Thunder Rolling Down Mountains didn't need a ghost shirt to protect him: when Heinmot Tooyalakekt was captured, he was a ghost of himself already.

Every night, Rina cooks dinner for her brothers and father. She washes their greasy clothes. She washes their greasy dishes. She smells all their boy smells in the close house. She hears the whoops and yelps of the young ones in the yard when they play Cowboys and Indians. They shoot each other with slingshots and arrows. They come home with tiny wounds and she wipes away the blood with alcohol. They fight with their feet and fists before the games start, because the brothers and all their friends want to be Cowboys. And why not? They know their history. For every good day the Indians had, the whiteman took another million acres.

Leora steals a postcard of Comes Out Holy on display at the World's Fair. It's 1904, the Louisiana Purchase Exposition in St. Louis. Comes Out Holy sits astride his pinto pony, wearing a union suit beneath his breechcloth so the clean ladies and pretty little girls won't faint or shriek when they see him.

Leora gives Rina Sitting Bull the sad warrior who nearly starved with Spotted Eagle, Sitting Bull the generous chief who never owned more than twenty horses. At the Trading Post, Leora sells Sitting Bull the red devil, star of Buffalo Bill's Wild West Show, another Indian on tour, another hero in a costume.

Sitting Bull the tamed savage autographs his own pictures for a dollar. He charms women of every color. One pale girl presses a coin into his palm and murmurs. Fluttering lips brush his cheek, and the Indian who claims to speak no English shakes his head and smiles. Another coin, another whisper — he demurs, then acquiesces: that cutthroat Sioux returns the coins and sells his tender kiss for nothing.

No image captures or reveals Sitting Bull the prophet, Sitting Bull before he danced, feet stained red, blue stripes like sky across his shoulders. This Sitting Bull sat very still while his adopted brother used an awl and then a knife to cut fifty pieces of skin from each arm, wrist to shoulder. He prayed and chanted. Later, he dangled. Lariats strung from a pole tugged and tightened till sticks shoved through his chest pulled raw muscle inches outside his body. He danced on tiptoe. He stared at the sun for two days. He never closed his eyes; he never stopped moving. Pain was just an idea, a thing of the world. Sitting Bull let go of it. On the third day, he saw enemy soldiers dropping from their horses, bluecoats falling like grasshoppers, all their heads pointing toward the great Indian Village. A voice from above said: *I give you these because they have no ears.* And it was true: the dead ones would refuse to listen.

Sitting Bull's people left a picture of upside-down soldiers in the sand, and Custer's Crow and Ree scouts found it.

But Leora sells no postcards of this Sitting Bull who foretold victory in the Greasy Grass, who stopped the fight the second day, who spared Major Reno's weary men, who in mercy and in wisdom said, *These soldiers want to live, so let them.*

She finds the Crow scouts: Hairy Moccasin, Curly, Goes Ahead. They led Custer to the kill; they saw the signs; they tried to warn him. White-Man-Runs-Him said, *More Sioux in the village than all your soldiers have bullets.* But the soldier-chief didn't trust him. Custer knew Indians were bad with numbers. Indians believed no honest man needed to count above a thousand. He was afraid the Sioux might slip away, afraid he'd lose his one last chance for glory. Half Yellow Face, Custer's wisest counselor, prepared himself for death and battle. He saw their fate; he said, *You and I are going home today — by a trail that is strange to both of us.*

When Custer died, the Crows like little brothers mourned him.

The wind above the Jocko River blows hard, always. In late fall and winter and early spring, six pairs of pale long johns fill with air on the clothesline. They are bloated boys, gray and headless. Someone has cut off their feet and hands. Retribution? At a trading post in Dodge City, the bones of Indians can be bartered.

Who can blame Rina for needing to escape the dreams she has of her brothers and their terrible bodies? She doesn't want to find their skulls in the field, doesn't want to see the long bones of their arms and legs bleached and polished. She never wants to meet the man who carves Indian relics into the handles of knives. A soldier holds a blade to her throat while his furious children stab her.

Leora doesn't sell Big Foot on a postcard, but he's frozen in her mind, twisted in the snow at Wounded Knee, old man in rags, hands always bare, eyes always open. Ghost dancer, he looks as if he wants to stand, as if the buffalo have come at last, as if he'll rise to meet them.

There is a painting but no photograph of Crazy Horse who resisted the picture box, who clung to his faith until the day he was murdered. He appears just as he painted himself for battle: streak of lightning down his face, spots of ocher hail on his naked body. He was born in the Winter the Oglala Took One Hundred Horses from the Snake, but he died on whiteman's time, September 5, 1877. Little Big Man grabbed his arm; Private William Gentles thrust a bayonet into his belly.

No one ever made a postcard of Crazy Horse's only child: he loved the little girl called They Are Afraid of Her, but she died too soon, age three, of cholera.

Leora wishes she could make a drawing of Finds-Them-and-Kills-Them, the hermaphrodite who usually wore a woman's dress, but who changed to buckskin and breechcloth before riding into battle. At the Rosebud Valley, He-and-She found and saved Bull Snake. Leora calls the hermaphrodite Brother-Sister, Fearless Savior. Under her breath she chants *Finds-Them, Kills-Them* as she sells T-shirts and arrowheads, rabbit skins and eagle feathers.

Leora Pierce never finds the ones called Antoinette and Sebastien. Her mother and father were not pretty or famous enough to be sold on postcards. She traces yellowed photographs in books with crumbling pages. In the picture called *Métis family in a Red River cart*, she looks for her own face but does not see it.

She tries to remember her father's voice, but hears only the screech and squeak of wooden wheels, the yowl and whine of the ungreased axle. Beneath her, something snaps and splinters, the worn wood of that cart always breaking. Once a whiteman appeared in their camp. He had a cart of his own, but his was quiet. This man brought her father a piece of iron to reinforce the axle, strips of metal to rim their wheels. He carried oil to smooth the ride. He laughed; he said, *I don't know how you people stand it.*

In return for these gifts, he wanted the buffalo robe Sebastien Pierce kept hidden beneath a dirty blanket. To Leora's father, the last hide of a soon to be extinct animal seemed more precious than any piece of shiny metal.

He asked the whiteman, *What beast would pull a cart that heavy?*

They'd need two oxen, not one skinny pony.

How would we float the Yellowstone?

A river is a path for the breakable and buoyant, but water is a grave for the solid and sturdy.

Sebastien said, *I can always chop a cottonwood, but if my iron axle breaks, how will I replace it?*

He could steal coins and buy one. Steal hammerheads and melt them. He could pull rails from the iron road. Then this homeless man, this no-name Métis, could hang for his crimes, and leave a dangling image for his daughter.

In dreams, Leora never glimpses her father's face. He's under the cart; he's repairing the axle.

She remembers his wrists, but not his mouth or his eyebrows. He wore bracelets of hair and beads and feathers. Two thin braids. In this way, and in this way only, Leora touched Antoinette, her father's dead wife, her own lost mother.

I see the white house, there in the distance. Look, Frances, how our mother lives with her five brothers and her father the junkman, each child haunted by the ghost of a mother who is not dead, but who is still missing. If you run the film of Rina's life very fast, you can see the paint peeled by ice and wind; you can watch the dry heat of summer scorch and blister it.

There are three bedrooms in this house: one for Virgil and Leora Who-Can't-Be-Trusted; one for Jesse and Jonah; one for Gaylen and Lamar and Vail. There is no room for Rina, the firstborn. She sleeps on the couch. She keeps her clothes in a basket.

I see a rocking horse on springs in the yard. It must be baby Gaylen's. There's a wheelbarrow turned upside down. Three bikes on their sides, one pink, one green, one yellow. The cluster of houses where Rina lives is not a town. It is three streets one way, three streets another. The speed limit for three square blocks is ten miles per hour. Beyond that, drive as fast as you can: nobody will stop you.

Rina sees bikes in every yard: bent, purple, red, rusted. Left on their sides in the dirt, abandoned at every corner. Orange or black, none worth stealing. It looks as if every child has fled in hope or fear, or as if they have been raised up, lifted out of this place in a single moment. But of course they have not been saved. They are at school. In less than an hour, the yellow bus will stop, and the children will emerge, hollering and kicking, free at last, the ritual of capture and escape played out every day on the reservation.

Leora Pierce sells more George Armstrong Custers than all her Indians put together. The boy general of the Civil War was only a lieutenant colonel when he fell for all time at the Little Bighorn. Let the dead bury the dead, she thinks, but this one won't stay under. As a child dressed in velvet, he marched through his father's house carrying a toy musket. He cried, *My voice is for war!* And he's still crying. *Exterminate the savages.* He wants revenge, and he gets it. Show no mercy, make no fine distinctions between allies and enemies. *These hills are full of gold,* he says; *take them.* Even in black and white, he shines: glossy hair, tight body. His languid pose is a lie: inside, he's coiled with energy. *There's grass here for all your cows, and trees for all your houses.* He doesn't need to eat or drink. He rarely sleeps; he's not tired. Pretty boy, tempting soldier. The Cheyenne women found him handsome. They say the one named Monahseetah lay down with him, and her child was Yellow Bird, and this is how the yellow-haired soldier-chief became an Indian in miniature. The cadets at West Point called him Cinnamon or Fanny. He's not just blond — he's strawberry, and the skin of his cheeks is pink and delicate.

Nobody ever made a picture of his mother weeping, of the terrible scenes in her house each time they parted. He followed her from room to room, whispering tender words meant to comfort. Why didn't he learn? His sweet voice made her mad with grief. She swooned; she fainted. Kind servants carried her to bed, while her son, George Armstrong Custer, hero of the Civil War, seeker of gold, hunter of bears, slayer of Indians, stumbled out the door, sobbing.

Who can explain a warrior's weakness?

He loved dogs, but had them shot before battle to keep them quiet.

He loved birds, but killed a white crane to measure its wingspan.

He loved children. A fragile girl at a school for the deaf beguiled him with her graceful gestures. But in the snow at Washita, his soldiers trampled babies' heads and split pregnant Cheyenne women open.

He loved his wife; he made her a wig from his beautiful hair. Even before he died, it burned, and Elizabeth, his *Sunbeam,* his *Sweet Rosebud,* was inconsolable.

Vain, brave, daring — lucky till the day he died but foolish many times before that — he wasted the lives of his men while he emerged with nicks and scratches.

But Leora Pierce can tell you this: the wolves and ravens cared nothing for his beauty. When they dug him from his shallow grave, they tore him apart like all the others.

At the Trading Post, Leora wears a porcupine quill necklace made by an old woman in Heart Butte, three turquoise rings made by Navajos, and a leather vest with glass beads and feathers assembled in Hong Kong. Another joke, on America and all her separate peoples.

Leora's hair is long and coarse, even darker than our mother's. She braids it for the tourists. Not to please, but to mock them.

Some nights she comes home, but most nights she doesn't. She drives to Evaro or Lolo or Hot Springs. Sits in a bar or the hot healing waters. She soaks in the mud bath, a good place to go down, to enter the earth, to become one with it. She sleeps in her truck. *Like an Indian,* Virgil says. He means she is unreliable. He doesn't understand her reasons: buying the whiteman's whiskey is bad enough; buying a bed in his motel is unbearable. She keeps blankets in the truck, her real home, a 1936 Ford with a V-8 engine. Despite his anger, Virgil keeps it humming. It's a junkman's pride that makes him do it. She's comfortable. She likes knowing she can leave any time, that her blue truck — speckled with dust that looks like hail — is not a prison.

Leora refuses to sell Wovoka, the Woodcutter, Jack Wilson, the Paiute Messiah. She hides this ghost dancer behind postcards of the nameless ones: Mandan Woman, Shoshone Family, Flathead Child. But Wovoka comes to her in a dream, big man in a big Stetson. He rises from the dead, just as he promised. The Woodcutter bangs the roof of her truck so hard he dents it. This Messiah throws himself against the cab to rock her. Jack Wilson pounds the hood, and Leora Pierce blasts him with her headlights. In the sudden glare, Wovoka the man becomes an auburn bear and flees into the forest.

He's left a fogged message, a line of breath on her windshield. Apology, defense, poem, proposal? Leora doesn't know: his words disappear before she can read them.

Big Bear, Brave Bear, Falling Bear, Catch-the-Bear.

Don't ask Jack Wilson to name the dead. He's busy hunting rabbits. And yes, he's very sorry about the Sioux, but he didn't expect Kicking Bear to take him quite so literally. He only told his followers to dance, to work in peace with the whiteman. And why not? That's what he did. *My children, be patient.* He didn't really know how long Indians might have to wait for the rewards of the next life. A year, a decade, a century? When he said, *the next time the grass is high,* he was speaking metaphorically.

Delirious in a dream, fevered through the solar eclipse of a New Year's Day, Wovoka the New Messiah saw all the dead buffalo return. They roared; they thundered. They covered the plains, river to mountain. They trampled the whiteman's pitiful cattle. Wovoka saw elk and antelope, wild horses, laughing otters. He met his dead ancestors, and the ancestors said: *We will return if you can wait for us. The blind will see. You will be young forever. When the flood comes, the whiteman will drown while all Indians watch, safe and high in the mountains. Those who believe will live; those who don't will grow little. Some will turn to wood, and some be scorched by fire.*

Wovoka taught his Round Dance to the faithful of every tribe. Gladly, he entertained them. And yes, it's true, this Messiah's ghost shirt could not be burned by gunpowder — but the simple Woodcutter did not expect grieving Minneconjous and flame-scarred Brulés, hungry Hunkpapas and defeated Oglalas to try to walk through a rain of soldiers' bullets. He did not want them to stand in the paths of rapid-fire Hotch-kiss cannons. *Dance*, he whispered, *be happy*. That's all he intended. He never said, *Lie down in the snow*. He never said, *Be slaughtered*.

Mostly he was just a weather prophet who saw rain in days of drought, who made ice hang from cottonwoods in summer. Decades after the dancers died, he told President Wilson he could freeze the Atlantic and walk to Europe, that the Indians would use ice to help their president fight the Germans.

I'll say this for Wovoka and his delusions: when the Seventh Calvary butchered three hundred unarmed Sioux at Wounded Knee, that restless band of drunken soldiers was finally sated.

None of Leora's people died that day. They were far away, wandering town to town in Montana. Still, these ghosts blow around her, and she will not pardon the Woodcutter, though he rises as a bear and begs her forgiveness.

When Leora doesn't come home, Virgil makes jokes about his Indian wife to his half-Indian children. He gives her names: Leora Falls-in-the-Mud, Leora Who-Never-Sleeps-Here. Alone, in his room, he has another name: Leora Pierces-the-White-man. He wants her to sleep in his bed; he wants to feel her skin hot against him. If she finds her way back to Dixon one cold October night, she'll sleep outside, in her sons' tent in the yard, the one facing east, the one shaped like a miniature tipi.

She's safe in the circle, no edges to cut her. She can't sleep in the house with four corners. *Junkyard box, whiteman's coffin.*

What did Virgil expect from a woman born in a hole, a cold cave dug in a hillside? This was his father's final joke: *When I gave you a piece of the reservation, I never said you had to marry an Indian.*

Once he found Leora lying in the snow. She'd made an image of herself as an angel, and now she curled inside it. When she was warm enough to speak, she said, *I am Watkuweis; I have seen a man with pale skin. He was kind to me. He bought me from the Crees who bought me from the Blackfeet who stole me from my mother while my father hunted buffalo. I have been gone a long time. My child is dead. I have returned from a far-away country.*

In the dead heat of a long afternoon, Rina watches the dogs who rule these streets. Their barks sound like laughter. A tiny white one with black spots digs and digs, a hundred holes in the yard to hide all the bones she plans to steal. Small as she is, this dog knows how to knock over garbage cans. She can outrun the bigger dogs and hide every bone if the holes are ready.

A furry black chow that looks like a little bear lumbers down the middle of the deserted street. Three fat dachshunds waddle, dragging their bellies. Rina sees the silver husky with pale blue eyes, the ghost dog that whirls to snow or shatters in a shaft of sunlight. There's the three-legged dog who runs as fast as any other, who can't remember his missing limb or how he lost it. There's a shaggy border collie who loves to work, who goes out to the fields every day to herd the sheep, though they don't belong to her, or to any of the people who feed her scraps from their tables. There's a muddy spaniel chained to the roof of his own house, chained because he'll kill anything he catches: mice, bats, rabbits, dachshunds.

In Rina's yard, there's one last dog. He has a sacred, unspoken name, but he answers to Max, the name Rina's father gave him. This one's head comes almost to her waist. He's pale gray and crippled, hipbones crumbling. He struggles to his feet every morning. He hurts, always. His huge head and humped shoulders remind Rina of a buffalo bull, but he has a mane too, and a long tail with short hair, except at the end, where it's long and silky. The mane is a lion's mane, the tail, a lion's tail. He might be a mythical beast; he might live forever.

But this dog, her dog, eats grass. He grazes — a sick old cow with bony haunches. Tomorrow her father will take the shotgun from the closet, will clean and load it, will go out to the yard and call the dog who trusts and loves the whiteman. Tomorrow Rina will run outside to stand between her father and the dog; and in the end, Rina will take Max to the lake, his favorite place, where the osprey circles high above, where fish jump to tempt him. Here, where water turns pink at sunset, Rina will speak the dog's secret name, and he will answer in a voice that's human. He'll tell her to shoot. *Now, be quick — while I am happy.*

But today, in this moment, the dog is still alive, the bikes lie in the dirt, the playground is deserted. People are home, of course — adults, parents. They don't have jobs. So Rina is better than they are, despite what they think. Her mother works; her father has a business. Plenty of wrecked cars here, and Virgil Devere could fix them. Cars on blocks. Cars without tires sunk in the dirt. Cars without hoods, cars without engines. She sees a black truck that must have rolled, whose cab is smashed down to the level of the dashboard. Did the driver

fly free, drunk and limp as a jumble of rope, did he land un-
hurt and roll or unspool, did he wake, long and straight and
laughing — or did he lose his head, was it crushed into his
shoulders? Rina must know, but there are so many accidents,
so many flying boys, so many headless bags of wind on the
clothesline, that Rina can't remember.

On the bluffs above Ravalli and Dixon and Moiese and
Charlo, dwarf pines cling to the hillsides. The banks of the
Jocko River are lush with birch and poplar, cottonwood and
weeping willow. It is early spring; only the first buds show. The
long, delicate limbs of the willows trail in the water, brilliant
yellow. Here a boy with black hair waits for Rina. It's twilight.
Imagine a blue sky streaked with green. Imagine how the river
reflects it.

Tonight Rina will tell Baptiste Thomas, her first lover, that
she wants one thing: her own life. Tonight, for the first time,
they won't kiss, and the boy will stare at the stream, his face
unreadable as the ripples on the surface, his heart already
gone, tossed out, lying still as stone at the bottom. He will not
cry when she leaves. He already knows that sorrow, like the
wind, is relentless; tonight and forever he will let it blow
through him.

Rina Devere will keep her promise in ways neither she nor
her lover ever dared to imagine.

One day, she was a girl hitching north to freedom who saw
a sign and stopped and married our father. She slept. And in a
dream, her mother died, frozen only ten feet from her own
truck, lost in a blizzard. She wanted to find Leora's imprint
and lie down in it forever, but she woke and it was true: her
mother was dead; Leora Pierce had driven her truck into the

river. Rina's new husband, who wanted to love her, who could never understand what she refused to tell him, held her in her dreams, and she was hot — her skin was on fire — and the air filled with wild music, the popping strings of a burning piano. When Rina Zimmer woke again, she was the mother of two fair-skinned daughters. She found freedom now by swimming hard in cold water.

What I have left is a wooden box full of stolen postcards. I have no images of Leora herself, no photograph of our mother Rina as a girl or as a woman.

Our grandfather Virgil came to Rina's funeral with our uncles Lamar and Vail. I remember the grease under their fingernails and the grease in the lines on their palms. Our grandfather clutched a brown felt hat; his jacket was too small, his boots muddy.

He did not speak to us. He did not touch us. It was the first and last time we met him. I read his lips when he whispered to our father. He said: *She was always in a hurry to get away and now she's done it.*

Frances, I see our mother in the kitchen of the white house on the reservation. She studies at the table. Her brothers sleep in their two rooms. Her father lies alone in the dark, awake, but silent. The shadows of black leaves flutter against the house. They might be the speaking hands of ghosts, but the girl who loves sound does not read the signs of her ancestors. Perhaps she is conjugating French verbs. Perhaps she translates a psalm to Latin. Sometimes she stops to murmur; she longs to make her cadence perfect. But if a coyote howls, she will open the window and answer.

I want to touch her shoulder. I want to warn the girl who is not my mother: *Rina, we will lose every tongue; we will be betrayed in every language.*

⊰25⊱

M Y S T E R I E S

There are fifteen mysteries in the life of Jesus and his Blessed Mother: joyful, sorrowful, glorious. I recite them: *annunciation, visitation, scourging, crucifixion, resurrection, ascension.* I am a hearing child who loves words, the repetition of sound, the magic of rhythm. I am mesmerized.

Who made us?

God made us.

Who is God? Does God see us?

What is mortal sin? What is hope? What are angels?

I am only nine years old, but already I know all the answers. *How many kinds of grace are there?*

A white dress hangs in my closet. *Little bride.* I think this. I touch it in the dark. I am ready for the wafer to become the body of Christ in my mouth; I am waiting for God to dissolve here.

Later, I have mysteries of my own:

How does the disease of a horse enter a girl's body?

Why does the brain swell?

How do you learn to say *encephalitis* if you can't hear it?

Why does my mother love the water?

Where does my sister go when she opens the window?

If holy wine turns to blood, why is Frances drunk with it?
When she speaks, why does my sister turn away from me?

I have my own catechism.
What is faith?
A father cries out in the night, and a deaf child hears him.

☩26☩

T H E   C O Y O T E   A N D   T H E   C R O W

The father and his deaf daughter could stop everything if
they knew that the children are here in the motel, footsteps
away. This morning, before it is light, there is still time to save
them. Yes, it's true, the old man's hearing is as keen as it ever
was: even now, the scuttle of a pack rat digging under the
porch or a raccoon scrambling across the roof would wake
him, but the motel is a hundred yards away, down the narrow
path and through the trees, and so he sleeps, ignorant as his
daughter.

Together, they shall be blameless.

Flint presses his naked body to the cold glass of the sliding
door. Rain drips from trees; water breaks on stone at the shore.
Stupid to use the crowbar. All he had to do was wait, pull the
old man from the car. But he couldn't wait — the man's quivering mouth made him explode. He wanted to shatter that face.
He wanted to shatter himself.

Valves open, veins fill. Pounding waves make his blood rock.
He is sick with sound. Each surge roars, chest to skull. He
doesn't need the stethoscope. He wants to sleep somewhere

safe and small, a hole underground, lined with feathers and moss, his own dark nest, moist and warm.

This morning, he touched his sister's soft belly. He touched her thighs, her white arms. He wanted to live inside her pale skin — hidden, unformed — a shapeless thing, curved close to her heart. He needs her to forget the old man on the road. She won't forget. Brutal boy. She knows him now. When he touched her, she pretended to sleep: legs rigid, eyes closed hard.

He figures he has one chance: get Cecile home before Mother hears the news on the radio. She'll call the sheriff by noon. Give him up. Gladly, he thinks, and why not? Easy to betray her first child. With her new husband, she'll have a new son. Frances Bell can send her bad boy back to God; she can wish him unborn.

He remembers a story his mother told him long ago. Once upon a time a crow laid two eggs; once upon a time the coyote ate them both. Foolish bird, the crow flapped and squawked. She hissed at the coyote: *Eat me if you're so starved.* She offered her neck. She laid her body down. The coyote thought of her smooth eggs, slick and warm inside their shells, golden and good as they slipped down his throat. The chicks they might have grown to be filled his belly and his heart.

He looked at her: black feathers, black eyes, sharp beak, bony skull. She was all crack and pluck — wrinkled hide, stringy meat — too much trouble to break, too much work to chew. He told her he'd rather gnaw a pair of old leather boots. He said, *I am what I eat; your babies are part of me forever now.*

She looked him straight in the teeth. He said, *You're my mother in a way, so you should love me as your son.* With a yip and a yelp, he turned to go. The childless mother saw the feathery plume of his long tail and the sheen of his silvery coat.

How did the story end?

Flint can't recall. He finishes it for himself. It's not that hard. The crow despised the coyote. She would, of course, and she's not alone. Ranchers hunt them from airplanes or plant tubes of cyanide with bait in the ground. They use traps and guns and dogs. Once Flint saw the gutted body of a coyote staked to a fence, left as a warning by the road.

The crow laid three more eggs. Kept her faith, guarded them well. One day they hatched, and the skinny coyote heard the chicks' tireless squawks. When their mother flew away to find them live crickets or a warm mole, the coyote shook the tree, and a featherless nestling fell straight into his mouth. Empty though he was, he could not bite down. He dropped the nestling in the woods. Words had given shape to thought: the crow was his mother after all, her chicks his own flesh and blood.

He ate only the dead: fish washed up on the beach, beetles on their backs, a festering horse. Sometimes he'd rather starve. On those days, he swallowed pebbles to fool himself. Full and heavy with stones, the coyote stumbled through the forest. At night he prayed to the bird gods, eagle and owl. He wanted to be saved, to be eaten alive, to be torn apart.

The shivering boy who tells stories to himself wraps a blanket around himself. He knows that bird gods pay no attention to the prayers of a coyote. They do not see him reeling through the trees, belly swollen, long tail dragging the ground. When he walks into the metal trap, only his mother the crow hears him howl. She thinks it is a trick at first, but he wails all night, through morning, till dusk.

When she comes to him at last, he whispers, *Mother dear, clever darling.* He shows her his bloody leg. *Use your beak,* he says. *Open this steel jaw and save me.*

She's smart enough to peck the spring. *Little wolf,* she says, *I know you.* She keeps her chicks tucked tight under her wings. *Trickster, all you want to do is eat us.*

He could make promises. Tell her how he filled his gut with stones to spare them. He could swear in his own blood. There is plenty of that now. But he doesn't even try. Why would a bird trust a coyote?

His voice is very faint. He says, *Please stay. I'm afraid to be alone here.*

She won't comfort the enemy.

She's teaching her children to fly. Black and bold, their raucous cries wild as laughter, they flutter; they leave him.

He is dying in a dream. He feels fat chicks inside his body, the ones born of all the eggs he's ever swallowed. They rise up in his throat, and he spits hard to free them. One grateful brother pecks the joint of the trap till the tight teeth pop open. Three sisters clutch him in their claws to fly him high over treetops. He sees his foot far below, snared and torn by bright metal.

He doesn't care about lost limbs: who needs to walk the earth if he has wings to soar above it?

He sails toward the green edges of twilight. Thin, blue clouds float across the tender face of the moon, three-quarters full, but sad and weary. This is his father's face, his father who comes too late, who cannot speak, who wants to love him.

In the morning, the coyote is still alive on the ground. Birds circle in the pink sky, drawn by his smell, thick blood, sour flesh. The trapper checks his line at last and finds this ragged creature. Five dollars, that's all he'll get, a pitiful bounty. The coyote's pelt is his only proof — one more killer killed — he's hardly worth a bullet. But the man is merciful and quick, his aim true, the shot easy.

Yes, Mother will call the police and describe him well. Not a coyote but a dirty boy wearing some other child's too big jeans and sweatshirt. Robbery, assault, deadly weapon. Intent to do bodily harm. Words make truth. Nobody says these words: scared, stupid, starved. They won't let him out at cighteen or even twenty-one. They'll send him straight to Deer Lodge, ten years at least, fifty if the doctor died alone on the road last night. Flint Zimmer will be an old man before they free him, weak and crippled, incapable of hurting anybody, teeth gone, muscles wasted. Or he'll be a young man in a box: stabbed by prisoners, beaten by guards, shot climbing a wall. There are choices, he knows, ways out of every prison. There are lightbulbs to break, and blue veins waiting to be opened.

But today he wants to live for at least a few more hours. He won't strip and bend. Won't open his mouth. Won't spread his toes. He won't be sprayed and shaved today if he can get Cecile back to Creston.

He shakes her. He's a rough boy, not her tender brother, not a lover or a child who wants to live inside her body. He says, *Wake up, it's time, we're leaving.*

⨯27⨯

A W O U N D E D C O W

Frances has been lying on her arms. They flop, numb and useless. Just a bad dream, she thinks, something about Cecile, something about Caleb. A wounded cow staggered through her kitchen, and Caleb said, *I'm almost done here.* Outside, Cecile rolled snow to build her lumpy hunchback. She stuck branches in his head. Antlers. Three crows pecked at his skull, then complained that he was empty.

Her hands buzz, hot and swollen. As soon as she can will her fingers to bend, Frances lights a cigarette. Caleb Vaughn, first husband, gentleman butcher: he'll come to your house like a country doctor, slaughter your cow in your own field — so you can see it. And if a calf breeches at three o'clock some February morning, you can call Caleb to help you. He gives life, or takes it. Whatever you need that day, he'll do it.

But his hands on her, dried blood under the nails, Frances couldn't bear that. After Cecile, she found ways not to have his children. They were black clots and water swirling. They seeped into the ground; they flowed to the river.

Last night comes back in fragments. She won at darts, she won at pool — deadeye, like Daddy. She took bets and flirted. Even drunk, she whipped the boys. She won five shots of Cuervo. Lucky lady, she laughed too loudly, showed teeth and gums, felt her lips stretch so far she couldn't close them. Gil Wiley said, *Keep smiling*. He fondled her knee under the bar. He said, *If only*. In his truck, he kept his hands warm inside her coat, underneath her sweater. When his big tongue filled her mouth, she couldn't think; she didn't want to. She would have gone home with him. *Just drive*. But he sent her on her way. A decent man? Maybe bored, maybe tired. Respectful of her, or loyal to Dexter? He walked her to her car, and she staggered like the dumb cow wounded in her kitchen. *I'm almost done here*. He kissed her again — no tongue this time — very politely. She drove away, like a good girl. She plunged into the ditch. Yes, she fingers the sore bruise on her forehead. So all this must be true, all this really happened.

And Cecile, was she in the yard, building that snowman? No, that was some other day, before. Yesterday the rain beat him. He's nothing but a hump of ice now. No crows perch in his antlers. Frances is glad he's melted. She never liked that ugly cripple, bent by his own weight, pocked, dirty. No eyes in his shrunken skull, and still he'd watched her. Like an owl, he could spin his head to see in every direction.

The stairs, the bath, the unmade bed, the dark kitchen.

Is it true?

She hears Dixie. The dog is under the porch, whining. She hasn't eaten for two days now. Is this love? Dixie pulls out her hair in tufts. Leaves her rump and legs raw from all her nipping. Desire like hers will kill you. She laps at the wet grass or opens her mouth in the rain, but she won't drink from her bowl; she won't take anything from Frances. Yesterday Cecile crawled under the steps and coaxed Dixie to suck a wet rag. She was filthy as the damn dog, and Frances said, *Get your butt in here.*

Frances told Dixie, *I'll call him tonight, let you talk to your darling.* A lie, she never called Dexter. Just as well, his voice without his body would make the dog frantic.

This morning Cecile stood in the open doorway. Yellow coat, wet hair — she looked watery, a girl in a glass tank, half floating. Damp wind blew through the house, and Frances said, *Close the door; Mommy's freezing.* The days jumble. Cold hands circled her wrists and ankles. Mommy, freezing. Little fingers covered her eyes. She couldn't swim to the surface. Her own mother spit in her mouth. From the bottom of the lake, Rina said, *Water is heavy this far down; water is everywhere, and like God, it wants to crush you.*

She remembers three men in her father's kitchen. Finally one of them said, *We found her.* In this way, Mother died a hundred times. A thousand. Will it be like this again? Day after day, Frances woke, not quite certain. *Shush, just a bad dream; close your eyes and think of something pretty.* That was Mommy's voice. Every morning, Frances struggled to the surface, gasping. When her mother's bloated body bobbed up beside her, she woke into the dream that was her life forever.

11:16. She calls Caleb, the only one who will help her. Who might think, but won't say: *You deserve this.* She imagines him in the shop, already bloody. He wipes his hands before he answers the phone, but still leaves fingerprints. When did they last speak? Flint's hearing — five years ago. Then, as now, she wished she could love him. The kind ones wound you with tenderness. They leave you staggering in your kitchen. Better to find a man who won't ever smooth the hair from your forehead, who won't kiss your neck with soft lips, who won't remind you, who won't kill you with his words: *Sweet dreams, my darling.*

Five years, but she whispers his name, and he knows her. And his voice, *Frances?*, makes it real. Their daughter, missing. *Please,* she says. She hasn't told him, but Caleb, because he's Caleb, says, *I'm coming.*

⚛28⚛

L I T T L E   W O M A N

Frances finds the damp blue dress crumpled on the floor behind the toilet, the dirty yellow coat on the floor of the closet in Cecile's bedroom.

So, she was in the house, it's true, not a ghost or a dream. She stood in the gray light of the open door, the wet day behind her. Frances jerked, half waking. She said, *Come here; lie down; be a good girl.* She made a space for Cecile, though the couch was narrow. Cecile came close and stared. Cecile said, *Where's Dixie?*

Frances finds her purse dumped in the hallway — cash gone, keys and license missing. Does the little girl think she can pretend to be her mother? She's stolen pink lipstick and bright blush, a bottle of red fingernail polish. Cecile, still alive, here, but gone now, and the car is gone too, so the boy must be driving.

She walks through the house for the third time. The mud on the stairs is Cecile's mud. *Sweet heart, darling.* The screen door flaps in the wind. *Jesus.* The dog howls from under the porch, half starved but not missing. *I'll call him, I promise.*

The phone rings and rings. *Please, not yet.* She doesn't want to know anything until Caleb gets here. Nine rings, eleven. Finally she picks it up, but it's only Sloan from the pawnshop. *Are you coming?* Even now she can lie. Car won't start, dead battery. She says, *A neighbor's on his way to jump me.* She thinks of Bob Estes three houses down the road. Yes, he would jump, any time she asked him. She thinks of Gil. Last night she almost had a lover. But this morning she's sick and pregnant, used up at thirty-one, the mother of a delinquent boy and a missing child, the owner of a stolen vehicle, the keeper of a delirious dog who won't come out and won't stop crying. She tells Sloan, *Give me an hour.* The truth can wait, always; Caleb will be here any minute, and Caleb will answer the phone the next time.

29

OTHER MYSTERIES

He did not plan to steal the car. He wasn't even sure he could drive it. This was Cecile's idea. One more mystery in the life of a child. He can't explain, and even if he tries, nobody will ever believe him.

Add kidnapping to his list of crimes. Give the boy another twenty. Make it life without parole. When you discover the revolver is gone, describe him as armed and dangerous. Consider him beyond redemption.

What time did you get home?
Why did you wait so long to call us?
The sheriff's deputies keep asking Frances the same foolish questions. Caleb squeezes her hand. The room at the station is too bright. She can't stop blinking. She's wide awake but strangely calm, already sedated. Every time the thin deputy calls her Mrs. Vaughn, she corrects him.

They've put it together: missing girl, furious boy, old doctor. They want photographs and descriptions. Four foot seven, fifty-eight pounds. This must be true. It says so right here on Cecile's report card.

The younger deputy is thick and serious, shirt too tight across the chest, shoulders bulky. Frances thinks of Cecile, her exact size — this man could crush her. *When did you see her last? What was she wearing?* He has a note pad to record her answers. *Yesterday, before school; I'll show you.*

When they take her back to the house, the deputies see the blue dress, the yellow raincoat, the dirty little socks, the muddy footprints. So they know, very small — Frances is not lying. The dumped purse is still in the hallway. *How much cash did you have?* Maybe twenty, maybe a hundred. She can't remember. They check the canister and the nightstand and the closet. They look under the bed. Only the revolver is gone, .38 caliber, she thinks — a Taurus? *We can call my husband and ask him.*

Yes, Dexter Bell will want to know his gun is missing.

Outside, behind the woodpile, they find the boy's clothes: hooded sweatshirt, fingerless gloves, black denim jacket.

Do you have any idea what they might be wearing?

She hears the dog somewhere far away, whimpering.

Where's Dixie?

Tied under the porch, muzzled with a red bandanna.

Now she remembers. She did this. How could she? She's *sorry, sorry, sorry, darling.* She crawls under the porch though Caleb tries to stop her. She's sobbing now, her face in the dog's muddy fur. *Jesus, somebody, help me.*

Caleb is on his knees beside her, untying the rope, unknotting the bandanna. She doesn't confess. They think the boy did this — such a small crime to add to all the other crimes, so what does it matter?

Dixie knows she's safe at last. She trusts the man who wraps her in a blanket. With her swollen tongue, she tries to lick him. She loves his smell: he tastes like her, an animal. He's gentle. He understands how thirsty she is. When he offers her a bowl of water, she laps it. Later, when Frances is finally asleep, Caleb will wash Dixie in the bathtub. He'll dry her with real towels.

Nobody, not even Dexter, has ever been this tender.

30

IN THE PHOTOGRAPH

Cecile is turning away, always in motion. You can't catch her. She blurs herself, a deliberate gesture. It's her class picture, last year, fourth grade. She doesn't want to be with these children. She doesn't want anyone to have her image. But Frances can describe her: blond, less fragile than she appears, determined. Here are the numbers on her January report card. How will they find her? She can hide behind a rock like a coyote. Vanish down a hole like a rabbit. Frances thinks of her legs and arms, how easy it would be to snap them. She looks at the tired deputy whose left eye won't stop twitching. She looks at Caleb's thick fingers. She looks at the other deputy, the one who bulges out of his uniform. Any man or even a boy could do it. She remembers Gil's hands on her, up her blouse, between her knees. He was the first to speak. *We should both go home, Frances.* She remembers warm water turning cool in the bathtub, how long she waited to check her daughter's bedroom. *Unnatural.* She knows it's true. At twelve-fifty-three she reported the child missing. It's right there in the deputy's report where anybody can read it: *Thursday, March 29, 1990. 12:53 p.m.* The numbers scratched on the page have made sins of omission a matter of legal record.

Mother's forehead badly bruised. Appears disoriented. Words are facts now, undeniable. *Claims she sustained head injury early this morning when car slid off road and she hit steering wheel. Sheriff's office has no record of alleged incident.*

They want her to describe the boy, and Frances sees him, red and squirming, a child in her lap, a baby. She sees herself, fifteen and motherless. The baby howls, and her father takes him.

Daddy never asks, *Who?* Daddy doesn't want to know when or where or how this happened. Father Demeron and Sister Marguerite suggest adoption, a good Catholic family, a young childless couple longing to love and protect him.

But the father of the girl refuses: Lowell Zimmer who owns a motel on the lake, who lives alone all winter with two teenage daughters, whose wife swam away one bright afternoon, this killer of cowbirds and savior of vireos says, *We take care of our own here.*

⇥31⇤

WITH HEARTS LIKE AWLS

What does the husband of a drowned woman understand about raising daughters? The autumn after Kina died, our father sent us to the nuns in Coeur d'Alene, and we lived as they did, cloistered. We were taught to love fasting, prayer, holy reading. We were instructed not to steal, not to covet, not to bear false witness. Murmuring was forbidden. I did not speak; I did not murmur. I understood that every secret was dangerous. There was the Word of God. There was one interpretation. We were obedient to the Reverend Mother, though we knew she feared our terrible imperfections. God had punished us; she had to wonder. She liked me best when I was sleeping, when the Word of God could enter me completely and without translation. Sometimes I lay in my bed, eyes closed, and felt her watching.

There were chants, meditations, prayers, lessons. There was work: ice to break and snow to shovel, floors to mop and potatoes to peel. Clothes to wash and wring and iron. There were meals to take in silence. There were vespers.

Ritual was meant to calm us. No time for discord, no time for panic. No idle moment for grief or pity or rebellion. Nobody asked what had happened to our mother. Who believes the stories of children? Mother in Heaven, Mother an angel. That's what the nuns told us. They gave us their images. Mother with her wings spread, waiting to welcome her children. How could they know? In the dream, she always had fins, no legs, just that powerful tail. If you tried to drag her to the shore, she flopped, gasping. She loved the water. She was sleek as a sturgeon, too heavy for clouds, too solid for Heaven. She fell, spinning. This was deliberate. With her fast body, she knifed the water.

What is hope?
Hope is language.
Sister Agnes taught me a hundred signs a day. She showed me grammar in space. When I made my first sentence in air, she clapped by waving her hands over her head and grinning. Applause for a deaf girl. I could say anything. So I signed, *My mother is drowning.* Agnes did not correct me. She understood: some things happen in present time forever. I signed, *Strawberries dipped in chocolate.* It was November, northern Idaho. That night Agnes came to my room and closed the door. Closing doors was forbidden. The strawberries were sweet, the chocolate black and almost bitter. A miracle. How had she done this? Who, before Agnes, had ever given me exactly what I wanted? She touched my cheek. She touched my shoulder. She kissed my forehead. That's how Sister Beatrice caught us.

The next day Mother Judith told me Agnes was gone. She'd heard her true calling at last. Exiled to Washington. *For my sake.* She meant to live on the Colville Reservation with twelve deaf children who needed her more than I did. Only a spoiled girl would think otherwise.

The Reverend Mother wrote her next sentence down so that I would understand her: *Sister Beatrice will teach you.*

I imagined twelve little Indians pretending to be airplanes in narrow hallways. They roared in the corridors; they'd found a way to hear something. They banged their fists and foreheads on windowpanes, then pressed their mouths to glass to feel vibration. They shouted into corners where they could catch their triumphant voices echoing. Before I came to the nuns, before my mother swam to the island, I had done this. In rage and delight, I threw myself into walls, I pounded the floor, I battered the windows. Frances covered her head with a pillow. Mother slapped me. Sometimes I went away for a few seconds. I felt dizzy and my eyelids fluttered. Sometimes I fell down in the kitchen and woke up in my bedroom. Then I had another word to learn, *epilepsy,* another word I couldn't say because I'd never heard it. Nobody was surprised. The doctor had warned my mother and father. *Common,* he said, *a complication.* My swollen brain again, more silent damage.

So, I was common. Imagine.

Once it happened in the woods, and I lay there half a day before my father found me. I hit my head going down; I broke my wrist landing. I was wet when I woke.

Had I been struck by lightning?

No, nothing divine or extraordinary. My own electricity had twisted my muscles tight, jolted my bones, left my body limp and throbbing. Now I was too weak to walk, and Daddy had to carry me.

No more wandering in the woods alone, no more swimming. My little sister was supposed to watch for clues I might be seizing. Frances hated this. Whenever she could, she ditched me. But at night we spoke in our secret language. I taught her my signs for *stone* and *rain* and *hawk* and *chickadee*. Hours before a storm, I could smell it coming. I taught her to read the sky. I told her how I'd learned to live inside my own body: I heard my heart in my skull; I sensed the pressure of my blood shifting.

We are all, and nothing.

Sister Beatrice signed with stiff gestures and no expression. She used a different language, not the one Sister Agnes had begun to teach me. This was English in sign, word for word, slow and clumsy. I could not say what I needed to say, though Sister Beatrice insisted it was a better way to communicate, easier for hearing people to learn.

Yes, it had this advantage.

My hands stuttered. I had nothing to say to Sister Beatrice. *Chocolate, mud, oil.* She had nothing to give. I refused to learn her language. In January, three fits seized me. Devil's work. The nuns sent me home, to the lake, to Daddy.

When I found his rifle under the bed, I unloaded it.

I flushed his pills down the toilet.

We kept each other alive that winter.

At night he called my name, or my mother's name, and I heard him. I am not lying. His voice hummed in my ribs, a constant trembling. I walked down the hall in my white nightgown. Was I asleep? I felt the light pass through me. My gown was gauze, pale as a moth's wing and just as delicate.

Were we lovers?

I can't answer in your language.

Frances despised the nuns and all their rules. She hated kneeling on stone floors, lying in a narrow bed, eating cold oatmeal without milk or sugar. She wrote me a letter. She said, *Save me.*

She opened her window at night. She climbed out and wandered. She turned ten years old on the eighth of February. She met boys in the ravine where they made exchanges. She brought them holy wine, and they all reeled with it. Sister Beatrice caught her in the chapel, stuffing herself with wafers, turning His bread to her body.

What are you doing?

Filling myself up with God.

What could you expect? We were bad girls, motherless.

Sister Beatrice slapped Frances four times, each blow hard and full of fury, driven by rage so pure it felt sacred. Later the humiliated nun lay face down on the hard floor, tearful and repentant.

Maybe God was fooled. Maybe Mother Judith and Sister Anne and Sister Tereza. Maybe all the faithful girls — Claire and Emma and Joan and Adelaide — understood this. Maybe Father Bennet helped Sister Beatrice explain it to herself when she gave him her confession. *Our Father, Hail Mary.* Words will heal you. *O my God, because you are so good, I am very sorry that I have sinned against you and by the help of your grace I will not sin again.*

Father Bennet told her to say these words until she believed them. Seventeen, eighteen, nineteen times. She was very tired. God smiled. Good Sister Beatrice fell asleep with His forgiveness, and the bad little girl, my own sister Frances, came home, to us.

I would like to say we were happy to be together, a family again, though the mother was absent. I will say instead that the snow was deep that winter, and the ice didn't melt from the lake until April.

⊰32⊱

ANOTHER WINTER

I know how I look when I seize. Once I saw a film of a woman writhing. She crumpled. Her body jerked on the hard floor; each jolt made her stiffen. Her eyes rolled white, and her lids fluttered.

I know what she felt after, how her bones ached, each one almost broken. I knew the shame of not remembering. She was wet, and maybe worse — a madwoman, a girl gone wild. I saw her mouth foam like a sick coyote's. Then she was scared and quiet, split lips crusted with spittle.

No wonder the nuns sent me home. No wonder my sister refused to watch out for me.

Imagine another winter, five years since the one in Coeur d'Alene, and my sister Frances is pregnant, belly swollen up huge and hard, little girl arms and legs still spindly. For the child who hears, the silence in our father's house must be unbearable. Nobody stays at the motel; we're closed October to April. There's no reason for either sister to go to school. Snow piles high on the road. The father plows, or doesn't plow, as he sees fit, as he wishes. He feels no need to go to town. Quite the opposite. The pantry's stocked, full of cans and jars and boxes: corned beef hash, pickled beets, green beans, lentils, powdered milk and powdered eggs, flour, salt, sugar, coffee. We are ready for disasters: blizzards, ice storms, nuclear fallout. We are prepared for sudden arrivals and departures. We are survivors.

In late November, wind takes down two trees, and Royce Beauvil appears with his chain saw to help his neighbor, our father, cut and stack them. He's a quiet man, keeps to himself mostly, the way our father likes it. But if ice should tear and crumple our dock, he'll give up a day this spring to help Lowell Zimmer repair it. If he hears the motor of the wooden boat sputter at dawn, he'll walk down the beach slowly — bringing not advice, but patience. In this way, he is more like a brother than a friend: he rarely needs to speak because he feels he has known you forever. If your wife swims too far one day, Royce is the one who will stay out on the lake with you longer than anybody. He'll let you believe you might find her, shivering on the shore, beautiful dark-eyed Rina, cold and embarrassed. He sees you are not ready, and his silence gives you faith, though it means nothing. He watches the lake and sky. He stays to witness. He does not expect a miracle. His god isn't like that. When he prays, he asks his god to give you the strength you'll need to endure this.

The mother of the pregnant girl, our mother Rina, has been gone five years, six months, seventeen days now. Nobody in this house has enough faith or madness to deny it. In February a freak storm drops three feet of wet snow in thirteen hours, and the father has to shovel it off the roofs to keep the house and motel from collapsing. It's midnight; he forgets his gloves. If you watch him up there, he'll scare you. One leg is two inches shorter than the other. He flew out of a tree when he was twelve — yes, flew, on purpose — and the broken femur never grew where it mended. This injury saved him from the war, but spared him no grief: he lost two brothers — one's parachute tangled on telephone lines in Belgium; one staggered, lost and wounded in the Hürtgen Forest. Lowell has learned to compensate on the ground, but the slope of the roof throws him off kilter. He slides, he stumbles. All this would be bad enough, but he seems oblivious. Royce Beauvil must see everything from his own house, a scene in a play, one lumbering fool on a roof with a shovel. Royce knows how work can make a man delirious, that snow is a force and not just a substance. The sadness of a lifetime can converge as you try to remove it.

Royce trudges through the white woods because the man teetering on the roof needs him. He comes with his own shovel and an extra pair of gloves. He doesn't yell at Lowell to get down from there, doesn't say stupid things like, *Plenty of time tomorrow*. Doesn't promise that his two strong sons will drive from town in the morning. He climbs the ladder. In the terrible, blessed silence of men, they work. It's necessary.

From the roof, Royce would be able to see his wife, Floris, standing in their bright kitchen, arms crossed over her thin chest. So he knows exactly what his kindness will cost him.

Anything the men might say about snow or cold or tomorrow seems obvious, so they hold their tongues and save their energy. The pregnant child stands on the porch, bare-legged, wrapped in a blanket. She wants to hear voices, the murmur and exchange of conversation. But they deprive her. At last they climb down, and she hears her father say, *Cup of coffee?*, and she hears Royce answer, *Got to get home now.*

So it is in our father's house.

Beginning in late February, he plows the road every time it

snows, because we have to be ready. We wait for the child to be born, the one who will not save us. Nobody calls, nobody visits. People are afraid of our family, of the girl with a swollen brain, and the girl with a swollen belly. Mostly they are afraid when they remember the woman who swam away one brilliant afternoon. Why didn't we see her? Nobody dares to ask, but they wonder, of course, *Did she mean to do it?* Anything is possible: our mother's desire makes us dangerous.

Those punished like Job evoke pity, not compassion. Then fear, then repulsion. Our neighbors wonder how long God will test us. They have to believe it is our fault, that they are safe, that we deserve misfortune.

My father's father was a minister without a congregation, a fierce Presbyterian, a mystic with no zeal for the work of conversion.

The Reverend Cyrus Zimmer fled to the mountains and built a shack to live alone there. If he was hungry or too cold, he might walk to town some January morning to visit his family, which is why my father — who had no father — had eight brothers and sisters, and why, by the grace of God, seven of nine were born in October. My father, the fourth child, was born in August, an exception. I imagine my grandmother Tilia climbing the steep path to her husband's shack. It's a mild day in early November. The ground is hard with frost, and there are patches of snow, but the blue sky is cloudless. She carries a basket full of bread and cheese and apples, her offering to the husband who will be neither glad nor sorry that she has come to visit.

He is a skinny man now, but tall and hard, and to her, still handsome. His green eyes burn with visions. Or so she believes. Her devotion is another mystery in my family, a love I can't explain, a faith my father never questioned. They were his parents. Strange as they might seem to others, to him they were unremarkable.

To make the sign for *faith,* touch the forehead with one finger; then close your fists, left hand over right, and make the gesture of planting a flag in front of you.

You see, every language is inadequate; no word can describe my grandmother's affliction.

I suspect the reverend's visions come from hunger, from staring at the sun too long, from refusing sleep and water. His red hair is long and tangled, his red beard a dirty mat, a lovely nest, always tempting. Flocks of birds worship him. They congregate to gather the threads of Cyrus Zimmer, those bright hairs he leaves everywhere. The little chipping sparrow, the noisy nuthatch, the fearless chickadee all line their nests with the glowing fibers of my grandfather.

He keeps a shard of mirror hanging on a nail, and Tilia will use this to straighten her hair before she starts down the mountain. But Cyrus never looks at himself that way. He uses the glass only to inspect a bite on his buttocks, or to reflect the sun and start a fire.

❊33❊

FIRST WINTER

It is easy to judge a life if you don't have to live it. Easy to think that the father makes the deaf child come and lie down beside him. That he clings to her in his grief, half forgetting. She is not his wife and not a woman but she is his and he is hers, and nobody sees how they live here. They are alone, the first winter. The nuns have sent the deaf girl home because her fits scare them. Benevolent women, they will keep the younger child in their care, will hold her distant and dear until the day Sister Beatrice catches little Frances stuffing her mouth with holy wafers.

The father does not come to his daughter's room. She believes she senses the rhythm of her name in the dark, but he does not call — and even if he did, she would not hear him. She chooses. She is the one who floats down the hall in her white nightgown. Who comes to him. *With deliberate intention.* She glides like a sleepwalker. Brings him water and flushes his pills and unloads his gun and hides it in the closet. She could sit on the edge of the bed. Like a good girl. She could wash his hot face and hot feet. Yes, he sweats. He tosses. And yes, she does sit; she does wash. But this is not enough for her.

Every language depends on the one who uses it. The word for *love* can be full of scorn or full of sorrow. You make the sign with an open palm or a closed fist, close to your heart or close to your head, soft and sweet, or hard and fast. Now, when I make the sign for my father's love, I strike my own chest.

Did he touch my hair?

Did he kiss my face?

Did he weep?

Did he whisper, *Darling?*

Did I feel his breath close to my ear and understand the sacred word his lips were shaping?

Yes, yes, yes, all this I am not confessing.

He was the one who stopped. Who locked the door. Who stood with his gun behind it. Who said to the deaf girl who could not hear him, *Go now, please; I'm tired.*

You think I am lying.

You think I want to protect him.

No, I want to go back there.

I felt his footsteps as he paced, so close, so separate, the locked door between us. I felt his hands against the wood. I said, *Daddy*. I said, *Please, let me*. Yes, I mean this. Out loud. I said. I said. I said. So he could hear me. Idiot girl, I raved. I didn't care that my voice was shrill and foolish. I felt his forehead against the door. He stood there, gasping. And the word in his brain was *no*, and the word stayed *no* forever.

I knew it was my mother's fault. She spit black water into his mouth. She said, *I'll drown you*. The dead are selfish. Don't tell me Mother is an angel. I know her. Her thick tail breaks the waves as she swims away from us.

⊰34⊱

In Summer

I could tell you something else: at night the window in our bedroom was often open, and I saw Frances climb out of it. Unhelpful as this information is, it seems important. I watched her run toward the woods. I didn't know who might be waiting. Later, she had boyfriends — men who stayed at the motel, or migrants who worked in our neighbors' cherry orchards. She flirted. She wore lipstick and mascara. Cherries sweetened in the dark, and my little sister ate them. She was beautiful, a miniature woman in a girl's perfect body.

I was not surprised when I lost her at the carnival. A deaf sister is a constant embarrassment to a pretty child. I made noises that humiliated her. Scared or startled, I might yelp or grunt. I felt these eruptions in my chest and belly. No wonder I loved the little pigs squealing in their cages. No wonder I befriended goats. Pygmies and giants, they came in every size but were not monsters. Some had floppy ears like spaniels, and some no ears at all, only pink holes, tiny whorls; I could look inside them. If Mother had looked inside me, would she have seen my brain swelling? Doctor Dees said, *You should have called me.* Did he blame her? I had lived through fevers before this one. The life of any child is dangerous. There's a swing over the gully, a rope and a stick tied to a fragile limb. If it breaks one summer day, you'll fall a hundred feet. Break like a doll on the stones by the river. This doesn't happen. You dig a cave in a hillside. Line it with rags and leaves. When you crawl inside, it does not collapse, and you do not smother.

Once I floated on a log with my mother. I had gathered hundreds of tiny stones and wrapped them in my towel. The cloth was soaked and heavy; then the log began to sink, and I was plunging to the bottom. I wouldn't let go of the towel. Those pebbles, long lost, seemed precious. Mother dove down to get me. Underwater, she spoke in sign, a premonition. She was still alive, and I was still a hearing child, but God in his mercy was letting me glimpse the future, so I wouldn't be afraid, so that I would be ready.

All this I survived, then a mosquito that fed on the blood of a sparrow carried its silent disease to me, and my brain swelled, and my fever raged, and I was changed forever from the inside.

Daddy said, *Watch out for each other.* He held my chin with his hand, made me look at him directly. He left us at the carnival gate. He said he would be back at ten-thirty. *Exactly.*

He asked me if I understood, and I nodded. How did we persuade him to drive us to Kalispell? Where did he go for three hours? Was I supposed to watch out for Frances because she was younger, or was she watching out for me because I was damaged?

Did my father trust me?

I'd had no fits all year. No strange flutterings. No wet pants, no mysterious injuries. Maybe I was healed. Maybe I would wake one day and hear my sister singing. Compared with Lazarus stumbling from his cave, the miracle of sound seemed like a small thing. But that night I was still deaf, and the spinning lights made me dizzy. So I went into the dark booth to visit the gypsy — fortuneteller, liar, our Madame Zahira. I gave her my money. Frances ditched me, it was easy. She didn't want the black-haired woman to tell her anything. What do motherless girls need to know about their future? Her future was here, in the field, but she didn't know it.

⊰35⊱

A Child of Two Fathers

Flint Zimmer. The two deputies are waiting for Frances Bell to describe her son. Black hair, green eyes, pale skin when he's just washed. Most times he's not. *My height,* she says, *five five.* Maybe a hundred and ten pounds if you weigh the boy with boots and mud. *Skinny,* she says, *but surprising, strong.* Like his fathers — he could hold her down. She felt each stone pressing into her back. She can count them even now. She felt their tongues. *Don't talk with your mouth full.*

They laughed in the same way. Brothers, two boys who had never been apart, Rudy and Clayton Kotecki. Flint had the same tilt to his hips, the same lope in his stride, the same soft mouth.

The night she ditched her sister at the carnival, she followed those brothers through the high grass. Sharp blades stung her bare skin. They gave her wine and cigarettes. She wanted to forget the legless man who walked on his hands, the miniature woman who wrote, *God Bless You*.

She wanted to forget the two girls joined at the hip. They wore identical pink dresses. Their long hair curled in dark ringlets. If you touched one, the other felt it. Nothing was secret. The tattooed man kissed the one called Frederika, and the one named Fern closed her eyes, swooning. Yes, two girls, one body. Frances didn't want to know her sister's life. She didn't want to feel it. The tattooed man repulsed her. He was old, maybe forty, almost naked, and the girls, Fern and Frederika, were only seventeen, or were they thirty-four, everything doubled? The man's body was covered with pictures. A dragon breathed fire on his back; three white birds flew across his shoulders. A thick serpent spiraled up one leg — she could see each green scale. Women danced on his biceps. They had huge breasts and tiny waists. Every time he flexed, they writhed: he owned them.

The legless man chased her into the field; the tattooed man held her wrists; the fat man lay on top of her.

Why did she go with the two brothers?

They were loud, and she liked this, their noise, their laughter.

She hated the silence in her house. Snow falling through pines all winter, waves breaking, ice shattering. On calm days in summer, Mother spoke underwater, deliberate and cruel.

So Frances couldn't hear the words, so nobody knew what she was really saying. Marie made signs with her hands, but Frances refused to read them. Daddy, who never did like to talk, now thought even less of it.

She can't see herself in the field. She can't describe her son to the deputies. She can't remember the faces of the Kotecki brothers. The wine was sweet, and the boys smelled of cotton candy. Where their fingers stuck to her skin, she can still trace them. Before the sky turned black, it was blue as glass, both dark and bright, as if the dome above were a window. Drunken girl, what could she prove? *Nothing.* Who would believe her? *Nobody.*

She kissed the younger boy on the ferris wheel. People saw this.

When she remembers it today, the fat man crushes her. He covers her with his loose flesh; it spreads till she can't breathe. He buries her. Later he rolls away. He can't walk. His bones won't support him. It's over, he wheezes, and she hears him in the grass, gasping. The boys have run back to their big truck where they drink rum and forget her. Three midgets and Miss Gloria the miniature woman sit in the field, her only witnesses. The legless man rests on the stump of his torso. He takes off his gloves. His fingers are long and very clean, like a doctor's, like a gentleman's. He says, *We'd like to carry you.* He's kind. He means this, but the midgets laugh in that terrifying midget way, all ripples and rills, ridiculous giggling. The woman with no arms has found the cigarettes. She strikes a match with her toes. She says, *You don't mind if I smoke, do you?*

Frances knows this is impossible. It's the dream that came after, more real than the memory she's lost, as real as the dreams of her own mother grabbing her ankles, dragging her to the bottom while her lungs fill with water. *I'm lonely; I miss you.* Rina should have thought of that sooner.

Frances blames God for everything. Was he deaf? She screamed his name. Why didn't he hear her? She would have spoken to him in sign, but the boys held her wrists till her hands went numb, till they flapped, useless.

The midgets laughed again this morning. Then she woke, arms paralyzed, hands buzzing. As the blood rushed back into her fingers, she understood, again, what had happened to her body, and her mother, and her children.

She could tell the deputies their names. She could say, *My son looks like them; ask the Koteckis for their high school yearbook.*

Clayton and Rudy are respectable now, grown men with good jobs. Clayton takes tourists on boat rides in Glacier Park. He has a little girl of his own. Last summer, Frances saw them together at a grocery store in Kalispell. He bought ordinary things: chicken thighs, hot dogs, white bread, orange pop. Planning a Sunday barbecue, no doubt. She smells charcoal and lighter fluid, sees a freckled wife in an orange blouse and yellow shorts. Frances imagines neighborhood kids running through a cold sprinkler. Their shrieks and yelps terrify her. The shivering girl who cries, who hides behind trees at the edge of the yard, whose legs are scratched and whose dress is torn — this one is Frances Zimmer who never grew up, who is trapped here forever.

She wanted to grab Clayton's wrists right there in the store. Squeeze his hands till feeling stopped. She wanted to put her name in his mouth, make him remember, make him spit it out. She wanted to stroke his little girl's head, twirl a lock of her silky hair tight around her finger; she wanted to hold that child still while she asked Clayton Kotecki if he could picture his own sweet daughter pinned to the ground by two big boys who looked exactly like himself and his brother.

Rudy Kotecki is twice divorced, an officer with the state Highway Patrol. He might stop Frances some night, catch her swerving or speeding down the lake shore. With his swirling lights and wailing siren, he might lure her to the side of the road. Would he think she was drunk? Would he ask her, very politely, to step out of the car? Did he ever know her last name? She's had three of them now. Zimmer, Vaughn, Bell — she's unrecognizable. No longer a delicate girl in a lavender dress with peach-colored roses. They killed that child in the field. They left her for the crows and coyotes.

Maybe Rudy Kotecki will be the one to find their son. He could shoot his own boy dead and still not know him.

In a small town, in a closed valley, your tormentors don't disappear — they just grow up, and their unremarkable lives destroy you.

A girl from the lake was nothing to them. She went to school in Bigfork or Polson. They were never sure; they never asked her. They lived in Kalispell — the city. They could forget any piece of that night if it made them uncomfortable. A lie becomes the truth if you tell it often enough.

When the Kotecki brothers tell the stories of that night to each other, they remember a horse with golden hair that weighed two thousand pounds. They remember the wicked gypsy woman who pointed, who cackled, who said, *You'll be sorry*. If they choose to recall a blond girl in a lavender dress, they see her riding a black pony on the carousel, rising and falling, forever turning. They wave and walk away. She is too young for them, too small. They are good boys, almost grown, decent young men who have no wish to love or touch or harm her.

Frances tells the deputies the facts, that's all. Wiry boy, skin unwashed. But she sees the red-faced baby Flint was: too angry to eat, he quivered, he squalled. She wanted to leave him by the lake or under the porch. She wanted to hide him in a nest of leaves deep in the woods. She wanted to bury herself. She just wanted the shaking to stop, for his sobbing not to be her fault, not to mimic her own cries the night his fathers took her to a field and laid her down.

Flint might be wearing Dexter's green canvas jacket. She offered it to him weeks ago, and now it seems to be gone. The clothes he steals are always too big. Look for a boy with cuffs and sleeves rolled. He will be spattered with mud — unless he's scored, unless he's taken a bath in somebody's house and found a pair of jeans that almost fit him. His face is thin. Don't be fooled; he's not fragile. His fingers are sticky, like his fathers' fingers. When she smelled burned sugar in the car last week, she knew it was the boy made of cotton candy.

Frances doesn't tell the deputies she knows the old doctor. One night, not long after Flint was born, Doctor Dees stopped by the house to see Frances and the baby. He'd called that afternoon. *You're on my way*, he said. *It's no trouble.*

He told her he didn't think she had enough milk. *Common*, he said, *with a girl your age and so small.* He'd brought a case of formula in the trunk of his car. He had two bottles. He called Flint *beautiful boy*. He told Frances, *Things will get better.* Tiny lies, meant to comfort. She wanted to say, *Please, take him.*

The doctor said, *Test it with your finger.* He meant the formula on the stove. He said it should be the same temperature as her own body.

That night, for the first time in his short life, Flint Zimmer was full. That night, he slept and maybe dreamed a sweet dream of himself. When he cried out before dawn, it was a soft whimper, not a howl.

Frances, I see you standing at the carnival gate with your deaf sister. It is one of those scenes in the play, one of those moments I can't bear if it is real. Your sister has washed your face and hands, has cleaned the knee you cut on broken glass as you crawled in the dirt, looking for your underwear. The music of the carousel torments you, like music in a box when the lid won't close. Even in the field you heard it, that one terrible song playing over and over in the distance. Your sister has given you her sweater so Daddy won't notice that your new dress is dirty and ripped at the shoulder. There is still hope in this moment: while you wait, you imagine a language that would make it possible to tell your father what has happened. But when he comes at ten-thirty, you can't speak. You stay mute as your sister. You sit in the back seat, in the dark; then you lie in your little bed, in the terrible silence of your terrible house. Your dead mother whispers from the lake. Your dead mother is the wave that pounds. She says, *Now you know, now you know, now you know me.*

THE STOWAWAY AND THE LOVER

Flint did not intend to follow his sister. He took Cecile to the road — to see her gone, to be rid of her. They walked half a mile to the E-Z Stop, a white shack at the side of the road where early morning travelers might buy donuts and coffee, root beer and peanuts. They waited here for Zeke LaCroix, though they didn't know him.

Fog drifted across the road and through the trees. They hid in the woods; nobody human saw them. Cecile wanted chocolate cookies soaked soft in milk. Flint needed fruit punch and cigarettes.

When the turquoise truck appeared, it was bright in the rain, and Cecile whispered, *Maybe this one*.

She was right. The man who climbed from the cab looked hungry, thin but solid, long legs, narrow hips — a man who couldn't float, who had no fat, whose bones were heavy. Zeke LaCroix: twenty-two years old and five years married, husband of a miserable wife and the father of three children.

He bought corn chips and Oreos, three pints of milk, a box of raisins. Later he thought, *She made me do it*. He hadn't smoked for three years, but he craved cigarettes. He resisted this temptation.

When he got back to the truck, a tiny, wet-haired girl stood beside it. *Get in*, he said. Tonight, when he's home, glad to be alive, glad to hear his own bickering children, he'll wonder if she asked for a ride or only raised an eyebrow.

He'll remember her thin wrists and soft skin, but who can he tell? Not his wife, not the sheriff. She surprised him. He touched her pale throat; he said, *I know you*. He meant she reminded him of his cousin Iris. The summer Iris was eight and he was eleven, he kissed her — not once, but many times — under the bed, crouched in his closet. Sometimes he still tastes her: dirt and salt behind her ears, lemon in her hair, sticky sap on her fingers. Is it a crime to want this? One day, in the woods, Iris let him tie her hands and touch her stomach. She whispered, *I'm your hostage.*

Now he's a grown man with a bloated wife and three kids crammed in a tin box of a trailer down in Polson. Twelve minutes, that's how long it takes to tie a knot. *Through sickness, till death* — a curse, not a promise. Zeke was seventeen years old that day, half a man, half ready. Three minutes in the back seat of Cristel's Pinto plus nine minutes in the church and he was married.

Sometimes at the edge of sleep, he sees his hand on his cousin's flat belly, her skin so white she seems translucent. He could tell the sheriff, *The girl in the truck had skin like that. I could have put my hand straight through her.*

She never said her name. She could have been anybody.

He's learned this lesson: if you love a thing too much, you'll lose it. He thinks of things he's lost: a pair of cowboy boots, black lizard; a suede jacket with fringe; a .766 caliber air rifle that took BBs or lead pellets; his own freedom. He thinks of the house that's not a house, a narrow box with four beds — and the wife who's not a wife, who only sleeps with him when she wants to get pregnant.

When he describes the girl, he'll say, *She was too hungry.*

He had to pull over a second time, at the grocery store just north of Bigfork. He bought apple juice and chocolate-covered peanuts. Did she tell him what to buy? He can't remember. She waited in the truck — she said, *I'm cold; leave it running.*

Later, he'll understand how lucky he is that the boy couldn't drive a stick shift.

Missed the bus. He knew she lied. No kid from the lake goes to school in Creston. But he didn't care; all he wanted to do was please her. When he's interrogated, first by the deputies and then by his wife, he'll say, *Help. I was trying to be helpful.*

He pulled over near the school in Creston, but she'd changed her mind. *I need to go home, I forgot my school books.*

He said, *I thought you lived on the lake;* and she whispered, *No, visiting Grandma.* He'll never guess that every time this girl says *Grandma,* she pictures a wolf in bed wearing a bonnet.

When Zeke dropped her at Dutch Hill Road, he discovered the stowaway, a filthy boy who crawled out from under the tarp in the truck bed. *Boyfriend,* he thought. He felt like a father now: she was too young, and he wanted to ground her for a month, keep her safe as his prisoner.

My brother, she said. Another lie? What reason did he have to believe her? She smiled a little closed-mouth smile, lips smeared with chocolate. He reached across the seat to wipe her mouth clean, but she leaped from the cab; she said, *Sorry.*

He didn't hear about the doctor till almost eleven, that poor old man, robbed by two children. He was at work by then, building oak cabinets in Burke Lundeen's kitchen. Burke's wife Constance heard it on the news and was so upset she had to find Zeke to repeat it.

Just kids — a boy and a girl. She hoped to God she didn't know their parents. *What a heartbreak, imagine.*

He did imagine: they could have robbed him the same way they robbed the doctor. Left him at the side of the road. *Idiot.* The boy could have beaten him with the crowbar, caved his skull after he broke his window.

And who would be to blame if this had happened?

He saw his own finger tracing a line down her throat. Yes, she let him. She leaned close and crossed her legs, like a little lady. She ate and ate, stuffed her mouth so full she could hardly speak. She gulped milk, and that's when he touched her. He said, *You're real,* and she nodded, as if she understood, as if his need to know didn't surprise her.

He was right about the boy, and the crowbar. If Flint had kept it, if he'd had it in his hand at that moment, he would have shattered the back window to get at the man and his sister. How could she let this stranger put his finger there, in the secret hollow of her throat, in the one place where she was most tender? She smiled at him; she moved closer. They drank milk from the same carton. She ate his cookies and his corn chips. She loved him because he fed her. And all that time, she knew her brother was in the back of the truck, starving. She knew he never smiled at anybody. Once upon a time, he lived as a prisoner in a hole. He carved her name in a heart on a wall with his fingernails. Until he bled. She knows how it hurt him. But he didn't stop, because he needed her there, in the cell, in his blood, on his fingers, in his mouth — he could taste her.

That was long ago, another life. This day, Flint Zimmer walked the earth, a free man. When he bit his lip, his blood tasted like copper. He gripped Cecile's thin arm as the man sped away. Icy rain burned his face. There were rocks in the ditch; he could crush her, but he didn't. She had a voice, soft and high, and he began to hear it. The rain turned cold again. The rocks in the mud grew silent. She'd stashed broken cookies in her pocket. *For you; I saved them.* She had raisins and apple juice — no fruit punch, she was sorry. She had another pint of milk. *Here, I'm not thirsty.*

So it was that the boy forgave his sister.

So it was that two children walked down the muddy road to their mother's house together.

❄37❄

T H E   E V E N I N G   N E W S

6:08. Frances Bell is on the evening news, pleading, *Come home.* As if she believes this is still possible. Bruised woman in a bright box — your children would howl if they could see you: stringy hair, sore eyes, gash of red on your lips. I can read you at last, every word; I hear you in my head, Frances.

Not like the nights in our father's house when you turned away, when I couldn't see what you were saying. *Pass the salt, storm tonight, dog on the road, owl this morning.* I didn't care what it was. I only wanted your voice in my head, the sounds I could imagine. But you spoke to him alone; you punished me.

Did you blame me for the silence in our house, for the absence of words, for my deafness? Did my signs on the beach that day distract you? We had a secret language then; only you understood me. If you'd watched Mother instead, do you think you could have saved her?

I suppose you blame me for everything: the tear in your favorite dress, the black pony, the miniature woman in a box, the Tilt-A-Whirl. I let you go. I should have followed. But I knew you would hate me for that. We never could have guessed what I might spare you — not only that night at the carnival, but every night of your life that followed.

Yes, I was afraid for you. I ran from tent to tent. From the fat man to the bearded lady, from the squealing pigs to the spotted cows. I hoped to find you on the ferris wheel, high above it all, where the man trapped in the tank of water and the quivering horse and the dwarf in her box wouldn't scare you. I said your name out loud, I swear; I kept telling people I'd lost my sister. I described you, your blond hair, your lavender dress with peach-colored roses. For you, I spoke, but nobody understood me. I was one of the freaks, a babbling fool. I should have had a tiny head and a tiny brain. People laughed; I saw them.

Frances, I knew, I knew what was happening.

You can't turn away from me now. You are caught in that box. Pixels, pixilated. A thousand colored dots, an illusion of your face in my television. You look whole, but when I sit close to the screen, I see the thousand places you are broken.

I read every word; I know you. But your voice is a child's voice, the one you used when I was nine and you were seven, the last time I heard you.

You say, *Flint, please, don't worry about the car; I forgive you. Forgive.* Could you do this?

Do you blame me for going to our father's bed? Yes, even after you came home, I did this. I left you alone in our dark room. I heard his voice. *Cross my heart.* He pleaded. *Hope to die.* I swear it was his whisper. I had to go. In a dream of myself, I floated down the long hallway. I was air, I was nothing. He grabbed my wrist. It wasn't what you thought. He was as afraid of the dark as we were, afraid of her, what she'd done, what she wanted. *Turn on the lights.* He begged me. I read his lips with my fingers. *Give me the gun.* I knew what he meant to do. *For rats, for burglars.* Liar, liar. *Give me my pills, just one more, I need it.* I had to stay. She'd shown him how, and every night she dared him to follow. He held me, yes, so tightly I could barely breathe; he clung to me in his sleep. I kept him alive, that's all. He needed me this way, a girl with real skin, warm and dry, lungs full of air instead of water.

God, it's true, he should have come to you, to us. He should have said something. He didn't have to be deaf and dumb just because I was. But he couldn't speak. He was drowning. He couldn't explain; he couldn't help us. He could only call to a deaf girl and pray she would hear him. There was no comfort anywhere, except in the lake, in the water — that was what she wanted, for us to swim toward the island one by one so that she could drown us.

It took all my will not to do it.

Frances, forgive me. I was a child, like you. I was afraid we'd lose him. She'd taught by example. I'll tell you the truth: she was only twenty yards from the shore and a mile down the lake when they found her. Her white bathing suit was snagged on a stone at the bottom. When they cut the cloth, she bobbed to the surface. She was nowhere near the Island of Wild Horses. That was just a dream we had when we loved her, when she was everything. Nobody could swim that far in cold water, not even Rina.

You think you should have watched her. Believe that if you want to. But I say we are not to blame. She chose this; and because she chose, nobody — not you, not me, not even God — could have saved her.

If we'd watched, if we'd run down the shore, if you'd called her name, she would have chosen another day. She would have done it in the bathtub.

And you wonder why I don't speak.

There is no language to contain this knowledge.

Who made us?
Rina made us.

Our mother created the world we know, where anything is possible.

When I see you say, *Come home; I forgive you,* I want to tell you: *It's too late, darling; what's done is done, what happens, happens.*

⊰38⊱

H O M E

Cecile did come home that morning. She stood in the doorway, a real girl, not just another one of her mother's visions. She wanted to sleep in her own bed, to be warm, to be silent, to wake some other day with no memory of the doctor. She'd eaten too many cookies too fast, and now she felt dizzy.

Her hunchbacked snowman was nothing but a shrunken-down hump of himself, a dirty mound, unrecognizable. Dixie cried, trapped somewhere. Three fat crows strutted across the yard, the only creatures on this earth who weren't miserable.

Inside, Mother sprawled on the couch, an ashtray full of butts and the open bottle of whiskey beside her. If the last cigarette had fallen from her lips, the house might be in flames at this very moment. When Cecile closed her eyes, she heard her mother's unborn baby weeping.

Frances woke and saw the child in the yellow coat, standing like a watery ghost in the doorway. Mother said, *Come here, lie down; be a good girl.* Cecile remembered Dixie biting herself and thought she understood why the dog had done this. It was too late to be good. The doctor's gray car was gone from the road this morning, so somebody must have found him. *Lie down with Mommy.*

Mother made herself small, but there wasn't room on that couch or in this house for Dexter and Flint and Cecile, no warm place for a crying dog, no safe bed for a howling baby. She stared at the mother on the couch, the bruised woman who lay so still, who closed her eyes, who muttered in her sleep, who never answered when Cecile asked, *Where's Dixie?*

Cecile remembered another time she'd come home later than Frances. Mommy was drunk that day too, but wide awake, waiting. Mommy grabbed her arm and twisted. Mommy smacked her head so hard Cecile's ears buzzed and her eyes went blurry. When she wrenched herself free, she ran to the car and Mommy chased her, but Cecile was quick: she locked the doors; she rolled up the windows. Mommy pounded on the glass and yelled. Mommy kicked the door. She could have gone inside for the keys. But she didn't. *Fine, freeze your little butt. What do I care?* Cecile read her lips through the pane, and in this way, she heard her.

Yes, it was cold; it was winter. No snow, but the ground was hard, the yellow grass frozen. Mother went inside the house and locked the doors, front and back. *Two can play.* Later, Cecile let Dixie in the car. She put her face in the dog's fur, but she didn't cry because Dixie wouldn't let her. Dixie licked her face. Dixie kept her warm enough, and it was hours after dark before Dexter came home and saved them.

Where's Dixie? That's all Cecile wanted to know when Mother opened her eyes this morning. It seemed important, as if the dog's life and hers were wound up tight together, as if the dog could tell her what to do, or explain what had happened.

But Mother couldn't wake enough to understand or answer, and when Cecile looked under the porch, the muzzled dog cowered in the shadows.

She didn't see Dixie, and she couldn't think of another reason to stay, so Cecile went back inside and dumped her mother's purse in the hallway. She took the driver's license just for spite and the lipstick just for pleasure. She took the carton of Kools from the freezer. For Flint. She poured whiskey on the carpet, so Mother would smell it when she woke, so Mommy would think she herself was the clumsy one who'd spilled it.

She found fifty-seven dollars in the wallet and another twenty-eight in the drawer of the nightstand. The 9 mm pistol was there too, but she didn't take it. She never liked the big black gun. She didn't trust it. Without its magazine, a pistol like that still might be loaded. She'd heard what had happened to a kid up in Whitefish. That boy waved his father's gun. The magazine was safe, pulled out, in plain sight, there on the counter. Brent Keeslar held the pistol to his head and pulled the trigger. He was grinning when he died. Two friends and his little brother watched him. He never understood about the bullet in the chamber, the one his father forgot, the one he had left there. *Daddy.* More proof: even an absent father can kill you.

She took the little revolver from the canister. She understood this gun. She could see when it was empty. She took the box of hollowpoints. *Just for emergencies.* Those words made sense; everybody used them.

She peeled off her wet clothes and changed into jeans and a faded sweatshirt. She took Dexter's jacket and a pair of Mother's jeans for Flint. He liked the green jacket, but refused to try the jeans. He'd rather be cold and wet. So let him. They could crank the heat in the car — as long and as high as they wanted.

She gave him the keys when she got outside. She said, *I'm ready.*

Now that he had his chance, Flint didn't want his mother's car. He wasn't even sure he could drive it. The last time he'd driven, he was only ten, free for a year, and Grandpa took him out in the El Camino every night all summer. The steep gravel road made the wheel jump. Grandpa said, *Tap the brake gently.* The first time Flint drove, he had to sit on Caleb Vaughn's lap. Dust in the air held the gold light of sunset. Caleb whispered, *That's our blessing.* They followed straight roads between farms. It was easy. He saw the peaks of barns and the steeples of churches, black against the brilliant sky. *Silhouettes.* He didn't know the word until that night. *Silhouettes.* A pretty word to trip the tongue, but Caleb taught him how to say it. The blue Mercury was dark as midnight sky, and shiny.

Mother rolled down her window. Her long, light hair blew around her face and tangled. He was driving. *A natural.* Cecile slept in the back, lulled by the rumble of the road. Nobody cried; nobody cursed him.

Why the fuck are you waiting?

That was Cecile, now, in this life. He was behind the wheel again, and he couldn't tell her he was scared. Couldn't say, *I don't know if I can do this.* It wouldn't make sense. He'd tried to steal the doctor's car just yesterday. Yesterday, when he was thinking moment to moment, not imagining the future. He was following instructions, trying to get things exactly right, the way the dancing car thief at Landers had shown him.

But he did remember, everything: the grip of the Mercury's steering wheel, the vibration of the seat, the roar of the engine. If only his mother would wake, if only she would fly from the house, wild-haired and fluttering, he wouldn't have to do this. He could stop now. He could sprint down the road. He could abandon his sister in the car. Let her swear her little head off. He could outrun his silly mother, leave her far behind and very small, leave her yelling, *Don't you dare come back; I'll call Beckett down at Landers.*

At last, a promise she could keep.

And he'd really go this time. It didn't matter where. He could live in the junked car above the lake. It wouldn't be that cold. He'd steal a sleeping bag and a tarp from a summer cottage. Or he might vanish completely. No need to drive or hitch, he could walk, follow the railroad tracks or the river. There were a hundred trails, a thousand. Even a tight valley has passes. He could take any one and disappear and not be lonely.

But his mother slept and slept.

She didn't burst from the house.

She didn't save him.

Cecile said, *Just do it.*

He remembered Caleb's legs moving under his legs, brake to gas; he felt the man's muscles. Now his own legs were long. Yes, a natural. He jolted into reverse. *Give him a name, make us a family.* They were moving. If he drove fast enough, maybe he could forget every precious word Caleb Vaughn had taught him.

LOST CHILDREN

From Swan Lake to Ovando, Flint was cheerful, almost giddy; he hummed with the girls on the radio; he kept time by tapping the steering wheel. Cecile painted her toenails bright red, and the wet polish looked delicious. He amazed himself: his body remembered — if he watched the lines, he could do it. Then Cecile rolled down the window and her long hair tangled and he thought of his mother and he wanted to drive off the road, wanted to punch the gas and jerk the wheel, wanted to lunge toward the river. When his grandmother called, he almost answered. But Caleb appeared again; Caleb whispered, *Easy, easy.*

They had to stop for gas at Townsend. In the shop where Flint paid, he saw a whole family, a thin man and a pretty woman, a blond boy dressed like a miniature cowboy, a tiny girl and her tiny doll in matching red outfits. Riding Hoods. He thought, *I could eat them.* In the fairy tale, the wolf ate too much, got too full, and grew groggy. The huntsman caught him snoring, full of Grandma, full of Little Redcape. The man slit the wolf's belly and found the woman and child inside, still alive, wet, but undigested. He filled the sleeping animal with stones, then sewed him shut with crude stitches. He never had to waste a bullet. When the rock-heavy wolf woke and tried to run, he fell down instead — and it was this fall that killed him.

The mother felt the girl's forehead. *You're flushed,* she said. *Do you have a fever?*

No, him, said Little Redcape. She meant Flint. She meant his thoughts burned her.

The man ruffled his son's hair. *Need to use the bathroom, pardner?*

How could they talk this way; how could anybody in this world be so soft and oblivious?

Cross a border. Flint has taken his mother's wise advice. He is trying to do this. At 6:08 the children are fifty-two miles north of Wyoming. So close, but he hasn't chosen a direct route — he doesn't even see it. Still, he believes they will make it. He could have headed west this morning, passed through Idaho to Washington. They could be in Oregon by now, three states removed. No one would track them.

But the sky is clear this far east, and Flint takes this as a sign that his decision is a good one. He keeps hearing the man who said, *Casper, like the ghost, friendly.* The chance he missed weeks ago has come back to haunt him. So it has to be Wyoming. He remembers how it looked on the map in the classroom at Landers: a big square, mostly empty. A safe place for a boy who wants to be nobody.

Fine, Wyoming. I can understand his reasons, the limits of his imagination and experience, but he should have gone south when he had the chance, through Missoula or Deer Lodge or Livingston. He's just passed Laurel, and even here he could have done it, avoided his fate, but he's stubborn or possessed or just plain tired, and he keeps heading east because the only map he has is in his head, and he wants to stay on this fast road, Highway 90. It will take him to Sheridan tonight. In Sheridan, they can sleep.

He wants to sleep now. He slept for twenty minutes at a rest stop and it scared him. Sleep is death: every time the wolf snores, the huntsman finds him.

He ate two hits of speed and drank three cups of coffee

back in Townsend. Now his stomach hurts and he's jittery, and he eats his last hit though he knows the Dexedrine won't help him.

He's both wired and exhausted. Muscles in his legs cramp; his hands lock on the wheel. Once, he blinks too long, and the tires spit on gravel. Cecile's sleepy too, and bitchy. Yes, like a wife, like a mother. She complains, hungry again — he can't believe it. She yelps when he swerves. As if that will help, as if he needs her to remind him. She's wearing Mother's red lipstick and black mascara. *Little whore.*

He wants to love her again, the way he did yesterday, the way he did last night, before the man in the truck touched her neck, before she let him.

She's whining. She wants to go home. Like a baby. He can dump her any time, hit the brakes and shove her out. If she doesn't stop soon, he'll do this.

6:11. There is a store outside Billings where seventy-seven televisions flicker. If the children could get there in time, they would see seventy-seven visions of their mother, Frances Bell, all different sizes, blown up or shrunken. The sound is off, but she keeps talking.

Sweet sister, if they saw you this way, would they laugh, or pray, or fall down weeping?

It doesn't matter. They aren't there yet. And they won't stop. Why would they? They'll never know how you looked tonight, how you begged them, how you promised love and forgiveness, how you lied to yourself and them, how your strange faith allowed you to pretend they might hear you.

Frances, nobody hears us.

⊰40⊱
T W I L I G H T

The children have left the world of whiteman's numbers. There are no miles to count, no hours. Flint's turned south at last, crossed the border to enter another country, tribal land, home of the Crows, the Absarokees, the reservation his great-grandmother's grandmother thought she'd escaped years before she turned twenty. He doesn't understand: shortcuts sometimes take an entire lifetime.

The map in the boy's head is unreadable. He thinks he sees two black lines, narrow roads splitting the Crow Nation. He knows for sure that Wyoming is on the other side, and that he will be a free man when he gets there.

His spine buzzes, a hum from bone to brain that sets a thousand indecipherable voices chittering. Three hits of speed and the coffee that washed them down made his heart flutter all day. Adrenaline surged, then left him toxic. Tonight, he's crashing. The pulse in his temple flickers, each throb a splinter of light, too fast and shallow to flush his brain with oxygen. He grips the steering wheel with both hands, but still can't hold himself and the car steady. The speedometer quivers below thirty and keeps slipping. He doesn't notice that the gas gauge just hit red and slides toward empty.

But this warning wouldn't change his course. There's nowhere to stop, and no turning back now. He's gambling on the reservation, betting his life, shooting for the border.

Frances Zimmer took one last ride at the carnival before she followed two brothers into a field. The crazy airplane looped her upside down and sideways. When she stepped off, she almost fell, and Clayton Kotecki put his arm around her. She reeled from the ride, sick already. It was easy for two boys to lead her in the wrong direction. Near the gate, she saw a man chained in a tank of water. His thighs bulged. Only a leopard-print loincloth covered him. When he smashed his face against the glass, his flat lips made him hideous. He knew everything, but didn't care. Why should he? A drowning man has his own troubles. He chose Frances from the crowd — because she looked afraid for him, because she stared, wide-eyed and pretty. He mouthed the words *Help me*.

Twilight. Every time Flint blinks, he loses his focus. He says, *I can't see*. He tells Cecile, *Watch the shoulder*.

At this hour, in the basement of the Calvary Chapel in Billings, Lucie Robideau sits among the faithful hundred Brother Duncan says, *Jesus took the nails for you*. Duncan Tulane is only a mechanic in his other life, a grease monkey, but when the mumbling mechanic enters this room, the voice of the Lord makes him a prophet. If he told Lucie Robideau that she will be the one to find two lost children, the woman would be stunned with gratitude: she knows that the greatest blessing of all is not to be saved, but to be the savior.

Tonight Duncan Tulane does not speak to her alone. He doesn't even recognize this small, dark-skinned woman. The mystery of Lucie's life to come is hidden in the code of another language. Brother Duncan raises his palms to show them Christ crucified in air. *Not through his hands, brothers and sisters, but through his wrists, through his bones, so that he could hang on that cross for hours, so that he would not fall down, so that he alone could suffer for your sins. He took the nails through his feet, and his feet, by now, were dirty. All this he did so that you might know the mercy of his Father's spirit.*

Now I ask you to walk; I ask you to raise your hands for Jesus. Prepare yourselves to live or die. Show Jesus you are ready.

Flint could stop outside Pryor. A car pulled to the side of the road for the night wouldn't attract anybody's attention. In this country, darkness is absolute and comes suddenly. He passes but does not see a church called Soul's Harbor, a sign that says MEDICINE HORSE FOR SHERIFF. He passes shacks and trailers, a burned-out house high on a hill, a yellow dog, a white rabbit. Bright shirts strung on clotheslines snap in the dark, flags of surrender, but the boy cannot hear them.

At the edge of the little town, a hand-painted sign with a red arrow points east to Saint Xavier. The road south is dirt and gravel, and there might be signs drawn in the sand that show his future, but it's too late for Flint Zimmer to get out of the car and read them. He turns east, he follows the arrow.

Lucie Robideau does walk, with the others, twenty, then thirty, then fifty, and the Holy Ghost is big enough to fill all their pitiful human bodies. Brother Duncan touches her forehead with his thumb, a gentle touch, a nudge that leaves a mark like ashes. She falls down flat on the floor, and one by one all the others fall down around her. Some curl, some rock, some moan — but Lucie lies paralyzed, unable to feel her feet, unable to move one finger. The body that had been hers is numb; her frail, miserable shell is empty. She is alone with the Holy Ghost, alone with God, alone with her beloved Jesus. The others are alone too. Do they know this? She hears them, yes, but they are somewhere else, above or beyond her.

If she could move her arms, if she could roll, she would pass through their bodies, those illusions of bone and skin and muscle.

She speaks, she knows all things. The woman who was a stupid girl is now a genius, full of God, full of language. He gives her the gift of tongues. She is blessed, and nothing matters. She can say all she ever needed to say, all that is forbidden in the words of men, all that human beings wish to keep silent. She praises him as he loves to be praised, in his own words, with her own tongue, in secret.

When Frances Zimmer spun in the Tilt-A-Whirl, her blood roared. All the sounds of the carnival blurred to become one sound, and she thought the noise in her skull would shatter her.

Halfway between Pryor and Saint Xavier, the road bends and Flint drives straight. It's this simple. He sees the long curve but is too tired to pull and hold the wheel. The car spins out on gravel, jumps the ditch, and plows through a fence before sputtering to a slow stop in a muddy field.

When it's light, when it's day, when it's happened, Earl Troy, tribal policeman, will pace the length of the skid and estimate Flint's speed at less than twenty miles per hour.

The number reveals nothing. If a woman drowns, she drowns — why measure the depth of the water? But the children are unharmed. Only their noses are bleeding.

One headlight opens a tunnel over yellow grass; the rest of the world and the inside of the car are as black as the lake.

Flint revs the engine, shifting drive to reverse. The tires spit mud and dig into the field. It doesn't matter: the gas he has in the tank would take them only another seven miles. If Flint believed God had hands, he would ask to be lifted. But his god is deaf and dumb and blind and crippled.

He thinks of the hole at Landers — the blue room, the ice box — how secure it was, how narrow. He took comfort in the limits of isolation. Nobody to hurt, no hand but your own to harm you. He hated it then, but wants it now, a quiet place where nobody else speaks in any language.

In the cell underground, he made no decisions. Twice a day, somebody fed him. He was not responsible for himself. He was not responsible for his little sister.

Cecile wipes the blood from her nose with the back of her hand. Does she blame him?

Matins, confession, work, lessons — exercise, vespers, meditation: this is the safe life of a convent girl or a prisoner. Those who have no rights shall not be held accountable. Obliterate desire. Your will is your curse. Stifle it.

In the little window high above her, Lucie Robideau sees the sky turn dark, blue and more blue, the most beautiful color she's ever known. Only her mouth and her eyes and her mind move. She doesn't want to blink. She is afraid of that sky, afraid it will break if she doesn't watch it every second.

She hears others praying over the body that was once hers. Brother Duncan and Sister Kate and Brother Esmond — she can't say their names or recognize their faces, but she senses their true spirits; she knows them. Then Sister Rubilyn kneels at her feet, Rubilyn Donner with her ruby lips and her long red nails and her short red skirt and her bare white stomach and her tight striped top, just a tube around her breasts — this is how Rubilyn will look afterward; but now, in prayer, perfect in the eyes of Jesus, perfect in her own love of Lucie, Rubilyn Donner is holy.

The others rise or vanish; the others pray far away in their strange tongues, in their distant bodies. But Rubilyn belongs to Lucie alone; Rubilyn Donner has been sent by God to teach her the mercy of love without judgment. Lucie did judge — yesterday and the day before. Even tonight she judged, before she fell down, before she lay paralyzed, before the scorned woman Rubilyn lay hands on her in the blue light of the Father. Now Rubilyn the redeemed raises her hands and holds them suspended, inches above Lucie's body. She feels how they move, each place they do not touch: bare feet, naked arms. The fingers of these hands trace each rib; these fingers with their bright nails are the fingers of God, the hands of the Spirit, warm with the blood of Jesus, and Lucie Robideau speaks in God's language, to God only.

No words have ever come so fast; no sentences have ever poured like water. She sees herself at the blackboard, eight years old, a stuttering child. Teacher said: *You'll write it a hundred times before you go home.* There she is at ten, eleven, twelve — little Lucie locked in her bedroom. Grandmother said: *For your own good.* She would learn to spell. *If you sit still long enough.* Night after night, Lucie saw her face reflected in the window; she saw the dark yard beyond the pane, the yard where Jesus paced, where Jesus waited for her to finish her homework. Jesus said: *Patience, my darling.*

Flint Zimmer chooses to walk. He chooses to take the gun, though Cecile is the one who understands how to use it. He slips it in his pocket because he is afraid of whispering wind and skittering animals. He is afraid of trees that waver like dark women underwater. He leaves the headlight on, because he likes knowing it is there, behind him.

As their pupils open wider, the children see the shape of this land, the rise of distant bluffs, the steep slopes of folding gullies. They see silhouettes of rocks and cows and fences. Far, far away, swirling stars fall behind black mountains.

A coyote howls, and a cow wakes to moan her answer.

The accident has given the children one last jolt of adrenaline, and this is how they find the strength to walk, and this is how they keep walking. But the little girl trails behind, and the boy is too tired now to try to help her. If you asked him, he wouldn't know where he is going or why. He wouldn't have any idea how long this journey will take him.

Cecile is a hundred yards behind Flint, then three hundred, then a mile. She's guessing. On this road, ten feet could be an impossible distance, a boundary she cannot cross, a chasm.

For a long time, she could see him, even in the dark. Sometimes he turned to yell, to call her name. She watched him climb a hill; then she blinked, and he vanished. If he's said her name since then, she hasn't heard him.

Long before the sun rises, the circle of the horizon begins to glow and the whole blue sky opens above her.

⇥ 41 ⇤

MORNING

Lucie Robideau, one more motherless child, thirty-two years old, grateful servant of Jesus. This morning she's delivering food and clothes to the Pretty Eagle Catholic School in Saint Xavier on the Crow Reservation. It's a weekly miracle, and her only mission. She brings notebooks and pencils, erasers, rulers — small gifts, badly needed. Once she brought a box of unworn shoes, her greatest treasure.

Each week when she returns from Saint Xavier, her station wagon is empty and there are no boxes left in the basement of the Calvary Chapel in Billings. But if God created the world in six days, surely he can lead the people back again; he can help the faithful ones carry their cans of beans and jars of peanut butter, their boxes of oatmeal and powdered milk and baby formula.

Her red Ford is seventeen years old. Its steering cables are loose, and there's a slow leak in the radiator. Every day, Lucie must remember to fill it. Even a God like hers can't keep track of such details.

Rosana sleeps in the back, strapped tight in her carseat. Lucie Robideau has never had a husband, but Jesus thinks of his own mother and forgives her. Rosana's father lives with his shy wife, his three sons, his blue-eyed daughter. Once, while Keenan Violette sang in the shower, Lucie looked at all their tiny pictures in his wallet.

She hasn't seen Keenan for more than a year, not since the night she told him she was pregnant. Sometimes she misses the man, but that small sting is nothing compared with the sorrow she feels when she goes to stock shelves at Safeway and has to leave Rosana with Mrs. Rice for eight hours. Mrs. Rice, who has five children of her own, says it is dangerous to love one child too much, and yes, even Lucie knows her love for Rosana is a weakness. It is too fierce and too jealous, and it keeps her from loving God purely. But Jesus understands. *The poor will be among you always.* He meant it was the sinner Mary's right and privilege to wash his naked feet with her tears, to rub them dry with her long hair, to anoint him with sweet oil. Who dared to judge? His time with her, with all of them, was brief and precious. So Rosana's time is precious, because she is a child born to a woman without a husband or a mother or a father. She is a gift from God, unexpected.

Sometimes, when Rosana is asleep, when Lucie is alone or scared or angry, she prays: *Sweet Lord, have mercy.* Sometimes he comes quickly and she feels his body. He lies down next to her. He's bleeding, so she washes him, as Mary Magdalene did, and the washing makes her holy.

Sometimes he stays outside. He moves through the willows by the river, and she tries to follow him in her mind, but it's dark and she stumbles, and he says, *Go home, wait for me; I'll come when I'm ready.*

But this morning, as she drives across the reservation, she is not troubled in any way. She sings as she sang last night before Brother Duncan touched her head, before she fell to the floor, slain in the Spirit.

She can't remember even one word of last night's holy conversation. And it would be wrong to try, wrong to conjure God's language without his help or permission. Wrong to speak in the car, wrong to be overcome while she is driving. *Unless it is your will, Lord. Unless you want it.*

The Holy Ghost is mute today. God the distant father has returned. *Patience,* he says. This is how he always speaks. And Jesus whispers, *my dear,* to soften God's instructions.

Her whole life, tender Jesus has been enough. She didn't need the Spirit too. It was wrong to need, to want, to clamor. So Lucie Robideau sings in the ordinary words of ordinary men. Her voice is low and sweet, and she remembers to thank God for what happened last night, for the blue light in this morning sky, which reminds her of the blue window that didn't shatter, that didn't cut or pierce her.

By day, words come slowly. She can't recite, can't memorize

a single verse. But she can sing whole chapters, whole psalms: with music, words flow, a river of sound — all she has to do is float through them.

She flunked first grade and fourth. Grandmother sent her to her room night after night, but it did no good. Numbers never added up; letters tipped and jumbled. Grandmother took the ruler to Lucie's hands while Jesus stood right outside the window. He let the old woman stripe the child's palms. He said, *You can bear this small hurt. I promise.*

When Grandmother left her, Lucie curled on the bed, knees to her chest, uncovered. She dreamed. And in the dream, the bed was a lake; and in the dream, she lay on the bottom. She was not afraid. A hundred fish swam close and touched her. Each touch became a kiss, and where they kissed, her hot skin healed.

Every day, Lucie Robideau talks to Jesus, and every day, he is there to answer. She does not know when or how this started. His is the first voice she remembers, his the first face she saw over the cradle. Though he has disappeared, though he has faded with age and grown invisible, though his wounded body is only an image she conjures, she cannot recall a single night of her life when she has not heard Jesus whisper. His voice too is faint, has lost its fine edge and definition. But he is the Word. He is the thought that comes swiftly. He is the absence of fear. *And this, my dear, is how it should be.*

She's looked for the other one, her own father, Victor Robideau. Sometimes Grandmother says he's dead; sometimes she says, *I think he's in prison.* She doesn't know where. *Maybe Washington, maybe South Dakota.* He is to blame for her mother who drank too much, who swallowed too many pills, who slept too long, who choked on her own vomit. *Let that be a lesson.* Grandma Faye says Victor killed a man in a knife fight outside a bar, but another day, in the same story, Victor Robideau is the one on the ground — the other man has the knife; the other man's hands are uncut but bloody.

Lucie knows one thing: Victor Robideau, if that is his real name, has dark skin like hers, dark eyes. Lucie's mother was freckled and fair. Lucie has a photograph, proof of the woman's pale existence.

She cannot see her brown self in this picture. Her black hair is thick and straight, her mother's fine and red and wispy. Grandmother tried to scrub Lucie clean, tried to make her skin shine, but no soap or sand or prayer could work this miracle. Children on the playground chanted: *Go home to the reservation.*

She wanted to go. The house where she lived with her grandmother was close enough to walk across the border to the Crow Nation. When she was small, she thought her father waited on the other side. She imagined him in a bright green shirt and a black hat, but the sun was always in her eyes, and her father's face remained mysterious.

One hot summer day when she was nine, she did walk that far, seven miles, alone. A tribal policeman found her and brought her home to Grandma Faye, who knelt, who grabbed her shoulders, who said, *My baby, where were you?*, who waited till the man was gone to shove her down the hall, to kick, to strip, to scrub her.

Grandma said, *He's not that kind of Indian.* Lucie wondered, *How many kinds are there?* Now she knows: too many to find her father. Like nine hundred thousand other dark-skinned men, Victor Robideau has vanished.

Every time Lucie visits her grandmother, she has to forgive her for scraping her skin raw, for swatting her palms, for telling lies, for crying, for saying, *I never meant any harm; I only wanted to protect you.*

When Lucie forgives Faye, Jesus forgives Lucie for her impatience. Faye is an old woman but still mean, a hunched little crone, crippled by arthritis. Grandmother was once strong enough to shove Lucie into her room, once quick and clever enough to pull the door closed, turn the key in the lock, and make the girl her prisoner. Now she's a skinny humpback with a cane who hardly has the balance to walk, but who still has the will to shake her stick and curse her daughter's daughter.

Lucie saw her last night, before the meeting, and Faye shamed her with words. Lucie may be thirty-two years old, a woman, a mother, but she is forever a child to Faye, one more failure of love, one more bitter disappointment.

Grandmother's house crumbles around her, the wood frame as sick as she is, as poor, as fragile. She called Lucie a fraud, a do-gooder. *But if you were truly generous,* she said, *you'd stay here tonight and clean your grandmother's kitchen.* She said, *That, my dear, would be an act of mercy.*

And if Lucie were charitable and full of love, she would buy Faye a new television. The old one is black-and-white, its screen tiny. With its antenna taped on top, it brings her noise and flickering light; it keeps her company. She leaves it on all day. And any day now it will blow or fizzle.

Once a week, Lucie brings groceries. Pound cake, tea, milk, sugar. It's all Grandmother will eat. She dunks the cake to make it soft. *It's all I want. My teeth hurt.*

Lucie Robideau can sing and sing; she can fill this car with her own voice and the words of the Apostles, but in every space, in every pause, Faye's voice rushes up to silence her. *Selfish,* she says, *just like your mother.*

IN ANOTHER COUNTRY

She spots the blue Mercury in the field just before dawn. There is no one else on the road this morning, so Lucie Robideau is chosen. *Whatever happens, I'm beside you.*

She leaves Rosana asleep in the carseat. Though she is afraid of what she may find, Lucie prepares herself to lay hands on anybody, no matter how long dead, no matter how damaged. She looks in the Mercury, front and back. She walks around the car five times, each circle wider than the one before it. No one lies in the grass. Nobody here is bleeding.

The sun rises over the bluffs. Jolted by light, Rosana howls, and Lucie scrambles back to the station wagon to stroke her face, to hold her close, to whisper, *Shush, you're okay, we're okay, it's nothing.*

Minutes later, when Lucie sees a little girl walking down the long road, she thinks, *I must know her.* But why is the child here, between Pryor and Saint Xavier? Why is she alone so early in the morning? Lucie thinks, *She could be my own daughter, or a girl like me, looking for her father.* She corrects herself even before Jesus reminds her, *She is my child, and she is me, though I do not recognize her.*

If this blond stranger rode in the Mercury that smashed into the fence, where is the driver? Where is her mother?

Here, Lucie. You. This is the answer.

She is not afraid. The child is alive. What is there to fear in this moment? Her life is a prayer, and the prayer now is simple: *Dear Lord, let me help her.*

When Lucie stops, the little girl opens the passenger door

and climbs into the station wagon — as if she expected Lucie to come, as if they are sisters who fought long ago, but who no longer remember why or when their trouble started. This morning, all is forgiven. Lucie says, *Did you have an accident?*, and the child shakes her head, too tired to speak.

Lucie nods. She means, *Okay*. She means there is time. She has patience. Patience now seems infinite. She pulls out slowly, ever careful — as soon as they are moving, she feels a rush of words, a watery pattern of comfort, a rising wave in her chest. She knows it is God, his Holy Spirit. She understands that he is offering his explanation in words that have no translation. The child needed her, or she needed the child, and now they are together, and they are both safe, and the sun rises in the east, and the unbroken circle of the sky is endless.

The girl closes her eyes and sleeps. Rosana sleeps. Lucie's children are calm at last; everyone is out of danger.

When Lucie sees the other child, she is not surprised. She knew he must be here somewhere, the one who drove the car, the one who crashed it. She did not find him in the muddy grass, so she kept her faith and waited. But she did not expect him to be so small, or dark, or narrow.

For a moment, all desire leaves her. She looks at the sleeping child by the window and wants nothing. When the sun strikes the girl's face, when the sun glows in her yellow hair, when this child is suspended in golden light, Lucie Robideau sees how the wounds of men might be healed.

She slows down to stop for the boy, and the girl wakes, and there is one word, a cry, and the word is *no*, and the girl turns, and her bright face falls in shadow.

Why one lost child wouldn't want her to stop for another, Lucie Robideau cannot imagine.

No. Again the girl says it.

Lucie hears and understands, but the warning makes no sense, so she does not heed it.

She sees the boy, the black-haired one, thin and sick and tired. She swerves to the shoulder. Even if she knew what Flint has in his pocket, even if she saw the gun in a vision, she would stop; she would try to help him. She trusts her God to watch over her. It is right to help children, the abandoned, the weary. No harm will come to her in an act of mercy.

The one in the car finds three more words: *Don't. My brother.*

The girl locks her door, then twists to lock the door behind her. The boy can't get in on her side.

So is Cecile to blame?

She'll have the rest of her life — five years or fifty or a hundred — to replay these moments out of time on the reservation, on a road where her past bends to meet her future, where every blade of grass and every drop of water and every molecule of air speaks one separate word of her history.

Flint pulls at her door, furious. He wants to get it right this time. He wants to redeem himself. He doesn't know that Lucie Robideau would take him anywhere. All he has to do is ask. She would keep his secret. She has secrets of her own. She'd take him across any border — Canada, Wyoming. If he'd let her stop in Saint Xavier to deliver the food and clothes and notebooks to Father Vincent, she'd take him all the way to Casper. If he'd leave her thirty dollars for gas, she'd give him everything else she has in her pockets: a prayer card with a picture of the Sacred Heart to bring him comfort in times of sorrow, a watch without a band to tell time in the whiteman's world. She'd give him twenty-two dollars for food and the silver cross she wears on a chain for protection. She'd give him the maps from the glove box, a pack of gum, a bottle for water. She'd give him hope. She'd give him her blessing.

There's only one thing Lucie Robideau won't do. She won't get out of the car. Because Rosana is in the back, and she would rather die than lose her daughter.

Flint does not see the baby, only the woman and Cecile. He pounds on Cecile's window, but she won't help him. He runs around the front of the car. He stumbles. He's a clown, and he sees this. He opens Lucie's door wide. He says, *Get out, now, I mean it.* He wants to prove himself to Sten Gunderson, the man who held a pistol to his head all those years ago, the man who sent him to Landers in the beginning. He wants to prove himself to all the invisible boys who follow him everywhere. The bad ones taught him to steal and burn while the good ones stood and mocked him. He wants to prove himself to Dexter Bell, who said, *Give him twenty bucks — I'll pretend I never saw him,* to the judge who said, *For your own good,* to the teacher who said, *Hopeless,* to the mother who said, *It's too far to visit,* to the sister who said, *Why the fuck are you waiting?*

The woman won't get out. She's stubborn. And she's strong, heavier than he expects. He tugs, but she doesn't give. He slaps, and she turns the other cheek. Yes, really. He knocks her so hard she lurches forward, but then she turns again to look at him, and her face is soft or surprised or forgiving, and he hates her for this, for her mercy, for her refusal to move, for her stupidity, for her failure to close the door and hit the gas. If she's not going to get out, why doesn't she just leave him? And his hand is on the gun in his pocket, and he says, *I'll shoot you.* A ridiculous boast. He doesn't mean now. He doesn't mean this instant. But the gun is going off, as if words themselves have squeezed the trigger.

The little gun, the Taurus, the .38 caliber with the bobbed hammer, the gun from the canister loaded with five hollowpoints, the feels-like-a-toy-in-your-hand gun — that gun is in his pocket. He's just going to slide it out. He's just going to show her. *Easy, easy.* The gun in the hand, still in the pocket. He just meant to wave it. So she'd move. *Goddammit.*

Now this has happened.

Somehow the gun has exploded.

And somebody is screaming, somebody is crying; somebody's swearing, and the woman, the foolish woman, is praying. Is she? Is that what he hears, this babbling? *Shut the fuck up or I'll kill you.* Even now the gun is still in the pocket of the jacket, but he tilts it up and she kicks him and the gun is going off a second time. He didn't mean to shoot, he didn't want to shoot, but it's his finger on the trigger and she looks at him, amazed, eyes wide open and she's not praying now, not saying anything, all sound has stopped; the unbelievable voice of the gun has silenced every creature in the world. If she had just gotten out when he asked, if time would only spin in the other direction, big time to little time, back in time fifteen seconds. God, are you no longer capable of even the smallest miracles? Still she sits there. She won't move, and now the gun slips out of his pocket, and the third shot is deliberate.

He drags her from the car onto the pavement and she won't die. She stares. She sees him. And he feels her thoughts: *My son, my child.* He knows her question: *Why have you killed me?* And he hates her and he hates this life and he hates the god who made him. Then he's in the car, shifting hard, punching the gas.

Where's the friggin' gun?

He's dropped it.

All the sound stunned out of him, all the sound that stopped when he pulled the trigger, all the words and cries this ground has ever heard come rushing back at him: buffalo hissing, wolf howling, child whistling, sister wailing, tires ripping, woman praying, old man chanting, cricket chirping, mother cursing, crow squawking, ice man melting, the whole earth moaning — a stream of sound, a torrent, sound without sense, sound without mercy.

Then it's there. It condenses. It is one sound in the back seat: a baby crying.

How can anything that small yell so loudly? If he still had the gun, he'd stop the baby's squalling. But the gun is on the road a mile back, with the woman.

He can't stand it, the terrible noise, the pinched red face in his rearview mirror. Less than two miles from where it happened, he slams the brakes.

He turns to Cecile, though he looks surprised to see her.

He says, *Get rid of it.*

What does he mean?

You, now.

Every word is a stone he swallows.

Every word hurts him.

She sees her chance and takes it. Cecile Vaughn climbs over the seat to release the screaming baby from the carseat. She's strong with terror. She pulls the child free and opens the door. With Rosana in her arms, she steps into the rest of her life and starts walking back toward the child's mother.

Gone now, forever, the sister he loved but doesn't love, the sister who forsakes him. He doesn't care. How can he? The one on the road is dead or dying. She's bleeding out. He's done it. He's killed himself and Cecile and the woman with three bullets.

He floors the pedal and flies blind into the blaze of sunrise.

❧43❧

CATECHISM

Who made Flint?

We did, all of us.

You, me, Rina, Cecile. Our father and our father's father. Our grandmother Tilia who climbed a mountain to lie down with Cyrus Zimmer. Caleb, Dexter, Royce Beauvil, Floris. The boys at Landers who tormented and taught him: Dale Geyde who stole cars, Martin Ortiz who raped his cousin, Evan Jewell who dangled in the bathroom. Sten Gunderson and all those who scorned Flint for his first crimes. All who feared his filthy fingerprints. Those who tried to love him, and those who wanted him locked away for half his life, sealed tight in a prison or a hole where they wouldn't have to see him, where they could pretend he'd disappeared, that they were safe, that their children and Flint Zimmer had nothing in common.

Who made Flint?

Those who judged and made decisions, those who witnessed and did nothing. Nathan Dees and Lucie Robideau who wanted to help him. Zeke LaCroix who gave him a ride but didn't know it. Those who spoke their minds. Those who stayed silent. We are all connected, victims and perpetrators, allies and adversaries: Custer, Sitting Bull, Buffalo Bill. The Crow scout Half Yellow Face, the Cheyenne woman Monahseetah. The ones who knelt in the snow, the ones who flew to Canada. Our mixed blood spills on the ground; our mixed blood swirls in our bodies. We are the place where enemies meet. We are the place where everything happens.

These truths I hold to be self-evident: the hunter shall be hunted; the betrayed shall betray us.

Who made Flint?

Those who tried to stay alive, those who committed self-murder. All those who had no ears, all who let themselves be slaughtered.

Who made Flint?

Those who taught by example. Those who taught by contradiction. Baptiste Little Knife who let himself be called Baptiste Thomas, who loved our mother but could not keep her.

Who made Flint?

White Deer Sees who fled her ancestors to marry the Métis, to become homeless. Antoinette who died of influenza, who abandoned Sebastien, who abandoned their child. Leora who could not sleep in a house with four corners, who deserted her daughter, who left Rina alone to feed five hungry brothers.

Who made Flint?

The junkman who built a child from spare parts and jolted him to life with electricity.

Who made Flint?

The junkman's father who gave one son his ranch and the other son a scrap of land on the Flathead Reservation.

Who made Flint?

We did, we did — we did. All of us. He is ours, together.

We all touched him, whether we knew it or not, whether or not he recognized us.

His crime is our crime.

In the end, we must ask the murderers to forgive us our trespasses.

I see you in the field, Frances. The lights of the carnival flash in the distance. I see Rudy and Clayton Kotecki, the two brothers who made Flint, and I think: those begotten in violence come to their rage with full hearts and empty bellies.

How will we find redemption?
Mourning for our merciless enemies.

⊰44⊱
M I R A C L E S

Lucie Robideau wants nothing.

Rubilyn has found her. These hands open her body; these hands spread the ribs to touch the heart, without pain. To caress, without desire. Her blood spills into the blue light above her; her blood turns the blue sky violet. Her body swells, numb and huge and cold, no longer flesh: her body is a cave of snow, a child's dream, a night to come, closing around her. The wind speaks, the heart flutters. If these are the last words, she wants to follow sound. But if they are only the ghosts of noise, echoes in ice, she wants to let go of them.

The sky bursts, red and blue; the window shatters; a thousand shards cut her in a thousand human places, and the voice she tried to hear and not hear, the voice of wind and tree and water, this voice is Grandmother's voice: *Selfish. Just like your mother.*

Is this what God most wants to tell her?

The rasp of her own breath is a rattle of stones thrown by children in a schoolyard. *Rosana.* They danced around her years ago. They chanted: *Go home to the reservation.*

She is home. *Rosana.*

God gives her pain with the word, white hot, each bullet a glowing knife that cuts through bone and muscle, spleen and spine, bowel and esophagus. God helps her remember. *Pitiful, human.* And Jesus says, *There is not much time, forgive him.* Lucie doesn't know if he means God, or if he means the boy who shot her. She would weep if she had the strength, because she can't forgive either one of them, not because of her own pain, not because she fears her own death, but because God has let the boy steal the child.

She sees herself far away, sitting in the shade of a tree, green leaves thick above her. It is summer, the one to come, and she is living. Three yellow butterflies land in the grass, each one as big as her open palm. God has sent them to amaze her. God has put Rosana in her arms, so Lucie rocks and sings — gently, gently.

When she opens her eyes, the white trees at the side of the road are bleached bare; the butterflies close their wings and vanish.

Jesus who sees everything, who knows her fear, says, *Trust me, I'll find our children.*

He leaves Lucie alone with God the father who is neither comforting nor angry. He watches blankly. The Holy Ghost must be somewhere in this wine-dark sky, but the one who gave her voice last night leaves her mute this morning.

⚜45⚜

OUR SAVIORS

Earl Troy, tribal policeman, three wives and seven children, six still living and one with the ghosts dancing. He's the only one on the road between Pryor and Saint Xavier, the only one close enough to find Lucie Robideau this morning. He checks his watch, 8:07, whiteman's time, his shift is over; but as long as he's in the cruiser, Earl Troy is on duty.

He lives in a one-room house, a shack with a privy behind it. He can piss off the steps, under the stars or in broad daylight, and there's no wife at the window to say, *What are you doing?*

Is this freedom?

Last night a woman in Wyola knifed her husband and the man shot her — flesh wounds, nothing serious. Earl had to cuff them both and drive them up to Hardin where the man's wounds were cleaned and stitched while the woman got sober in lockup. In the end, they forgave each other and cussed him: he was the enemy.

Earl Troy loves all his wives: Wanda, Simone, Pauline; and he loves his children: Trevor and Leonard, Simone's boys, grown men, both married to white girls, both living in cities. He loves Wanda's twins, Leann and June, fifteen and not identical: June could be a boy of twelve, hair cropped short, quick and skinny. Leann looks like a woman of twenty. Last time he visited, she kissed him on the mouth as she always did, but this time it scared him. He loves Willie, the boy who will be a dancing boy always. He loves the little girls, Pauline's Lorelei and Kateri.

Yes, Earl Troy loves them all, but he can't live with anybody except the dog, Kita, the old retriever who dug him out of the snow one winter, who found him by his smell, who bit his numb hands softly, who licked his face until he woke, who brought him back to life, though he thought he wanted to die that day, a good day to die; he was laughing when he fell down, drunk and stupid. He loved the snow. It didn't hurt him. But it did hurt later, after the dog led him home, after he tried and failed to build a fire. His bones ached. Wind whistled through the shack. The skin of his hands and face cracked raw where the ice had burned him. He thought he would die this way, sober and sorry. He shook — he couldn't stop shaking. His own body turned violent with quivering, trying to keep itself alive, trying to jolt him. The dog lay down on the bed beside him, as close as she could get, almost on top of his body. She kept him warm enough to survive till morning. Now she was slow and crippled: the two of them shared this pact with sorrow.

Sometimes, on Earl's days off in July or August, Wanda invites him and his other wives and all their children to her house just off the reservation in Roscoe. He brings steaks for the women and himself, buffalo meat that he buys in Billings. He brings hot dogs for his daughters. Pauline roasts potatoes and corn in the coals, wraps them in foil and puts them down in the fire. Simone fries bread. At dusk, the three women lie on blankets, watching stars, waiting for meteors. They love one another, and this, he thinks, is a miracle.

The girls sit on the porch, whispering secrets and eating watermelon. They spit seeds, a contest, so he joins them, but Kateri, his youngest, who is only six, always wins. That quiet child, polite and pale, who says she wants to be a nun, who seems to know this already, this same child always spits the farthest. She could whoop, she could gloat, but she doesn't — she's a good girl, shy and pretty like her mother, and despite her wish to marry Jesus, Earl hopes that she and all his daughters will find men who love them, men who can live in houses without putting their fists through walls as he did.

This morning, in the police car, he thinks of the watermelon seeds, and a warm night last summer. If his daughters don't find men to love them, he hopes they will love one another as they did that night, with love that needs no explanation. He remembers the women murmuring in the grass, and he thinks, *Yes, maybe this is better, after all, maybe they don't need me — or any man*, and his sudden knowledge makes him both sad and grateful.

Earl Troy finds the blue Mercury, its tires dug into the mud of the field, its single headlight still faintly burning. 8:19. Someday, when he's old, when he retires, he'll smash the watch with his heel. Today he's trapped by time: he'll have a report to file.

He finds the story written in mud and begins to translate. By footprints he knows that the driver was a woman in a man's shoes or a boy without substance. The marks are wide, but shallow; this one's light and moves quickly. The passenger was a child in sneakers. A young girl, he thinks, she leaped through mud and left three half-prints.

Somebody else came later to look in the car. A small woman who walked in five circles.

The plates start with the number seven, Flathead County. Earl Troy knows the number for every county in Montana. He keeps track of who drives through his country, tourists mostly — for every two Indians on their way to Plenty Coups' log house, a thousand Anglos appear, all on their way to the battlefield where most are stunned and some still grieve for Custer and his slaughtered soldiers.

Earl Troy knows this land. Every bend in the river whispers

its name if you listen. He knows the depth of the water and the stones at the bottom. He knows where rolling hills fold into treacherous gullies, where you can lose three ponies or three wives, though they stay close enough to smell you. In the hills, he can lead you to a herd of white cows. In the valley, he'll show you the black ones with white faces. The cows belong to whitemen, but the Indians still keep a herd of scrawny buffalo. He could drive this road in absolute darkness. If you blind-folded him and made him walk, he could tell you exactly where pink rock from the center of the earth bubbles up and breaks the surface. He knows where the ground holds enough water for cottonwoods to grow, where the chickadee lives, where the mountains look like castles.

But he cannot guess where these people are, or why they've come, or if he'll find them. Just children, he thinks, runaways, lost now. He could make a call from the radio in his car, check for reports of stolen cars or missing children. But he waits. He sees from their tracks that they're okay. There's dried blood on the dash and the doors, a few fingerprints and the wipe of a hand. Bloody noses. He finds no sticky trails of red in the greasy grass, no dragging foot, no deep mark in the mud to show where a soldier fell or staggered.

If he's guessed right, if they're runaways, he wants to know their story before he sends them back to Flathead. Not every child should go home. If these two are walking, if they've stayed on the road, he'll find them.

So he won't be home on time this morning. Maybe noon — if he's lucky. He wouldn't mind so much for himself, but Kita is there alone, shut inside, waiting. Waiting is intolerable for the young; but for the old it's even worse — like dying.

He watches the odometer, trying to imagine how far they could walk. The damp mud had a thin crust, so he guesses the kids went off the road sometime before three this morning. Depending on their luck or stamina, they could be anywhere by now: Wyoming, the Black Hills, Billings; they could have crossed the border, heading for Lame Deer, Cheyenne country, a separate nation, beyond his jurisdiction. No way to know if they caught a ride last night. The one who stopped and circled their car might have found them minutes later. If he doesn't catch them between here and Saint Xavier, he'll make that call to the Flathead sheriff.

Five point two miles from the Mercury, he sees something moving on the road ahead. *A dog or a deer, nothing human, not a child* — is this a prayer to some forgotten god, or is he certain? The shape is still more than half a mile away; and because the sun is in his eyes, because he's forgotten or lost his dark glasses, he can't be sure what he's seeing.

He remembers a dog he did find, half coyote, half husky. She looked like a little wolf, this crossbreed. Her front legs ran in the grass, but her back legs were completely stiff, paralyzed. Some pissed-off rancher had shot her in the spine. *Sheepkiller.* He left her in the ditch to die; he didn't waste a second bullet.

The animal's eyes opened too wide, whites showing. She'd been lying in the grass for hours. Earl Troy was still a child, not yet a policeman, not even close — he didn't have a rifle or a knife or an awl or a pistol. He didn't have a vision of himself in the future. The closest shack was at least a mile away. The trailer where his mother lived was three miles behind him. The dog pleaded, *Save me.* He had only his hands and the rocks in the ditch, and this is how he was going to have to do it.

It was her ear that killed him, her ear turned back, almost inside out, to expose the pink whorls, and he thought, *I shouldn't see this.* It was too intimate, too dangerous. He looked away while he touched her ear; he was just going to cover it with his hand, pull it down, but she snapped her head too fast for him to move and she bit him hard — she drew blood from his arm, and it was this pain that gave him the courage he needed.

She took two blows to the skull. He was screaming. She snapped at the air, her mouth bleeding. Why had he fought with his mother? Why had he come here? He couldn't remember. The dog was his punishment — or his salvation.

The third blow calmed her, the fourth broke her skull open.

He went home, covered with her blood, and his Christian mother forgave him for all his crimes, for the sins of pride and anger.

All this he sees in an instant: as if a boy still kneels on this road, and Earl Troy has torn the air to watch him.

If he finds an animal this morning, he'll just shoot it. If it's a deer, he'll have to drag it to the ditch and call for a truck. If it's only a dog, if he can lift it alone, he'll wrap it in a tarp and put it in the trunk, then try to find its owner. But Earl Troy knows that whether or not this body is claimed, chances are good that he will be the one to bury it.

If he's wrong, if it's human, if the one in the road is a drunken man, he'll take him home or to the mission, give him someplace safe to sleep. And he'll be kind, and he'll speak quietly, because he who almost died in the snow, he who was saved by the dog named Kita, he who put his fist through the wall in his wife Wanda's bedroom, he who can only live in a shack with an animal, he has no right and no reason to judge anyone.

Earl Troy is slow to see and slow to understand.

He does not want to believe that the creature in the road is not a dog or a deer, not a drunken man, but a wounded woman.

He knows Lucie Robideau. When he stops, when he kneels, he wipes the blood from her face with his bandanna, he says her name, *Lucie*, and he says the Lord's name, *Jesus*. He does not believe in her god; the name Jesus is only a word to him, a gentle curse of amazement. He knows Lucie for her work, for the gifts she brings to the school, and though he does not trust or even like her god, he believes the work she does is sacred.

He holds her head in his lap. He is stupid with grief. He says, *Hang on. I'll call a chopper.*

He has to leave her to do this, has to set her head back on the pavement; he has to stand and walk away, back to his car, back to the radio.

If she could speak, she would ask him not to desert her. She'd tell him it is too late. She who is prepared to leave her poor body knows this. She would tell him each second now is precious, each moment splits: a minute is the lifetime of all their people, a stone near her wrist is the whole world. His face is the face of God, and she loves him.

He returns centuries later, and the words he speaks are incomprehensible.

He can't stop weeping. He loves her more perfectly than he ever loved anybody. He would exchange his life for hers, take his beating heart from his chest if he could save her. His wives' names, his children's names, his mother's name, his own name — all these, forgotten. There is the road, and the grass, and the sky, and the sun that has risen, and the day that some god has made for ever and ever.

He who holds her now, who loves her, knows she is bleeding

out. He knows she means to leave him on this road, that she has moved beyond pain, and he is afraid for his own life, afraid because he does not know who he will be after, when she is gone, when he is abandoned. Still he speaks in the whiteman's tongue, still he uses human language. *Stay with me*, he says, *they're coming.*

Though her eyes are open wide, he understands she cannot see or hear him.

Does she whisper? Does she speak? Is it possible?

He thinks he hears one word. *Jesus?* As if to ask him.

He starts to tell her who he really is; he struggles back to his own name, to the limits of words, the prison of language. Earl Troy, tribal policeman. And even as he remembers the name, his name, he realizes it means nothing now — nothing.

He has no reason to define himself. No reason to speak a truth from this world. No need to deny her god. Truth is for the living. Argument is for the ones who will survive till evening.

She is not among them.

He will not burden her with facts.

If she wants him to be her hero Jesus, he will be her Jesus. It's not that hard: all he has to do is whisper: *Yes, I'm here, my child.* On another day, he might have said that Jesus is a whiteman's lie, a savior sent to give you hope while the whiteman steals everything, while the whiteman chops the earth to pieces, while he destroys your god and slaughters your buffalo, while he poisons the wolf, while he kills your faith in one another. She is brown-skinned. She is golden. And though she lives in the whiteman's world, by her own blood she must understand their history: the whiteman keeps god in his pocket; the whiteman uses Jesus like a coin to buy anyone he wants here.

But this is a day to die, not to argue. So he lets her god stay. He becomes Him.

Blind Lucie, deaf Lucie, she can't form a word, still she prays in another tongue, inside, in silence. Still she sees in another world, in another time, into her own body where Rosana is a single human cell and then a child in an instant, where Rosana is her and they are whole, then in a moment separate. She sees her body will go one way, and Rosana's go another. Jesus who can raise the dead could slow her blood. But he doesn't. She cannot ask. He will not explain. And if God let Jesus die, why should she be special?

Everywhere, every hour, doctors perform miracles with bodies. In a hospital far away, they fill one man with the blood of twenty others. With hollow needles, they take the marrow of a brother's bone and inject it into the veins of his sister. Liver, heart, kidney, lung: they can exchange anything inside you.

Even now, while Lucie Robideau dies on the road, doctors somewhere do this. You don't need to be a saint to live. You don't need to be the son of God to heal.

Forgive him. There is not much time.

She knows now that Jesus wants her to forgive the boy who shot her. If Jesus is here, if he has come back to her, then Rosana is safe. He promised he would be with Rosana as long as she still needed him.

God the father gives his child Lucie one last vision. Mercy comes in a different way for each person. Some will be raised from the dead, some sealed in the cave forever. For Lucie Robideau, mercy is memory. She sees the man from her church, the one who burned his hand with hot oil last winter, who grabbed for a smoking pan, who dropped it as it exploded. She sees his terrible flesh, his skin in flames, his body crackling. They all prayed for this man together. Later he told them that Jesus had watched over him every day in the hospital. Jesus, who understood the limits of pain, comforted him in his suffering, in his passion. Jesus murmured like a lover while a doctor in Billings sewed the blistered hand inside the man's own chest. This is not a story Lucie imagines. This is the truth; this really happened. The doctor said, *It's our only hope with burns this bad; sometimes your own body can heal you.*

Lucie Robideau who was once slow, who so often failed, who could barely read words printed on a page, who could not add columns of numbers or fathom their mysterious meanings, this same woman in her new and brilliant blindness reads her own dream, and is saved by her own vision.

She is the body; the boy is the hand. They are one. He is her. She must open her own chest, her own heart; she must sew him inside where her own grace might heal them.

Jesus, as he rises, as he lifts her, says, *Yes, my darling, you are everywhere.*

CATCHING THE COYOTE

Hunters converge: the Absarokees and the Cheyennes; sheriff's deputies from Custer County; highway patrolmen from Wyoming and Montana. They block every border, the ones between states and the ones between nations.

No longer armed, no longer deadly, Flint Zimmer drives too fast to steer the old station wagon. On a dirt road south of Saint Xavier, he skids through mud and gravel. He rides the Tilt-A-Whirl. Desperate boy, he pulls hard to correct his spin, and the car is a crazy airplane, rolling upside down and sideways. Three doors burst open when the ride stops, but Flint Zimmer keeps flying.

Once upon a time, in a prison for lost boys, a little car thief danced his crime. That quick child loved to play the trickster. Bragger, actor, sweet deceiver — Dale Geyde never performed the pirouettes of chase and capture.

Flint lies in the damp grass, the dead yellow grass, pounded flat and buried deep beneath drifts all winter. He remembers a child long ago who rode a bicycle down a dark highway, who sailed into high weeds one cold night in November. Like him, that boy woke, amazed to feel cold dirt between his fingers.

This time, he's broken: two ribs cracked, left lung punctured, right ankle twisted, pelvis bruised, cheekbone fractured, eyes swollen, face and hands lacerated.
Miraculously conscious.

He remembers now: that awful crying. Cecile slammed the door and left him; Cecile chose the baby. Whose baby was it? Some stranger's. A man in a truck touched her throat with one finger, and she didn't bite him. She never loved Flint enough. She was always unfaithful. *Sleep, little brother*. She is bigger than he is. How did this happen? They lie in her narrow bed and her skin is warm and her mouth is soft and her hair is silky and now, even now, he closes his eyes to let her kiss him.

The stunned woman says, *Why have you killed me?* The baby howls, Cecile vanishes. He feels the gun jump in his hand. He hears three explosions. Did he do this? No, just a cap gun — powder under paper, not bullets — he's too small; he slips the toy gun into a leather holster. The real gun hides in his pocket. The revolver fires itself before he can touch it. Just a bad dream. Like the dream where he torches the boat, and flames on green water thrill him. This dream comes often and always leads through that hot tunnel to a cool blue room with cinderblock walls. He throws himself to the floor. And again, and again — six times or sixty?

Is this how it was? Is this why he's broken?

The guard helps him stand, the guard helps him fall. This might be another way to say it.

Three great birds hover. Big enough to block the sun, loud enough to fill the world. They have blades instead of wings. They chop the air to pieces. These three land in the greasy grass. They are the triangle; he is the center. From gaping holes in their bloated bellies, they spit barking dogs and crouching men with rifles and shields.

They have found him. They have come to deliver him from evil.

Shattered as he is, he finds the will to kneel. The snarling pack surges toward him and the men shout, but the roaring birds and yapping dogs are too noisy: he cannot grasp human orders.

God gives him strength.

He transcends pain.

He rises to meet them.

The leader of the pack leaps. This black dog with golden ears and a pale gold stomach weighs seven pounds more than Flint Zimmer. He's coiled. One body blow to the chest — that's all it takes. The muscled animal knocks the wounded child to the ground, then clamps the bare throat to hold him. Three slender females rush forward, snapping like turtles, speaking a silent language. They are well trained. Merciful in their own way. With their sharp teeth, they grip his wrists and one ankle. If he struggles, they could kill him. He knows this. The dogs speak in low growls to him only: *Lie still*, they say, and he obeys. Their jaws clench, but their teeth do not puncture.

The men who follow are less gentle.

They wear vests to deflect bullets. They bring fear to deflect compassion. They shield themselves with words: *brutal, remorseless, murderer*. They are on him.

One hooks chains to the dogs' collars and pulls hard till their mouths open. One kneels on his back, splintering ribs already fractured. The boy can't breathe. The dogs shimmer: morning light burns through the hair of their legs — yellow, auburn, silver. The dark one bursts to flames, and the child on the ground sees through him.

The man who squats on top of Flint, who pins him flat, who shoves his face into the mud, this man weighs more than the three sleek females put together. The dogs nip and groan while the man presses the last gasp of air out of him. Flint tries to speak, to beg, to surrender, but his own name is the only word he can murmur.

Somebody twists his arms to cuff his wrists, and still the one who kneels won't stand, won't release him. Another shackles his ankles. The fourth man kicks his head and hammers two words into him: *Little motherfucker.*

The boy spits black blood, and the first man rises, finally satisfied. Flint's chest heaves. The body wants to live. Air, there's one breath inside one lung, and the body fills with light and the boy watches his kicked head roll away from him, through the yellow grass, down the gully. He wants to laugh because his empty skull looks so surprised and so foolish.

⚜47⚜

WHOSE CHILD IS THIS?

Frances, nobody reads this part of the story. Our captured boy, this battered killer, will deliver no eloquent speeches about his own grief or the long suffering of his people. But the child knows sorrow. Yesterday, he wanted peace and tried to flee; he gave up his own country; he prepared himself for exile.

In the play of his life, Flint Zimmer is never one thing or the other. From the head of a wise chief springs the furious half-grown warrior. That vengeful child says: *I have done it; I have killed; now you will have to fight them.*

Through the years of his long flight, Flint Zimmer learned one lesson many times: every ally turns betrayer, every tribe refuses refuge. In the end, even your own people will not claim you.

Sometimes he ran. Sometimes he wandered. When he came to our doors, we fed him once, but denied him shelter. Our houses were too clean, his pants and boots too muddy. We withheld comfort. When he burned, we did not sew him inside our chests; we did not give him time to heal. We were afraid of this strange son, so we cut him out of our bodies and saw too late that the wounds we carved would never close, and the blood we spilled would flow forever.

We threw him down a pit with wild boys. We locked them all in tiny cages. We tossed them scraps of meat through bars, or sprayed them with cold water.

Our bad boy became a mute prophet. He stamped a vision of his future in mud and snow, but failed to heed his own warnings. Like a soldier without ears, he fell into the camp of his enemies.

Terrified hunter, pursued Indian — in the play of his life, our son is the only actor. He wears a blue coat and black boots. He wears a wolf's hide; he wears baggy jeans and a torn jacket. He keeps changing masks: first dark, then pale. Now the victim, now the killer.

He stands naked while two guards shave his skull. He stands shivering while the one with powder disinfects him.

We see at last that neither skin nor blood defines Flint Zimmer: he is the homeless one, the child without land, the boy who lost his family.

We taught him well, Frances.

We put the gun in his hand. We said, *Don't use it.*

We showed him where to aim. We turned our backs and he shot us.

⽷48⽷

ON BLEEDING OUT

The first bullet grazed the thigh, and the wound was hot, but not serious. The second tore the spleen.

Be not afraid: for I have redeemed you. I have called you by your name, and you are mine.

Lucie Robideau turned to face her attacker. *When you pass through the waters, I will be with you; and through the rivers, they shall not overflow you: when you walk through the fire, you shall not be burned; neither shall the flame kindle upon you.*

How will you die?

Lack of oxygen.

No matter who you are, no matter what you believe, this is the answer.

The third bullet pierced the chest.

If you weigh 126 pounds with your fluids still contained, a six-pint bleed will probably be enough to arrest the heart. If a bullet tears a vascular organ — the lung or liver or spleen, for example — there is not much time for a savior to appear. Repent. Hope for a miracle. You might lose consciousness on a reservation road and wake up tomorrow in a hospital in Billings. But if a bullet or a blade severs the carotid artery, the iliac, the aorta, pray fast: you have less than a minute.

If you are Lucie Robideau, if your wounds are multiple, if your blood has soaked your shirt and jacket, if the torn vessels of your chest are bleeding into a hole in your esophagus, if your blood is pooling in your stomach, if your hands are too small to stop it, but too large and human to reach inside and repair the damage, you have less than an hour to live, to dream, to believe, to love the man who comes, to pray for the daughter who has been taken. You have forty-seven minutes to curse God. Don't do this. Time is precious. Forgive him, as he forgives you when you say, *Why have you left me here like this? Why did you let him take Rosana?*

Think fast. The pressure of your blood drops quickly. How much have you lost? A cup, a pint? Could you hold your blood in your own hands, could you drink it now and live till evening? If marrow pumped into the vein can find its bone, why can't the blood you swallow find its proper vessel?

The body is fierce, but limited: your pulse flutters; the heart seeks its own rapture. A pump cannot understand that no matter how quick its strokes, there is no way to replace your losses. You breathe hard to compensate for lack of oxygen; *you know not what you do;* your lungs heave, trying to saturate what blood is left, but it is not enough; it is not enough; and the man comes and you call him Jesus and you are calm and nothing hurts and you forgive the boy and the pressure falls and there is not enough blood to carry oxygen to your brain and you sleep and the vessels collapse and the furious hammering slows and your breath is a rattle and a gasp and your body contracts and you vomit blood and your pulse drops and your heart is tired, so tired, and you vomit again but you do not feel it; you do not see the man covered in your blood; you do not know whose hands hold you, and nothing hurts, nothing hurts, nothing hurts now and forever.

⊰49⊱

CATECHISM

My sister's children have made our family famous. You can read our story in the daily news. Our faces flicker on your television.

Bruised and swollen, chained to a hospital bed in Billings, our brittle boy is unrecognizable.

What are angels?

The ones who dare to touch. The ones who stitch wounds and set bones. Who drain fluid from the chest. The ones who come three times a day to slip a metal pan under a boy's buttocks. Who do not judge, who touch his body without fear or love. The ones who wash him.

In a courtroom seventeen days later, Flint Zimmer is strong enough to stand at his arraignment and enter the plea, *not guilty,* a small untruth that gives his lawyer, Mr. Tom Lovett, public defender, time for bargains and investigations, time to read the case, time to interview his client. But anyone who buys a newspaper in Billings or Kalispell or Great Falls or Missoula sees a color photograph of a thin killer in an orange jumpsuit, a shackled little man fragile enough to shake his chains, slight enough to slip through them.

If you study that image, if you read the history of a boy's crimes, from burning boat to murdered woman, if you imagine his grimace is a grin, I suppose you have reason to be relieved when you learn that this ruthless killer in chains, this preposterous child, will be tried as an adult and not a juvenile.

Once upon a time, a woman drowned in a lake wide as a sea, and the people who loved her became new and strange to one another, but the lake was still a lake, and what was familiar saved them. Before my father sent his children to Coeur d'Alene, before the nuns sent me home again, I scrubbed the tiles in the motel bathrooms, I washed sheets and towels, I mended pillowcases. I bleached the stains from the sinks. I scoured the toilets. I did not complain with my hands or my body. I was teaching my father how to survive. When I vacuumed the carpets and made the beds, I was telling him he didn't need a wife because he had a daughter.

At twilight, swallows came by the hundreds. I remembered the liquid ripple of their cries and felt the air sing around me. My father walked along the edge of the water while I stood on the dock, and we were together this way, because the birds had come, and their quick flight made a pattern like music. My sister pedaled her bicycle up and down the highway. Even if we'd called her name, she would not have answered. When storms rolled down from Canada, when rain swept over the mountains from the Pacific, Rina rose up from the lake spitting sea birds. I heard them in my sleep, and their voices woke me. I was always right: in the square window of clouds, I saw bursts of gulls flapping against the wind, using their huge hearts and all their strength just to stay in one place, and I knew that this was how we too would have to do it.

One bright summer day, a woman with dark hair and strong legs swam away from her husband and her daughters. A woman they loved too much, a woman besieged by their clamoring and staggered by their mute insistence, this woman chose the lake and the cool waves and the songs of wild horses.

That August, cherries sweetened in the dark. Who would have believed we might live to witness ordinary miracles? And so it is again, cherries ripen and we eat them, and our lips are dark with juice, and the insides of our mouths hold every secret.

It is almost September when Cecile Vaughn, eyewitness to murder, testifies against her brother. *Is this the gun, is this the jacket, how many shots, did he aim the third time?*

The boy will never tell his own story. Where would he begin? With the voice of a sturgeon, with a Red River cart, with carousel music?

These are not mitigating circumstances.

When Flint sees his sister in court, does he know her?

Her mother has taken her home where she sleeps in her soft bed night after night, where she throws sticks for the dog to fetch, where she crumbles graham crackers in milk and pretends she is a child. Today Cecile Vaughn wears a pink dress and white anklets. Accomplice or witness? Her role shall be defined by language, by the needs of the law, by our own desires. This morning I curled her fine hair. My sister said, *That's what you can do to help me.* I tied a lavender bow; I touched Cecile's small face; I made the sign for *pretty.*

Nobody wants the girl to share Flint's crimes — not even me, I confess it. *Who stole the gun?* Nobody dares to ask her.

If the boy is all bad, we can be safe again: we can cut evil out of ourselves.

Doctor Nathan Dees might speak the truth if he could bear to face it. But in kindness and in shame the good doctor says, *I think he made her do it.* He stares at the girl swinging her legs, and refuses to believe a child so sweet and fair could have molested him.

Zeke LaCroix says, *She was hungry and afraid.* He will not let himself remember Cecile the tiny woman, Cecile who leaned close, who ate chocolate cookies, who made him ache, who made him want to touch her. She was not afraid. He was. His finger on her throat quivered. He will never speak of it. Each small lie, each omission of truth, makes the next lie necessary. He needed the girl too much. With his touch and with his love, he made our boy more desperate.

On the charges of attempted car theft and aggravated assault in the case of Doctor Nathan Dees, Flint Zimmer, the firestarter and the thief, is found guilty. On the charge of unauthorized use of a motor vehicle in the case of Frances Bell: guilty. On the charge of car theft and deliberate homicide in the case of Lucie Robideau: guilty. On the charge of using a firearm during the commission of a violent crime: guilty.

Once upon a time, none of this had happened. Who we were then, I cannot remember. One long night in March my sister and I waited for word of our children. Caleb had gone home to his other wife and his three obedient daughters. I was the one who sat by the window in my sister's room, who saw the dark becoming day while she lay sleeping. When she woke, she did not ask, *Where's Caleb?* In our houses, people vanish and reappear without warning. Our father stood in the doorway, silhouette of himself, a man's frail shadow. I was afraid; I saw him old in an instant.

Did he sense the truth already?

Does knowledge come from the word, or from the body?

Frances and I had hours to live in hope and ignorance, just as we had lived that day when the men in boats looked for our mother, when we still had grace, when our God still had mercy, when we were small, when we were stupid, when we were good and full of light, when we prayed to sweet Mary, mother of God, and she gave us her son, and Jesus loved us.

We forgot only this: he had to die to prove it.

When does grief begin? Does suffering start when another dies, or only when we hear of it? Imagine our unfathomable innocence.

I have learned that murder makes strangers intimate. In late September those who knew the woman and those who failed to love the child gather again to see Flint Zimmer sentenced. Today, the state shall seek and find its retribution.

Cecile Vaughn, that gray-eyed child, wears a pale green dress with yellow swirls. She's shined her own shoes. I see her face reflected twice as she sits between me and my father.

Wanda Troy, Earl's second ex-wife, rocks the child who was saved by Cecile. Rosana Robideau who is not yet two years old will know her mother Lucie only through the stories we tell or by the radiant light of her own visions.

My thin-faced sister is swollen huge with the son who shall be good, who shall be called Jacob, who shall be safe, who shall be protected, who shall not be torn or seduced by his hungry siblings. People stare, amazed by this woman, Frances Bell, who would dare to bring one more violent child into their world.

She teeters, ready to burst. It could happen any moment.

Dexter Bell, soon to be the proud father, holds his wife's arm, and helps her walk, and keeps her steady.

Caleb Vaughn, that kind, befuddled man, will never comprehend his first wife or first child. What is mercy without understanding? When he tried to love my sister, I wanted to tell him: *The passion of a motherless girl will destroy you.* In signs he could not read, I might have said: *Dear brother, water breaks stone, and is broken upon it. Leave us.* Now Caleb the skillful butcher sits in the back of the courtroom with his hat in his hands and his narrow tie knotted too tightly. He wanted to give the boy his name; he thought the word itself might save him.

Some testify and some stay silent.

Rubilyn Donner remembers the last night of Lucie's life. *I saw her filled with God. I touched her, and she trembled.*

Duncan Tulane helped her load the station wagon at five o'clock the next morning. Lucie Robideau sang as they worked, a high, sweet song; she had made music of Paul's words to the Corinthians: *Although I speak with tongues of men and of angels.*

I had forgotten her name, Brother Tulane says, *and I was ashamed to ask her.*

Earl Troy stares at his open palms, as if he hopes to find an answer written on his hands, as if at last he'll see and grasp it.

Who among us can measure the loss of a day, a life, an hour?

Lucie's crippled grandmother says, *She's all I had. What will I do without my Lucie?*

Who is wise enough to weigh the suffering of a dying woman, or the misery of those who survive her?

Black-haired, blue-eyed Keenan Violette — Lucie's faithless lover, Rosana Robideau's elusive father — bows his head and seems to pray but says nothing. He makes no claim in any court of law: his betrayal and his loss are unspeakable. Will he ever touch the smooth cheek of his daughter, will he whisper his own name and tell their secret? *Rosana, my love, you are not an orphan. You are the rose and the violet, and you are mine, now and forever.*

The doctor who examined the body of Lucie Robideau describes her wounds, the loss of blood — thigh, spleen, esophagus

— the brief pain, the shock, the body's wisdom, the flow of endorphins from the brain, the bliss, the delusions, all the logical reasons a woman this damaged might have seemed unafraid, why she might have smiled and grown calm, why she might have mistaken Earl Troy for Jesus.

Who will speak for Flint Zimmer? Who will tell a tale of a crow and a coyote? Who will say there was once a summer night when a child sat on a man's lap and drove into the sunset? Who will whisper that once upon a time the boy who lived in this boy's body repeated the word *silhouette* until it was holy? Who will describe the one who slept under the porch, rolled up wet and cold in a scrap of carpet? Who will tell the judge and God and these witnesses we see gathered before us that he smelled his mother inside her car, and the scent of torn petals and damp hair and spilled whiskey made him dream that she had kissed him?

Jeannette Dees confesses: *My husband's lost twenty pounds. He can't sleep with the window open. He won't drive alone. I take him to work and pick him up in the evening. He's a pediatrician who's afraid of children.* She looks at her husband in the third row of the courtroom. *I'm sorry,* she says. She turns to the judge. *He asked me not to tell you.*

Frances Bell never speaks in defense of her child. How could she explain? *I wanted to love him. I tried, but I couldn't.*

We see the photographs again, the body of a woman torn open.

What good would it do if Cecile made the sign for *brother*, if she said, *When he fired the gun, he did not know that this would happen.*

In the bright light outside the courthouse, Caleb Vaughn tells a reporter, *What did they expect? The boy grew up in prison.*

Floris Beauvil, who never forgave Flint for fire on water, tells her neighbors, *My husband's a fool — or a better person than I am.*

Sten Gunderson says, *Five years ago I caught that little son of a bitch in my house. I could have told you then something like this was bound to happen.*

To me, alone, my father says, *He won't survive without hope.* I read his lips when he murmurs, *Sometimes a man needs to lie down in the grass or walk beside water.*

In sign, to myself, in the dark, I say, *Imagine this silence.*

What is mercy?

Ninety-nine years for the murder of Lucie Robideau. Eighteen for the assault of Nathan Dees, who could have died, who looks that fragile. Ten for taking Lucie's car, plus six months for borrowing the Mercury from Frances. Two months for stealing a crowbar that shattered a window. Four months for stealing a revolver from a canister; ten years for using it to kill a woman.

To be served consecutively. One hundred and thirty-eight years. With the stipulation that Flint Zimmer will not be eligible for parole until he has served at least thirty years of his sentence. Thirty years until he stands alone under stars or falls asleep in the hot sun with his sister. Thirty years until he wakes and strips and dives into the cold water. Thirty years until he rises, ecstatic.

Remember: parole is a privilege.

Thirty years. If he can be good. If he can obey every order without question: *Do not pass food or medication or your handkerchief to another inmate. Do not speak in line at food service. Do not press your ear to the wall. Do not try to communicate through the air vents.* Thirty years. *A knock will be considered a*

*signal. Signals are Class II Infractions for which you will be
written up, for which you face a month's detention.* Thirty years.
*Do not use slang when speaking to a staff member. Do not scar
your own arm or try to draw an inky dragon. Do not attempt
to feign illness in order to avoid work or procure medication. Do
not set fire to your hair or your mattress or your toilet paper. Do
not braid a rope from the shreds of your blanket. Do not attempt
to hang yourself. If necessary, the state will murder you by lethal
injection.* Thirty years. If he can stay alive and in his senses. If
he can eat and dress and wash and keep believing he is a person. If he can sit in a room one day and swear by Jesus who
died on the cross that *Yes, a lifetime in a cage among exiles has
reformed me.*

Who will he be at forty-six? A man who went to prison as a
child, a boy of forty-six who has lived ten years on the outside.

What is mortal sin?
One that takes away the life of the soul.

Flint Zimmer hears his sentence without a flicker. If he feels
for himself, if he's sorry for Lucie, or Cecile, or Rosana, if he
regrets the grief he's caused his mother, or the pain and suffering he's brought into the life of one good doctor, his frozen
shoulders do not betray him.

No remorse, Judge Loren Whittaker says. *I never saw it.*

Nobody asks: *Did you consent to kill Lucie Robideau?*
Consent? The word of the church has no place in the courtroom. Did the gun ask permission? Did the boy agree to do
its bidding? Did a cloud pass overhead to say: *These are the
consequences?*

Lucie Robideau is dead. Three times Flint Zimmer pulled the trigger. There is not one moment of my life when I wish to forget this. If I let her go, who will teach me to love the boy who is her murderer?

Every cut on Flint's face has closed and healed. The bones of two cracked ribs have mended. Both lungs fill with air. He breathes; he moves among the living.

When he turns, I do not see the fine white scars that mark him. His eyebrows arch like a woman's. He looks surprised. Is he? Terrified or deadly, who can read him? He tosses his head, but his hair is shaved too short to fall forward. He limps. Perhaps his pelvis or ankle or ribs still hurt him. Or perhaps he is numb to all pain, and it is only the shackles that hobble his footsteps.

Alone in his cell in the county jail, Flint Zimmer lies on the floor, shivering. The bed is too far, a foot away — he cannot reach it. Tomorrow a white van and three officers will come to take him to the state prison in Deer Lodge. He's not a boy tonight; he can't go back to Landers. His crimes have made him a man, and as a man, he is responsible.

Did it happen the way they tell it?

He has one hundred and thirty-eight years to ponder these questions: *Why was the gun in my hand, why was the hand in my pocket?*

There is proof he can't deny: residue of gunpowder on his fingers. When he puts them in his mouth, he thinks he still tastes it.

There are witnesses: his sister who has betrayed him but who would not lie; Rosana Robideau who saw everything but who has no words to tell her story.

There are photographs to sway the judge and jury. When

Flint closes his eyes, wet blood on the pavement flows thick beneath him.

Who was that woman on the road, and what was she trying to tell him? Is it true what they say? Did she talk to God in his own language? He pulls his knees to his chest and holds them close. If he cries, his keening voice is high and soft, beyond all human hearing.

⊰50⊱

T H E   L I V E S   O F   B I R D S

In my father's house, we are quiet. I do not mean that the girl is mute and the man has lost the habit of speaking. I mean our hearts are slow, our pulses stutter. I mean our breath is shallow, and we set our feet down softly in the hallway.

Weather saves us. We are cold in October. Tamaracks on the hills turn golden, and the wind shakes the brittle needles until they fall around us. The lake is gray or green or blue and broken. At night, it rocks us. In a dream my father and I dream together, Rina wakes wet and shining.

Geese pass overhead in great flocks. They know the land beneath them, the length of every lake, the winding path of every river, the exact distance between farm and forest, the line where the swamp becomes a meadow. They honk, I suppose. For my sake or his own, my father pretends he cannot hear them.

Early one November morning, we take the chain saw and the ax to the woods and cut three dead pines. For half a day we saw and strip and split and stack. In this way, a father and a daughter promise each other they will survive another winter. Where a fire blazes night after night, they shall be warm together.

Flint Zimmer lives in a prison inside a prison. For melting a plastic spoon into a hard point, for filling his pockets with dirt, for possession of one broken mop handle with splintered edges and five aspirin stolen from an inmate with arthritis, he's earned himself thirty days detention.

At his hearing, at his jailhouse trial where there are seven witnesses and three judges but no lawyers, he will not tell the hearings officer why he made a spoon into a weapon. He does not explain that he intended to pack the dirt in a sock, then dampen it and let it harden. He cannot say how the mop cracked, or why its long splinters seem so precious. He will not confess that the prisoner whose joints ached was willing to exchange five aspirin for one pulpy apple, three sugar cubes, and half a cigarette. *Do not borrow, purchase, loan, or steal property belonging to another. Exchanges of any kind are forbidden.* It's right there in the yellow book, the one called *Guide to Adjustment.*

Do not strike, wound, or assault anyone, including yourself. Every answer leads to another question. If he says, *I needed protection,* he will have to name the man who whispered, *Better find yourself a husband, baby.* Was this a threat? *Love letters or threats must be reported.* He has choices: he can be a boxer or a slave, fight every man in the joint, or submit to one and find shelter. He can live like a wife: clean a cell, make a bed, run errands; he can make trades for his lover: give up his cigarettes, his sugar cubes, his coffee; he can turn his face to the wall and close his eyes until the day a younger, prettier boy arrives, until a boy less used catches his husband's fancy.

Flint Zimmer is all bone and tiny muscles, five foot six, a hundred and thirteen pounds, a killer, yes, but still slim in the hips and willowy as a dancer. *Look at him; he's candy.* With his scruff of beard and faint mustache, he looks like a pretty girl in a costume. *How long do you think it will take us?* Two hours, or four minutes? For reasons you cannot comprehend, a guard might close his eyes while three men pin you in the shower. They'll turn you inside out while water pounds your buttocks. Whatever happens here, happens and happens forever. The men who touch you one night are free to eat breakfast with you the next morning, free to grunt or curse as you eat, free to make the sound of a wet kiss, free to spit in your food, free to touch your leg under the table.

Do not attempt to feign illness or injury. Those who fail to report for meals face ten days detention.

Flint knows how easy it is for a guard to be oblivious. The week he arrived, two inmates with baseball bats killed the one named Pileggi within a hundred yards of a tower. Why didn't the man in the tower shoot? If the body lay in plain sight, why did it take the yard officers forty-five minutes to find him? Kidnapper, rapist — the particular details of Pileggi's crimes made him unpopular. Was Pileggi a snitch? The guards let the prisoners think so.

Flint remembers Evan Jewell, that fat boy who hanged himself at Landers. And when was that? A lifetime ago, a decade? Did it happen last night? Flint saw him this morning. And then he saw himself, naked, dangling, purple face, white body. His fingers tingle. He wants to skip a stone across the lake at twilight. *Just one more time, then you can lock me up forever.*

It's true he needed protection — if not from three men with trembling hands, then from himself, from his dreams and his imagination. *Some people experience the following emotions and symptoms as they adjust to prison: difficulty getting to sleep and staying asleep; dreams and nightmares; excessive worrying; obsessing; feelings of sadness and regret; brief periods of depression; feelings of loss; obsessing; fears of how other inmates will treat them; obsessing; feelings of anger, resentment, and revenge; obsessing.*

What do they mean when they say *brief*? As compared with thirty years, or in relation to a hundred and forty? *Better get yourself a husband, baby.*

On November third, Flint Zimmer torches his shirt and singes his mattress. In this way, inmate number 37703 secures himself another month in isolation. Did he mean to lie down in his own fire? He filled the block with smoke, and the men on his unit had to sleep with wet towels over their faces. For thirty days he's safe in lockup. He learns the simple truth: in prison, punishment and protection have the same dimensions. He measures his cell by his footsteps, heel to toe, twelve by seven. He can touch the ceiling with his palms flat. The lightbulb is bolted behind a Lexan shield so that a frenzied boy experiencing feelings of frustration or loss or revenge cannot break it. Lights pop on at six and off at ten. Regardless of what you are doing. *Obsessing.* Men have left messages on these walls. *Be Not Afraid. Jesus Rules.* They have carved hearts and swastikas. They have listed the Stations of the Cross. They say: *This is number ten.* Yes, you are stripped of your clothes after you fall the third time. *Your body is your temple now — better learn to live inside it.* The bed is a concrete slab and a thin mattress. You are allowed to keep a toothbrush and toothpaste. The guard will bring you an electric razor twice a week. *If necessary.* You have a metal toilet and one roll of toilet paper which you tear to tiny pieces and use to stuff the holes of the air vent.

If you don't, it's too cold to sleep and you spend the night thinking. The window is not a window. Diffuse light filters through a four-inch slat at the back of your cell. You cannot see past it. *Translucent.* Another lovely word to hold in your mouth, and you will have all the time you need to comprehend its mysterious contradictions.

On the ceiling, a prisoner who may have been experiencing a brief period of hopelessness or rage or depression has etched these words for your contemplation: *Murderers and thieves who compare themselves to Jesus deserve to be crucified.*

There's a slot on the metal door that the guard can open. When he taps his keys, be quick: he wants your hands to cuff them. And so he shall. When he's done, withdraw them. Stand back while he opens the door. He has a chain for your waist because you are dangerous. You grin. *Dangerous.* You love the thought; you cannot help it. The cuffs lock snug to the chain. You might run or roll, but you shall not strike anyone, including yourself. Three times a week, this is how you walk to the shower. You are safe. Jesus rules. In the yellow book that is guiding you toward adjustment, the words say: *Respect your body. Keep yourself and your living area clean. Exercise regularly. Shower often.*

On December ninth, after six precarious days of freedom in the main population, the insolent boy disobeys the direct order of a staff member: Flint Zimmer refuses to enter the shower; while being stripped and dragged, the prisoner spews and spits and flails — the inmate in question uses obscene and abusive language. Afterward, the boy has a broken nose and a bruised pelvis. One guard has a long scratch down his arm and a welt below his left eye. Did Flint do this, or did the man come home late last night and fight with his wife at three in the morning? Do wives ever come here to confess? Is a prisoner ever found not guilty?

For crimes real and confabulated, inmate number 37703 is transferred to Maximum Security, where the rules are the same as detention but the sentence is indefinite. He eats and pisses in his cell. The smell of the body is constant. Twenty-three hours a day he can lean against these walls and rub his skin raw on cinderblock. One hour a day, he's in a kennel, a wire cage big enough for three men or three animals. There are six cages in the courtyard. This is his time outdoors; this is his exercise. One day he's out at nine in the morning, and the next day nobody unlocks his cell till four-fifteen, almost dark, so the boy gets twenty-seven minutes in the cold, but that's enough: he's tired of walking.

If he gets down on all fours, if he bares his teeth, if he growls, if he raises his long, magnificent tail, will the guards call for backup? Will they bring darts to put him to sleep or guns to put him out of his misery?

If you can restrain the body, you can tame the soul. Ask the tranquil nuns in Coeur d'Alene. Ask the girls who starve themselves to feel holy. Ask the guards who live like you, who spend half their waking lives in cages. Ask the saints who show the marks of the nails on their palms, who bite hard on their own flesh to kill desire.

One morning, Flint feels Cecile lying on top of him. But he wakes with his own hand on his own cock jerking. This is love in isolation. The weight of a girl is a trick of the senses: he's held fast by a wool blanket twisted tight around him, and the high, sweet voice of a child is only a guard in falsetto, mocking.

He wants to build a man of snow. With his bare hands, he wants to dig a hole in its chest and feel the cold, white heart melt through his fingers. He wants to sleep beside a furred animal: dog or cat, cow or coyote. He wants to scatter seeds and lie down and wait for birds to flutter softly all around him.

From the wire cage, he can see the walls of the prison on four sides and one patch of sky above him. This is his world now: if he's lucky, one hawk, one mourning dove, one free thief of a magpie might pass far overhead while he watches.

By May, the dangerous boy has grown docile: he rarely speaks, he eats, he washes; he does not spew or flail or threaten. When the guards taunt, when they call him dog-boy or Fido, he nods and smiles. In the kennel, he sometimes clings to the cyclone fencing. Touching the fence is not allowed. This is his worst transgression. He moves quickly to the center of the cage if the guard whistles.

On the twenty-ninth of June, for reasons never divulged to the prisoner, Flint Zimmer is delivered from Maximum to High Security. Freedom now means a cell with two bunks, and a man older than his grandfather for a cellmate. He is allowed one hour in the yard and one hour in the gym, but after the months alone, after the weeks of light so mercifully diffused in a world translucent, the blazing grass and brilliant sky blind him. He eats among men. Every voice is a violation. Sounds erupt: snorts, groans, curses. Who's that crying in the dark? *Shut the fuck up or I'll kill you.* The men smell of dirt and sweat; their air swirls around him. Whose breath is that, whose footstep follows? The crackling music of a radio and the gibber of laughter from a distant television make him want to weep or bang his head until the light in the sky goes dim, until his ears buzz, until his skin feels nothing.

The old man says, *Don't worry. It gets better.*

Why are there flowers here? He cannot understand it.

Someone has planted columbines and bleeding hearts and poppies along every walkway. Pink and yellow, red and lavender — who would do this? A prisoner with time to spare. Look at the man who digs: he was somebody else on the outside — husband, father, rapist, robber. Now his palms are dark with dirt and he kneels to tend his flowers.

Petals tremble in the wind, delirious, and the boy wants to go back to his cell, to the hard bed and the familiar wool blanket, to the pale room where he doesn't have to be afraid, where the heavy heads of orange poppies don't bend as he walks past them. White blood drips from each tiny bleeding heart, sweet hearts, lush and delicious — you could put them on your tongue; you could taste them, bite your own sweet lip; you could fill your mouth with a hundred hearts, a thousand — you could tear them pink from the vine and crush them. And if you dare to touch, will the gardener kill you with his yellow spade? If he turns as you pass and hears your thoughts, will he rise, does he know you? You want to run, but running is forbidden. Your heart runs; your red heart races. There is a tiny fist that hammers. There is a child's hand inside, insistent.

The old man is right. It does get better. The color blue becomes bearable. The wind doesn't hurt. If he stays in the middle of the path, the bleeding hearts and columbines can't touch him.

He answers a letter I wrote in December. He says, *Send $$ for my account. I need toothpaste and cigarettes.* He says, *I'm learning to spell. Yesterday I stood in the yard for fifteen minutes, and I wasn't afraid, but a magpie tried to steal my buttons.*

Is he joking?

He says, *My teacher is helping me write this letter.*

Yes, a teacher who gives him lists of words to memorize and use in sentences: *omit, believe, thief, breath, moral, mournful, panic, ridiculous.*

The lives of birds amaze him. If a sparrow flies over these fences by mistake, it is free to sing to the prisoner, and free to fly to the forest. He sings nine hours a day, twenty different melodies in a single morning, a thousand variations before sunset. To stop here and sing once costs him nothing. Three bluebirds pause on a coil of razor wire, warbling in a dream waiting to happen. The raven who struts along the edge of the fence watches the men in their cage without pity or judgment. The bird knows his mate's call. If he mimics her voice, she will hear herself and answer. So it is: the wise raven finds his true mate among hundreds.

Somewhere unseen in the thickets of distant fields, there is a nest the magpies have abandoned. It is wide and deep enough for four feral cats, a pair of foxes, five rabbits. Lined with hair and rootlets, it is a soft, safe place just the right size for a small boy and his sister.

If a wild canary flies over these fences, if she breaks her wing, if Flint hears her trills, will he be quick enough to catch her?

What is faith?

Two white-throated swifts mate in flight, somersaulting toward earth in a dizzy spiral.

C A T E C H I S M

Last summer, thistle grew dense behind our house, and my father and I spent three hours chopping. Now, where thistle twisted, a tangle of wild roses we did not plant has burst from red bud to pink blossom.

What is grace?

The mother of a child who died adopts the daughter of a murdered woman. Wanda Troy takes Rosana Robideau as her own. *In sickness and in health.* A mother's vows are sacred.

Once a week, Earl Troy visits each of his wives: Simone, Wanda, Pauline. He brings fish and bread, he eats at their tables. Sometimes he would like to lie down in their beds, to remember the shape of each woman as she curves against him, to hear a wife's secret words as he enters her. But he does not ask. He is afraid one friend might allow it, one wife who is no longer a wife might offer herself up to him in grief or pity.

In each house, he kisses each woman when he leaves her. He lays one hand on the head of each daughter: Leann, June, Lorelei, Rosana, Kateri. He drives to Billings and Great Falls to see his sons. He holds Malcolm, son of Trevor and Joelle, his first grandchild.

In this way, he prays without ceasing. He does not call it prayer. He does not realize that each word and each act is now sacred.

Sometimes he drives too fast, thinking he has to get home, thinking, *Kita is hungry*. It is July again, more than a year since he found and failed Lucie Robideau. He forgets for a moment that the dog who once saved his life is behind the house, buried since February. He forgets the frozen earth, how hard it was to break it. He imagines Kita on the bed, head on her paws, waiting. She cannot jump down to greet him, but she thumps her tail against the heavy blanket and smiles her dog smile. Though she is weak and crippled, though her eyes are now milky, her hair is still gold; and in this light, she shimmers.

What is hope?
A dying woman sews the burned hand of her murderer inside her chest and asks that they will be healed, that they will be whole, that they will be holy.

What is mercy?
A boy survives long enough to know his crime and mourn his victim. Through his grief for her, a child without faith shall become a man who believes that the woman he killed waits to deliver him.

How will we find redemption?
By seeking those we fear inside us.

⚓52⚓

S N O W   I N   A U G U S T

There's no way out of this story.
It must be told and told.
How can we know ourselves without it?

First there's the girl, Cecile Vaughn. She wanted to leave Rosana many times. She laid her in the ditch. She hid her behind a rock. She wrapped the baby in her own sweatshirt.

She covered her ears and tried to run away, but she was too tired. She saw cows and hawks and ravens. They spoke her name. Who can comprehend a child's visions? She imagined Rosana's head crushed; she felt her own stomach torn open.

Every time she pictured these things, she went back and lifted the heavy baby.

When Earl Troy found them together, Cecile carried Rosana on her hip and was walking slowly toward him.

In late October, one month after Flint Zimmer received his sentence, Cecile's classmates invented a new game. They called it *Execution*. The boys took Cecile into the woods, tied her to a tree with twine, and covered her eyes with a bandanna. Then two clever sisters with BB guns shot the prisoner. One pellet nicked her knee, one grazed her shoulder. Before the boys untied her and ran away, the younger girl whispered, *That's what they're going to do to your brother.*

Cecile came home hours later, lip split, legs muddy. Mother who hadn't slept last night, Mother who nursed the baby every two hours, Mother who was not drunk but was so tired, this mother lay in her rumpled bed, curled around her darling Jacob.

From the dark room, the mother who couldn't see her bewildered daughter said, *Is it late?*

And Cecile said, *Not really.*

Most nights, she slept under the bed instead of in it. She was afraid of fallen leaves, the way the wind swirled them upward. She was afraid of rain pounding on tin or dripping from dark branches. She stared at her little brother in his crib, but never held him. She was afraid of Jacob too, sweet milky breath, soft hair, tiny fingers. *What have you done?* Her body was the place where everything happened. Once upon a time, the arms that were Cecile's arms lifted a screaming child from her carseat. This was the thigh the brother touched. This was the throat, the belly, the eyelid.

Were you ever afraid?

Yes, always.

The body that was hers was there when the boy shot the woman. The hands that were her hands slipped inside an old man's pockets.

Tell it again.

These ears heard the baby sobbing. *Rosana.* The unseen child was a wave of sound. She cried in Cecile's sleep. She woke her. She had an exact weight, a shape Cecile felt imprinted against her chest and hip and shoulder. When her little brother cried, she wanted to smother the sound; she wanted everyone in the world quiet. Mother was afraid of her crimes and her intentions. When Cecile watched Jacob, Mother scooped him up and pressed him close as if eyes and thoughts might wound him.

Cecile Vaughn flunked fifth grade. On purpose? She was no better than her bad brother. A twenty-dollar bill disappeared from Dexter's wallet; a bottle of whiskey vanished from the cupboard.

Cecile knew that not one day of her brother's life would have been the same without her. Her hand was on the gun many times, and in her way she taught him. When he finally pulled the trigger, she alone was there to witness. She thought of all the broken windows, all the wide beds, all the big towels, all the whimpering dogs in strangers' houses. She helped him break china. She loved noise. She wanted to steal. She remembered the pitiful dolls. She pulled off their heads to look down their necks. They had nothing inside them. She twisted their arms and cut their hair. She stuffed them deep in the trash to bury them naked in garbage. She was five years old. She was never a good girl. She slit the belly of a cloth doll packed tight with cotton. She pulled the stuffing out and out, and still this doll kept all her secrets.

When she remembered the dolls, she remembered the woman, how the inside came outside, not soft, not white, not cotton. She remembered how kind Lucie was before it happened, how the light struck her face, how softly she spoke, how sweetly she sang when she thought Cecile was sleeping. She heard the sound of the invisible gun — invisible because it was still in her brother's pocket. She saw Flint's face, pinched red and unrecognizable. The sound made blood splatter the windshield, the dash, the seat between them — blood splattered her own hands, her mouth and eyes — the woman's blood was inside her, and the boy who was her brother dragged the woman out of the car, and the woman lay limp like a doll growing small on the highway.

Now it is September again, a year since Flint left us, since we left him, since he was exiled. The girl who refuses to read out loud at school, who will not copy her lessons in her notebook, who hates words on the page, who wants to pretend they have no meaning, who wants to forget all the words ever written about her and her brother, this girl reads the headline: FIVE DEAD IN PRISON RIOT. Inmates in Maximum Security have murdered one another. They have broken through chainlink fences with their bare hands and burned everything that would catch fire: mattresses, clothes, trash, blankets. They have broken glass and melted through Lexan shields. They have found the keys to every cell. They have freed their allies. They have stabbed and slashed and beaten and strangled informants, the ones held in Protective Custody — here, among them. *Some people experience the following emotions and symptoms as they adjust to prison: difficulty getting to sleep and staying asleep; dreams and nightmares; excessive worrying; obsessing; feelings of sadness and regret; brief periods of depression; feelings of loss; obsessing; fears of how other inmates will treat them; obsessing; feelings of anger, resentment, and revenge; obsessing.*

Two guards escaped through hatches onto the roof; five others barricaded themselves behind the steel door of a shower room. Only the prisoners are dead. Liars and snitches, thieves and extortionists, the betrayed betrayers of their brothers.

Five dead, four injured.

At school, a third grader with a stick says, *Did they get him?*

Flint Zimmer is not among the dead, not yet, not this time. He's safe, moved from Maximum to High Security in June where he walked afraid between columbines and poppies. Does Cecile know this? He has a job swabbing cellblocks. He is not among the murderers. No mop handles have broken in his hands; no long splinters have been found embedded in his mattress.

Cecile Vaughn lies under her bed, reading every word with a flashlight. The dead are not named: *pending notification of relatives.*

When Mother calls her name, she does not answer. When Dexter stands in her doorway, she sees his feet, but she is very small and safe and hidden; she is very still and quiet; she can hold her breath for a minute or more, like a swimmer, like a diver, like a prisoner playing dead so the men with shivs won't kick his head and slash him.

+——◄►——+

Halloween, a cold wind rattles the last leaves, and Cecile makes her own costume. She wears a cone-shaped hat over her mouth and nose, shreds the sleeves of a flannel shirt and pretends they're feathers. Little owl, she flaps and hoots around the baby's crib until sweet Jacob wails.

Dexter who is not her father, who is not bound by blood or law to love her, Dexter Bell who stares at her now as if she is a stranger, a child who has broken into his house, an intruder, Dexter Duane Bell who is sometimes kind and sometimes angry yanks Cecile out of the baby's bedroom into the bright hallway. He rips the silly cone from her face, and the elastic band cuts her — just a fine line of blood, cheek and ear, nothing serious, *You can't hurt me.* Long ago, on a winter's night, Dexter Bell rescued a sleepy child from a cold cave and carried her to her bedroom where he changed her clothes, kissed her mouth, rubbed her numb feet, and whispered, *Shush, just a dream, don't be scared.* Tonight, he sends Cecile to her room alone. No trick-or-treat, no supper.

We are her last hope. Frances comes to the lake. She looks at me when she speaks to our father. She lets me read her lips. She says, *Please, can you take her? Just a few months, I'm so tired.* She says, *Maybe she can go to school in Polson; someplace where nobody knows her.*

All these years, and my sister still doesn't understand that my father and I would do anything she asked us.

Imagine two motherless girls asleep in a room together. They do not speak of what they've lost because one is deaf and one wants to forget the secret signs they used last summer. These two sleep like stones cast into the lake. Outside, the wind howls. One hears it in her dreams and one feels it through the cracks near the window. One dreams she is a gull, flapping at the pane, trapped outside forever. One dreams she has drowned but not died and the fish open their soft mouths and touch her with their cool bodies.

Imagine a father who stands silently in the doorway, who watches them, who loves them, who is afraid of them, who cannot guess what they are dreaming, who has chosen to stay alive, who has willed himself back to being.

Imagine a wooden box full of postcards tied with a blue ribbon. Long ago, our grandmother Leora drew a picture of Stone Child, the Chippewa. Faded and folded, this Rocky Boy died before he finally got his reservation. Now he's old as stone, old as sky and mountain. Was he ever a boy? Did he kill birds with pebbles as a child? In Leora's crumpled drawing, his face looks worn by wind, his cheeks by ice and starlight fissured.

Swift Bear, Chased-by-Owls, Flying By, Cloud Man.
No Heart, Five Wounds, Looking Glass, Toohoolhoolzote.
Louis Riel, Wandering Spirit.
Blue Horse, Blind Bear, Black Kettle.
They died in the Greasy Grass.
They reeled at the Banks of the Big Hole.
They fell in the Bear Paws' clutches.
They swung from the gallows in Canada.
Their blood froze in the snow.
They were ice on the Washita River.

Where do we begin? The dead have gone to their Father, and their names must not be spoken. Still, they long to be remembered, to have the cadence of their stories pounded into the ground, each one in his own language. They want to echo from this earth. They want to sing through rocks and roots into the bones of all the living.

What can we ever know, and who will believe our stories?

I'll tell you the truth: I wasn't surprised when our mother left us. Every riddle, every song, every tale she told was a warning. Once upon a time, there was a woman who fought with her husband and ran away from her tribe. She walked two days through wind and snow. Is it possible to be lost if you don't care where you're going? On the third day, she climbed a hill and crawled into a dark cave, where she dreamed her body was ice, and she was trapped inside, but not yet frozen.

When she woke, she saw the eyes of wolves all around her. They had laid their bodies down to keep her warm; they had saved her. *Do not be afraid*, they said. Were their voices human, or did she understand their language? They brought her fresh deer meat, and she ate it raw because she was so hungry. Later, when there was time, she cooked and dried the meat. She made pemmican with berries. She tanned hides and carved awls to sew moccasins and dresses.

Do we forget our names if no one speaks them?

For two years, the woman lived among the wolves. She meant to stay forever, but one day the great wolf came to her and said she must return to her own people. He told her to walk to a herd of wild horses. *They can lead you back,* he said, *but beware: the stallions will try to keep you.*

The woman did as she was told. And it was true: when she found the horses, the stallions courted her. They had flowing manes and long tails. She saw no reason to resist them.

When she ran with the herd, her clothes became rags and fell to pieces. She was dark and covered with dirt; her black hair grew thick and tangled.

One day, hunters from her people's tribe came upon the herd and captured one thrashing creature and seven swift ponies. They did not recognize their sister. They roped and tied and dragged her as they would any other dangerous animal.

When the woman was washed, her people knew her. They spoke her lost name to call her back, but she refused to answer. They combed her hair and gave her fine clothes made of the softest doeskin. She could not be tamed. She lived among her people, yet apart, never again fully human, never again truly wild.

We are a strange family: my father, me, Cecile — the quiet child, the woman who will not speak, the man who learned long ago how to live beyond language.

Cecile listens to the voice of the water. She listens to crows who bark, who woof softly as wolves when they do not know she is beneath them.

I give her signs so that she can begin to tell her story in another language. Her left hand is a knife between the ribs; her right hand quivers near her face, fingers fluttering. With one long sweep of her arm, the brother who cuts the heart flies away from her.

How else can she explain?

She fears and mourns him.

She wants him dead. She wants him to come home and sleep beside her. Both desires are true. When she signs, there is no need to resolve them. Shapes in air cannot be permanent. One hand makes the rain, one the river — one falls, they flow together.

We live in the present. We speak only when someone watches and write nothing down: words are lies when we give them edges.

There are four questions I will never answer: *Why did my mother swim toward the Island of Wild Horses? Why did my brain press tight inside my skull one summer? When a father calls a deaf girl's name, how does she hear him? Was Cecile Flint's sweet heart or his hostage?*

She dreams him, ghost brother, thin enough to slip through bars, quiet enough to spill like water. When he shows himself to her, he is an old man with a bent spine and twisted fingers. He is harmless. Free or runaway? She does not need to ask. In this dream, nobody will try to hunt him.

He follows railroad tracks and laughing creeks, looking always for his lost sister. Wrinkled woodland creature, she is old, like him, but still small as her girl self. She crouches in the long shadows of dusk or early morning. Hidden, but not hiding. She is silent. She is waiting.

When they lie down in leaves together, he shows her a hundred scars on his chest and thighs and belly. They open like a hundred mouths. They say, *This is how I died; this is how you killed me.*

With his own mouth, with his last kiss, he says, *I don't forgive you.*

How long can she bear to live among us?

With her brother she crossed the border. She saw death. They killed together. Who but Flint will ever know her? If I make the sign for *love,* cross my closed fists over my heart, spell her name or call her darling, why should she believe me?

What is love without knowledge?

I have no answer.

I love my father above all others. Because I know his crimes. Because I know his passion. Because one bright day Rina dove deep and let her mouth fill with water while she answered the sturgeon in his own language.

After this, no man but my father could really touch me.

·

It's March, and Cecile has cut her hair close to the scalp. She wears faded jeans and a gray hooded sweatshirt under a black denim jacket. She's five feet tall but so thin she looks longer, a shadow winnowing through trees at twilight. Her boots leave shallow imprints on the muddy hillsides. First wolf, then doe, she moves through the woods with a loping stride, building her stamina. She is twelve years old. She thinks like a woman.

She knows now what happened inside the prison: cells filled with smoke and blood and water; the sprinklers worked, but the vents to clear smoke didn't. Two inmates survived by jamming the door of a laundry room with a broomstick. Another who knew the riot was coming painted himself red to fool his brothers; he held his breath and lay still even when they poked him with a broken mop handle. When it was finally over, when the prison's Disturbance Control Team had stormed the compound with tear gas, Cecile knows how the guards stripped and cuffed the choking prisoners. Blind men ran a gauntlet of shattered glass, and the guards in their double lines felt free to trip or kick while the ones with their hands cuffed behind their backs — the barefoot ones, the ones now naked — lunged forward.

If the guards were terrified and angry, who could blame them?

For seven hours, the naked men lay face down on a stretch of bare earth, *a no man's land* between Maximum and High Security. On that hot September day, their bare skin burned; they sweltered. There were no distinctions drawn between victims and perpetrators, no time to decide who among them had raged and who had crouched in his cell, waiting to be delivered. The night turned cold, and still they lay on the ground until their cuffed hands went numb and their cut feet stopped bleeding.

——— ◆ ———

When I say Cecile thinks like a woman, I mean she has been spared nothing. Though her brother did not lie on the ground that day, she feels his raw skin burning. When she closes her eyes to stop her visions, it is not the men who lie stripped and bloody she sees — it is all their victims: men stabbed behind taverns, women raped in their own kitchens. Then she sees herself walking down a dark road, and the sky is blue though the sun has not yet risen, and the woman with the child stops, and Cecile is the one with the gun in her pocket, the one afraid, the one furious, the one too terrified and tired to think, the one who shoots, who kills and is killed, who vanishes on the road, who ceases to be herself, who never was or is never again a child.

One night she stays out long after dark, but I feel her at the window. She watches the bright room where my father and I perform our parts in a silent play she cannot enter. She sees inside where everything is still and everything is passing. We are ordinary: the woman mends her father's shirt; the man crumples newspaper to build a fire. Perhaps she sees what we choose not to see, that the man who once carried his limp daughter out of the woods is now slow to stand, that he has grown thin, that his left hand trembles. Perhaps she understands that the woman who will not speak might one day need her.

If the girl decides to stay, if she believes she can come inside and sleep in her bed one more time, it is only because she knows she saved Rosana. When she lists her crimes — murder, theft, rage, betrayal — the life of Lucie's child is her only hope of redemption.

So we live, and now it is August.
Cecile rows her tiny boat across broken water. Wind from

the north chops the waves, and clouds roll down from the mountains. It begins to snow. Yes, in August. We live in a world where everything is possible.

In this spinning snow, the girl becomes a blue ghost, a gray flurry, a white wave, and then nothing.

I stand on the dock. I am a woman who has grown older than her own mother. I cannot see the one who swims or the one who rows after her.

Later Cecile sits at our table. Like a person. She eats with me and my father, this ghost girl who struggles to stay in her human shape, who feels herself slipping when she moves too fast through woods or over water.

Her hands are red, still cold when I touch them.
She lets me touch her.

What is grace?

A father and daughter and child live together in a house on a lake far away where it snows in August, where the voices of wild horses call from a distant island. Love here is a stone where waves are breaking. Love this hard is not a transgression. We learn to forgive ourselves and each other for our misguided passions. We do not speak in words. We explain nothing.

What is hope?

A child called Rosana cries in the night, and the mother who has adopted her is alive; Wanda Troy floats into Rosana's room, quiet as an angel. But this woman has flesh and substance, human hands and human arms to rock a child. She whispers the words that are not words, in a soft, sweet language, in a tongue of fire, in the mystery of sound between mother and daughter.

❈53❈

T H E   B I R D M A N

Once upon a time, Cecile, there was a man who was the husband of a drowned woman and the father of two daughters.
He hated cowbirds. He shot them from the trees. He walked
through the woods, looking for the nestlings of songbirds,
vireos and chickadees, warblers and finches, the hungry ones
pushed from their nests, the featherless ones that had fallen.
And though he knew they could not live, though he knew it
was impossible, he brought them home, he made nests of
grass and hair and silk and feathers, he fed them soft bread on
a toothpick, he gave them water from an eyedropper. He kept
his faith for all time, and for all time he tried to save them.

NOTES

1. The Landers School for Juvenile Offenders, a state youth correctional facility, is a fictional place, a composite based on several institutions in different states during various time periods. Landers is not intended to represent any single institution in Montana or any other state.

2. Wildhorse Island, referred to as the Island of Wild Horses in the novel, is a 2,160-acre island in the southwest corner of Flathead Lake in Montana. The island falls within the borders of the Flathead Indian Reservation, but is not owned by the tribe. When the Salish people were threatened by Blackfeet raiders, they swam their most valuable horses to the island. Because the island is so large, it was often difficult to find all of the horses, and some became wild. In 1939, two bighorn sheep were taken to the island. Today, the sheep population has swelled to nearly two hundred. Deer, coyote, raptors, songbirds, and waterfowl also find refuge on Wildhorse Island.

3. Creston, Kalispell, Bigfork, Columbia Falls, and Polson are all small towns in northwestern Montana. The incidents that take place in these towns and the people involved are fictional.

Cecile Vaughn's encounters at the Creston grade school, and on the bus she rides to and from school, are entirely imagined.

4. Many historical sources recount the story of Plenty Coups and his vision. The most comprehensive and passionate version I found is in *Plenty-Coups: Chief of the Crows* by Frank B. Linderman (Lincoln: University of Nebraska Press, 1957). The story Marie Zimmer tells in chapter 14 is based on Linderman's account of his extended conversation with Plenty Coups. Several of the italicized lines are direct quotations from Linderman's translation of Plenty Coups' story, and other italicized lines are Marie's extrapolation of the tale Linderman recorded. Frank Linderman was born in Ohio and moved to Montana when he was sixteen. He became intimately associated with the Crows and other Indian tribes. Plenty Coups considered Linderman a friend, a signtalker, and told him the story of his life and his people so that this piece of history would be preserved in written language. Plenty Coups refused to speak of the time after the mass slaughter of the buffalo.

5. *Of Wolves and Men* by Barry Lopez (New York: Simon & Schuster, 1978) and *The Company of Wolves* by Peter Steinhart (New York, Vintage, 1995) both provide compelling details about the campaign to annihilate the wolves of North America.

6. Hundreds of writers have spun their versions of the Battle of the Little Bighorn. Almost all historians agree that none of George Armstrong Custer's men survived the battle, which is one reason a definitive reconstruction of events is impossible. The controversial story of Custer's involvement with the Cheyenne woman Monahseetah (or Me-o-tzi) appears in *Custer's Fall: The Native American Side of the Story* by David Humphreys Miller (New York: Penguin, 1985). *Son of the Morn-*

ing Star by Evan S. Connell (New York: Farrar, Straus and Giroux, 1984) is one of the most fascinating and richly detailed versions of the battle, the people involved, and the events before and after this cataclysmic event. Both Miller and Connell evoke surprising and complicated visions of Sitting Bull and other Indians involved in the Battle of the Little Bighorn. Miller's account provides information rarely found in other sources.

7. Since American Indians did not use written languages, the spellings of their names vary widely. For instance, Linderman ⟨...⟩ Plenty Coups' Indian name Aleek-chea-ahoosh. Another ⟨...⟩sh. In most cases, I have ⟨...⟩t comprehensive source I

⟨...⟩ck Wilson, the Woodcut- ⟨...⟩t Dance religion appear in ⟨...⟩exts. *Black Elk Speaks* as ⟨...⟩ln: University of Nebraska ⟨...⟩ded *Knee* by Dee Brown ⟨...⟩s, 1981), *The Ghost Dance* ⟨...⟩mes Mooney (New York: ⟨...⟩host Dance: A Sourcebook ⟨...⟩ersity of Nebraska Press, ⟨...⟩ditations on this enigmatic

9. I found the story of Watkuweis, the Nez Perce woman whose words of caution and mercy to Twisted Hair may have saved the men of the Lewis and Clark Expedition, in *The Nez Perce Indians and the Opening of the Northwest* by Alvin M. Josephy, Jr. (Boston: Houghton Mifflin, 1997). The name Watkuweis means "returned from a faraway country."

[handwritten note: Sometime, our suffering begins long before we find our way in the world.]

[handwritten: post modern — storying play —]

[handwritten: admired Norman MacLean]

10. Indians knew the Little Bighorn Valley as the Valley of the Greasy Grass. Translators disagree about the accuracy of this name. In the Crow language, the expressions "rich grass" and "lodge grass" are very similar and are more evocative of the lush grazing in this area of the state now known as Montana.

11. Gerald B. Pileggi was murdered by two inmates with baseball bats in September 1990 at the Montana State Prison in Deer Lodge.

12. Inmates in the Maximum Security compound at Montana State Prison rioted on September 22, 1991. The events of that day, including the murders of five Protective Custody inmates, were widely reported in the days following the riot. *Riot at MAX: An Administrative Inquiry into the Circumstances Surrounding the Montana State Prison Riot of September 22, 1991* (Washington, D.C.: United States Department of Justice, National Institute of Corrections, 1991) provides a detailed account of the riot, the circumstances that contributed to the uprising, and the events that followed. The introductory page of the report includes this statement: "The contents of this document reflect the views of the Administrative Inquiry Team. The contents do not necessarily reflect the official views or policies of the National Institute of Corrections."

13. According to the members of the inquiry team (Jeffrey A. Schwartz, team leader, Clayton Bain, Stan Czerniak, Dennis M. Luther, Lanson Newsome, John Pfaff, Jr., and Mike Shafer) who compiled *Riot at MAX*, the Montana State Prison had serious systemic problems long before the riot. When I visited the prison in the summer of 1999, I was impressed by the professionalism of the staff, the concern for inmate health and education, and the variety of work programs available to inmates. In

my representation of the prison, I have attempted to fuse these disparate visions, to reveal the tension and danger within the prison during the early 1990s, while pointing toward more positive aspects. The violent uprising in 1991 led to important reforms in prison security, the articulation of grievance policies, and staff education.

14. The story of the woman who lived with wolves and ran with wild horses is recounted in *The Sioux: Life and Customs of a Warrior Society* by Royal B. Hassrick (Norman: University of Oklahoma Press, 1988). Hassrick heard the story from Brings the Buffalo Girl.

15. The epigraph of the novel is from *Young Men and Fire* by Norman Maclean (Chicago: University of Chicago Press, 1992).

ACKNOWLEDGMENTS

I am grateful to the Mrs. Giles Whiting Foundation, the Ohio Arts Council, and the Ohio State University for their generous support. Caryl Phillips offered his faith and friendship; Ruth Anderson and Annea Lockwood provided a sanctuary. My early readers gave me hope and helped me clarify my vision: Wendy Thon, Margaret Himley, Christine Flanagan, Laurie Thon, Mary Pinard, Alice Lichtenstein, Miles Coiner, Lois Ann Thon, Melinda Milner, and Mark Robbins — I thank you all. I am grateful to my agent Irene Skolnick for her dedication, and to my editor Janet Silver for her wisdom.

As I explored the world of this novel, the work of many writers gave me insight into my people. I am especially indebted to Kathryn Watterson (*Women in Prison: Inside the Concrete Womb*, Boston: Northeastern University Press, 1996); Oliver Sacks (*Seeing Voices*, New York: HarperPerennial, 1990); Edward Humes (*No Matter How Loud I Shout: A Year in the Life of Juvenile Court*, New York: Simon & Schuster, 1996); Sherwin Nuland (*How We Die*, New York: Knopf, 1994); Wilbert Rideau and Ron Wikberg (*Life Sentences: Rage and Survival Behind Bars*, New York: Time Books, 1992); Francis Bird Linderman (*Plenty-Coups: Chief of the Crows*, Lincoln: University of Nebraska Press, 1957); Evan S. Connell (*Son of the*

Morning Star, New York: Farrar, Straus and Giroux, 1984); David Humphreys Miller (*Custer's Fall: The Native American Side of the Story*, New York: Penguin, 1985); William L. Bryan, Jr. (*Montana Indians Yesterday and Today*, Helena, Montana: American & World Geographic Publishing, 1996); Dee Brown (*Bury My Heart at Wounded Knee*, New York: Washington Square Press, 1981); Peter Steinhart (*The Company of Wolves*, New York: Vintage, 1995); and Barry Lopez (*Of Wolves and Men*, New York: Simon & Schuster, 1978).

Matthew Pelikan delighted me with his love and knowledge of birds. I thank Sally Hatfield, granddaughter of Frank Linderman, for her interest in my work, and for her blessing. I am indebted to Norman Maclean for his inspiring journey and for all the wise and merciful words of *Young Men and Fire*.

I am grateful to all the devoted photographers whose passionate images helped me see what words couldn't evoke, and I offer special thanks to Edward S. Curtis, Don Doll, S.J., Rodman Wanamaker, Roland Reed, Mathew Brady, Alexander Gardner, David F. Barry, David Notman, L. A. Huffman, Charles H. Carpenter, Charles M. Bell, Norman A. Forsyth, and Clarence G. Morledge.

Linda Moodry guided me through the Montana State Prison and patiently answered my endless questions; Linda Walsh and Jack Powers allowed me to see the important work they do in mental health and education; and Kenneth A. Miller offered his knowledge of prison life with great wisdom and generosity. I could not have written the final chapters of this book without their help. Craig Thomas of the Montana State Board of Pardons explained the complicated and ever-changing guidelines for parole.

I thank Katie Hampton at the University of Montana for finding news articles on the 1991 riot in the Maximum Security compound at the Montana State Prison, and Rita Kraus of the Carnegie Library in Kalispell, Montana, for sending me dozens of articles on juvenile crimes in northwestern Montana. The Maureen and Mike Mansfield Library at the University of Montana loaned me a precious copy of *Riot at MAX: An Administrative Inquiry into the Circumstances Surrounding the Montana State Prison Riot of September 22, 1991.* I am indebted to Bruce Machart for the time he spent copying the information I would need, and for reading the manuscript of the novel with great care and curiosity.

Steven Cummings guided me to Randy Schwickert, and I thank both of them for their legal expertise. Randy Schwickert's thoughtful and compassionate answers to my questions about the intricacies of juvenile law have given me invaluable insight. I am especially grateful to him for the day we spent in juvenile court. The images of that day taught me more than I imagined possible.

I thank my favorite doctors — Laurie Thon, Eric Shapiro, and Reesie Johnson — for their subtle and detailed answers to my medical questions. Elizabeth Domholdt and Gary Shoemaker helped me understand the startling differences between various pistols and revolvers; I am grateful to them for their bold and precise instructions the day they taught me to shoot.

I am forever indebted to Janet Thon and John Cloninger for their tales of fish, guns, children, and animals. I thank you again, Jan, for the fiery image that illuminated the path I had to follow long before I understood where I was going.